P9-DEC-227

Something Like Gravity

Also by Amber Smith

The Way I Used to Be
The Last to Let Go

Something Like Gravity

AMBER SMITH

Margaret K. McElderry Books
New York   London   Toronto   Sydney   New Delhi

MARGARET K. McELDERRY BOOKS

An imprint of Simon & Schuster Children's Publishing Division

1230 Avenue of the Americas, New York, New York 10020

This book is a work of fiction. Any references to historical events, real people, or real places are used fictitiously. Other names, characters, places, and events are products of the author's imagination, and any resemblance to actual events or places or persons, living or dead, is entirely coincidental.

Text copyright © 2019 by Amber Smith

Jacket illustration copyright © 2019 by Mia Nolting

All rights reserved, including the right of reproduction in whole or in part in any form.

MARGARET K. McELDERRY BOOKS is a trademark of Simon & Schuster, Inc.

For information about special discounts for bulk purchases, please contact Simon & Schuster Special Sales at 1-866-506-1949 or business@simonandschuster.com.

The Simon & Schuster Speakers Bureau can bring authors to your live event. For more information or to book an event, contact the Simon & Schuster Speakers Bureau at 1-866-248-3049 or visit our website at www.simonspeakers.com.

Book design by Debra Sfetsios-Conover

The text for this book was set in Simoncini Garamond.

Manufactured in the United States of America

First Edition

10 9 8 7 6 5 4 3 2 1

CIP data for this book is available from the Library of Congress.

ISBN 978-1-5344-3718-0

ISBN 978-1-5344-3720-3 (eBook)

For Sam

PART ONE
june

CHRIS

EIGHT MINUTES. THAT'S HOW LONG IT TAKES LIGHT
from the Sun to reach Earth. That means every time we look
up at the sky, we can only ever see the Sun as it was eight minutes ago, never how it is right in this moment.

The next closest star to our Sun is Proxima Centauri, at
4.2 light-years away. That's 25 trillion miles. It would take tens
of thousands of years to get there. And the farthest stars are
millions of light-years away. Far enough that so many of the
stars we see don't even exist anymore; they've died in the time
it took for their light to reach us. All we can see is the past,
but only so far—13 billion light-years. Anything beyond that
is simply too distant, and the light hasn't had enough time to
reach us yet.

There's something about that. Something fascinating. Terrifying. Beautiful.

But sometimes I wish that for just once I could see into the future, not on an astronomical scale, maybe just two or three years into my own life. If I could know ahead of time how this will all turn out, whether I'll be okay or not, then maybe I'd be a lot less scared, a lot less angry, right now.

That's what I was thinking about in the backseat, as I stared out the window, watching the scenery on the I-90 turn like seasons, from suburbs to city to suburbs to country and back again. Until now, my parents had only spoken once in two and a half hours, and that was to tell me to turn my music down.

"Chris?" I pretended not to hear. *"Chris,"* Mom repeated, louder, twisting around in her seat.

My dad's eyes ticked up to meet mine in the rearview mirror.

I pulled my headphones down around my neck. That was all the response I'd give her.

She stared at me like she was trying really hard to see something in me, see some*one* in me. "Is this punishment?" she asked. "You're trying to punish me by doing this?"

"Sure," I muttered.

Monosyllabic. I learned that word when I was seven, as in Mom hated when I would give her monosyllabic answers instead of full sentences, which is why I used them strategically.

"I said I was sorry, Chris." *She hadn't, actually.* "You hate me that much?" she asked, and I could tell by the sharp edges of her words that I was making her angry. *Good.*

"Whate'er," I mumbled, smashing the word down to a single, compact sound. I hadn't spoken more than one-syllable words to Mom in two days, and I sure as hell wasn't about to start now.

"I—you—" she began, but stopped herself, realizing we'd had this fight a million times already, not only over the last two days, but the whole past year, and no one ever ended up winning. She turned to Dad instead. "A little help, Joe? I mean, really. God, she just—"

"He," Dad interrupted. "Okay? Can we just let it be?" He cut his eyes to her, not quite raising his voice. It takes a lot for him to actually get angry, but lately that quality has only seemed to enrage my mom.

"Let it be?" she repeated, this bitter laugh vibrating under her words. "Fine." She jerked herself around in the seat, crossing her arms and making a point to stare straight ahead, without a sound. But I could see her working the muscles of her jaws, clenching her teeth like she was chewing up whatever words were left over in her mouth.

Dad watched me in the rearview again, his eyes wanting to tell me something I don't think he knew how to say with his voice. That he was trying. That maybe part of him understood part of me. That he was on my side. Sometimes.

He looked forward again, rolled his head from side to side, and then readjusted his grip on the steering wheel, accelerating to just above the speed limit. I put my headphones back on and closed my eyes.

All I'd done was dare to leave my house. All I wanted was a little freedom, just a tiny amount of control over my own life.

Two days ago I woke up early, before my parents. The house was quiet and the day was perfect. I started getting dressed, laced up my running shoes. I was planning on heading down to the basement to use Mom's old treadmill, like I did most mornings.

But somehow, I walked out of the front door instead.

I took three easy steps down our porch stairs, then into the driveway, and then down the sidewalk. First I just jogged. Past our neighbor's house, then up to the stop sign at the corner. I was going to turn around.

But as my feet hit the pavement, falling into that old familiar rhythm, I ran. Ran the way I used to before school, back when they still let me go to school. I didn't mean to be gone for so long. Maybe I knew they'd be worrying, but I just couldn't care anymore. I couldn't keep living inside their fear, because, as much as I hated to admit it, their fear was contagious and it was beginning to become mine too.

Yes, I forgot to bring my phone, but that was an accident.

When I got back, they were waiting for me in the living room. They'd even called Coleton, my only remaining real-life, flesh-and-blood friend, who was sitting on the couch looking like he'd just rolled out of bed. I walked through the door, and Dad stopped, midpace, stood very still, and yelled, really yelled, "Where the hell have you been?" in a voice that sounded like a stranger's. Coleton stood quickly, and I distinctly remember the look on his face as he approached me. He came so close, I actually thought he was going to hit me, but instead he just stood in front of me and said, "You're good." I couldn't tell if it was a question or a statement, but I didn't have time to respond because he shook his head and elbowed past me, slamming the door behind him on his way out.

Mom didn't say anything.

She marched up to me with yesterday's mascara streaked in angry black lines across her cheeks, and pushed me. Shoved me, hard, against the door. And then she took a step back, and I remember it happening almost in slow motion. I heard it before I felt it. Like that sharp crack of the door slamming shut again. Except it took me a second to realize that sound was her hand against my cheek. A slap. The feeling spread like a million tiny needles piercing the side of my face one after the other. She had never hit me before; neither of my parents had ever hit me, not so much as a single spanking as a child. I don't remember if anyone said anything; I just remember Mom backing up slowly, looking at me as if *I* was the one who'd hit *her*.

I stormed up the stairs to my bedroom, grabbed my phone, and saw that I had forty-seven missed calls, eighteen voice mails, and twenty-nine text messages from the three of them.

That was when I called Isobel. Because she had promised me she'd be there if I ever needed anything. And I desperately did.

The chirping of the turn signal woke me. Then the rumble of loose gravel under the tires made me sit up. I looked around as we were finally pulling into the driveway that led up to Aunt Isobel's house, which used to be my mom's house too; it was the house they grew up in.

After ten hours of sitting in the four-door pressure cooker that was our family car, I jumped out the instant Dad shifted into park.

"Holy shit," I mumbled under my breath. This was really, truly the middle of nowhere. People say that, but I always thought it was an exaggeration. Not this time. Nothing but farms and fields and woods as far as I could see. I'd only ever seen this place in old photographs; it felt strange to be here in person. Exactly what I was expecting, yet nothing like it at all. The only thing that resembled civilization was the old, dilapidated house that stood in front of me, the place that would be home for the next two and a half months.

I had the urge to run again—to run and keep on running forever. But just then, I caught sight of Isobel on the front porch. She was wearing her nurse's scrubs and leaning up against a post that also leaned, supporting an awning that sloped too far downward to be structurally sound. Her feet were bare as she descended the steps, and as she came closer I could tell from her heavy eyelids and her casual smile that she was tired. She must've just gotten off work. But something changed in her face when our eyes met, like we were coconspirators and this whole mess, this whole fucked-up year, was all part of some elaborate plan that was working out perfectly because it had brought us together, right here, right now.

Isobel could make me believe in a lot of things.

She was holding her arms open, and as I walked toward her I remembered everything I loved about her all at once. And I felt less like running away. Isobel is older than Mom by three years, but still, I've always thought of her as the cool, young aunt. She's brave. Does her own thing and doesn't care what people think—like last year, how she streaked her hair electric blue, just because. Or when she got that bird tattoo when my grandma died.

I usually only get to see her once or twice a year. Thanksgiving and Christmas, or sometimes she'll make the trip for a special birthday or anniversary.

She'll come for bad things too. Like Grandma's funeral. Or like last fall, when I was beaten so bad that I was in the hospital—she was there then. She was also there when I got out, and she stayed with us for the six weeks it took for me to get better. She forced me to do all the painful physical therapy, and even let me hate her for pushing me so hard. She wouldn't let me give up. She made me strong again, even stronger than I was before.

"Chris, my goodness! Look at you, come here." She gave me a quick, firm hug. Not a long, drawn-out pity hug, for which I was thankful. When she pulled away, she shielded her eyes from the sun as she looked up at me, then took my chin in her other hand and said, like it was no big deal, "So handsome."

But before I could respond, Mom appeared right next to me, saying, "Hello, Isobel," her voice all tight and annoyed and disapproving.

"Sheila, good to see you." Isobel flashed a smile that was so much warmer than my mom deserved, but then she gave me a wink when Mom wasn't looking.

The three of us stood there, silent, as we waited for Dad to trudge up from the car, struggling to carry four of my bags at once. As he set them down on the ground and looked at Isobel, he smiled—a real smile—for the first time in a long time.

Isobel pulled him into a hug that lasted just a few seconds too long. Definitely a pity hug—poor old Joe and his nasty wife and his screwed-up kid that he doesn't know what to do with anymore.

Mom looked down at the ground and cleared her throat. As my dad and Isobel pulled apart, Isobel said, "How you doing, Joey?"

"Joey?" He scoffed. "Please, you make it sound like I'm twelve years old."

"What can I say? In my mind you'll always be a twelve-year-old." She clapped him on the shoulder and reached over to mess up his thinning hair, but he ducked away quickly.

Dad and Isobel graduated high school the same year. They used to date when they were my age, and that's how my mom and dad first met: Mom was Dad's girlfriend's little sister. It's hard to imagine any of them being my age. It's hard to imagine Dad with Isobel.

Isobel always said they were better as friends. And Dad never said much about it at all. They still had this sibling-like banter that always seemed to make Mom so jealous. All my life, she had made these little comments about it, jokes usually. But there was no humor in Mom's face now, as she leveled the two of them with her eyes.

Sometimes I wonder if my parents were ever really happy, if it was me who did this to them. Maybe there's something like the speed of light when it comes to love, too. Like they were doomed before they ever started, but it's just taken seventeen years for them to be able to see it.

MAIA

I DIDN'T EVEN KNOW GRAFFITI EXISTED IN CARSON, North Carolina. I saw it by accident yesterday morning when I was at the gas station filling my eternally deflating bike tires with free air. I usually rode there in front of the store, so I hadn't seen the back of the building until then.

A car pulled up to one of the gas pumps, music blaring. When I looked, I saw that it was all my friends, piled into Hayden's mom's old-ass Ford Escort, laughing and shouting with the windows rolled down. They were going to the beach, to the carnival we went to every summer.

They had invited me. They always invited me; they were good friends that way. I said I was sick. I wasn't sick, though. That's why I ducked behind the building with my bike, heart racing, waiting there until they left. And when I looked up, there it was: one of Mallory's photographs, except in real life.

I loved my sister. Even when I didn't understand her, even

when I hated her, I still loved her. Which I guess is the reason I woke up early today to be here, staring at the graffiti on the back wall of the only gas station in town.

I returned this morning with Mallory's camera hanging around my neck. There was this one sharp thread in the strap that poked into my skin, and I wondered if it had bothered her the way it bothered me.

Part of me also wondered if Mallory had spray-painted the wall herself and then taken a picture of it—that seemed like the kind of thing she might do. But in person, I could see that the letters were worn, faded from years of grime and weather. I brought the camera up to my face and squinted through the viewfinder.

My fingers fit into the smooth places that *her* fingers had worn into the body of the camera over the years. I took a step back, and then sidestepped to the right, back again, and a little to the left. And there it was. The picture my sister had once taken, framed exactly how she'd framed it. I looked down at my feet and adjusted my toes so they were pointing ever so slightly inward, the way she always used to stand. I was in the exact spot she was in when she took this picture.

I waited to feel something.

I don't ever take pictures myself—that was Mallory's thing. And I am nothing like Mallory. There wasn't even film in the camera, but I pressed the shutter release so that it made that sound—that *clap-click-snap* sound that always seemed to accompany Mallory wherever she went.

Mallory had had a way of seeing things that no one else saw. But after our parents divorced four years ago, when she was in ninth grade and I was in eighth, she became serious about photography. We were only eighteen months apart, but it may as well have been eighteen years, for all we had in common. She had plans to become a famous photographer, vowed to travel the world after she graduated from high school. She wanted to work for *National Geographic* and see her photographs in art galleries and stuff like that. She was going to do it too; she had a fancy internship all lined up in Washington, DC, with some up-and-coming magazine that was going to pay to send her overseas on assignment.

People in Carson just don't do stuff like that.

Most of the time I thought she was snobby and pretentious. This town, her life here, our parents, me . . . nothing was good enough for her. Even though she already had everything—grades, talent, friends, the adoration of our parents and teachers and classmates, beauty, brains, magic—still, she always wanted more.

I never understood it. Never understood *her*.

Which I guess is why I'm trying now.

I gazed at the words melting in hasty cursive script, studied the handwriting of the vandal, their capital letters mixed in with lowercase, the messy lines stacked like blocks one on top of the other. Not anything like Mallory's scribble handwriting. Besides, she would've taken up the whole damn wall if it was her.

wE doN't
sEE thiNgs
as thEy aRE,

wE sEE thEm
as wE aRE.
  —aNaïs NiN

I lowered the camera and tried looking through my own eyes instead. The words must've meant something to Mallory. But to me it just felt like a riddle. One I wasn't smart enough or edgy enough or creative enough to understand.

"Screw you, Mallory," I whispered.

I pulled the strap back over my head and stowed her camera in my bag, picked my bike up off the pavement, and glared at the wall one last time before pedaling away.

Off to Bargain Mart, my summer job, the one my parents said would be good for me. Not that they knew a damn thing about what was good for anybody. Not me, and especially not themselves. They've been divorced for four years, yet still live together. They say it's because of financial reasons, but I think it's more that they can't figure out how to actually leave each other. Because if they really left, then they couldn't make each other miserable anymore, and if they couldn't make each other miserable anymore, then they might have to actually feel the effects of all that has happened.

I had no choice but to pass my school to get to Bargain Mart. I had no choice but to pass my school whenever I wanted to get anywhere in this town. And when you pass my school, you can't help but notice the giant boulder perched out on the front lawn: the Carson High School, Home of the Gladiators, Spirit Rock. It had always been decorated with birthday wishes or sports messages like: WIN! GO! NUMBER ONE!

Six months ago the senior class repainted it in Mallory's honor. They let me help too, even though I was only a junior. Because, after all, I was her sister.

We decorated it with bright colors and pictures of white birds and feathers and hearts and crosses and flowers and teardrops, and one of her fellow art student friends even painted a picture of a camera and a volleyball. People wrote out messages like WE LOVE YOU, MALLORY; NEVER FORGOTTEN; TAKEN TOO SOON; and FOREVER IN OUR HEARTS.

The thing was, I didn't even want to help. I'm sure that makes me a terrible person, but what would I say, what *could* I say?

If you've always been defined not as a full-fledged person but solely as another person's polar opposite, and that person no longer exists, do you also cease to exist?

Those were the words I really wanted to paint on the surface of that rock. That was the question that had been on my mind, the one I knew I wasn't supposed to ask out loud. Not that I was some kind of loser, or anything. I was just average. Not popular, not disliked either. Not short or tall, thin or heavy, ugly or pretty, smart or stupid. I've always just done what was expected of me—no more, no less. So I grabbed the paintbrush that someone was holding out to me. The instrument was clumsy and foreign in my hand, and I smeared out a big, crude, blob-shaped heart. Average. Mediocre. Unremarkable.

They patted me on the shoulder and said I was strong and brave and such a good sister, and all kinds of things that weren't really true. It made them feel better to think certain things about me. They were the ones who needed to feel better, after all—they were her friends. They wanted to make me their friend too, like they could hold on to something of her through me. But it didn't take them long to see I was no substitute, no connection to the friend they loved.

Sudden death. That's what they call it when someone just dies and there's not a good explanation as to why, or at least not one that makes sense.

Apparently she was on fire in gym class that day—they were playing volleyball, and volleyball was always her game. She spiked the ball over the net perfectly time after time, they said, scoring point after point. We were told she was laughing when it happened, right before she suddenly stumbled and went down.

Fainted, they thought.

But she was already gone by the time the school nurse got there. She was gone before the ambulance came blaring down the road, before it came to an abrupt stop at the south entrance of our school. Already gone, as the paramedics rushed inside with their equipment. Gone as I watched it all unfolding from the row of windows in fifth-period chemistry—the whole class, even the teacher, had gathered to see what was happening.

Because nothing ever happens in Carson.

Sudden cardiac arrest. The autopsy showed that she'd had an undetected heart condition, an electrical problem. Her heart just stopped. It's extremely rare, they told us. Of course it would be.

· · ·

I was late to work again, so I was assigned to the clearance aisle.

Crouched in the overcrowded lane of miscellaneous junk no one wanted, armed with a pricing gun, I was retagging all the spring merchandise that was never going to sell. Sickening amounts of after-Easter candy, chocolate eggs and bunnies, marshmallow chicks, and egg-painting kits: marked down from 75 percent off to 90 percent off. Then the Mother's Day leftovers: cards, boxed chocolates with the fillings no one likes but for some reason they keep making anyway—like strawberry cream and that weird liquid cherry stuff that tastes like cough syrup—all marked down from 50 percent off to 75 percent off.

For hour after mind-numbing hour, I was at it. The sound of the pricing gun was nicking away at my concentration, never letting me think but never letting me really rest. Every last cell of my brain was emptying out into the monotony of the task, slipping from me and spattering to the shelves of unwanted holiday-themed leftovers.

This was going to be my whole summer.

When my lunch break came, I realized I had rushed out of the house, leaving the brown paper bag containing a cheese sandwich with mustard and a baggie of goldfish crackers sitting in my refrigerator back home. But thankfully, since Bargain Mart sells everything imaginable, from house paint to tires to toys, and makeup and cleaning supplies and food, I bought one of those Styrofoam cup-of-noodle soups, a banana, and a bottle of Dr. Bargain (Bargain Mart's very own Dr Pepper imposter) before heading back to the break room.

I was standing in the microwave line when three kids from my school came in and sat down at one of the big tables, talking loudly about a party that was happening on Friday. I knew all of their names—in a town of only 5,479 people, you tend to know mostly everyone's names—but I didn't really *know* them. They knew me, the way everybody knew me, as Mallory's sister, the sister of the girl who died last year.

I caught bits and pieces of their conversation: "Bonfire, in the woods," one guy said. "At Bowman's?" the girl asked. "Yeah, at Bowman's, where else?" the second guy answered. "Kicking off the summer right," the first guy added, clearly trying to impress the girl.

They talked about Bowman's like Bowman was a linebacker on the football team. But Bowman's isn't a person, at least not anymore; it's a place.

"Oh, hey, Maia," the girl offered when they saw me standing there.

"Hi!" I smiled my big fake smile, and I raised my arm to wave, gestured to my Styrofoam lunch, then the microwave, so they'd know I wasn't just standing there eavesdropping.

"So did you hear about the party at Bowman's?" the girl shouted across the break room.

"I think so," I called back.

"You should come," she said, then quickly looked to her right and left, as if she was silently asking permission, as if she had forgotten what happened the last time I was invited to a party.

No one said anything for several seconds, and then the

first guy chimed in, uncertainly, "Sure, I mean, come if you want."

"Thanks," I managed, also pretending I didn't remember about that party last spring. "I'm pretty sure I'm busy that night, though."

"Bummer," the girl replied, but I could see them exhale a collective breath of relief. It wouldn't do for a trio of underclassman to invite an unwanted guest to a party thrown by our newly graduated senior class.

"Yeah," I agreed, and sighed like it really was a *bummer*.

Thankfully, the microwave beeped just then, the person in front of me retrieved their food, and I could finally extract myself from this conversation. I turned away from them, placed my cup of noodles on the rotating glass tray, shut the door, punched in three minutes, and stood there, watching it spin around and round.

CHRIS

I STABBED AT THE CHICKEN BREAST, AND JUICE OOZED out of the puncture holes left behind by my fork, forming a puddle on the plate. Mom was cutting up her food into tiny bites, working the knife back and forth like she wanted to saw through the kitchen table itself.

Dad was on his second beer and so was Isobel. It seemed like they were silently racing each other. Only, Dad didn't normally drink, so he was already getting slow and goofy. Mom, on the other hand, *did* normally drink. If it was after seven o'clock, you'd be sure to see a glass of red wine attached to her hand and a flush to her cheeks that crawled up from her neck, lasting until she went to bed. But here, she adamantly refused as if it were suddenly a matter of principle. Instead, she had only a glass of ice water that was rapidly collecting condensation in Isobel's non-air-conditioned house, which Mom had already commented on several times.

"You'll need to update this place or it will never sell," Mom told Isobel. Mom was always giving people unsolicited home advice because she was a real estate agent. But this was not simple friendly advice; it was a judgment.

Isobel, ever cool and levelheaded, came back with, "Good thing I'm not selling, then."

Mom held up her hands in front of her, like she was some kind of martyr surrendering a fight, even though she was the one who was trying to get it started. It's always unnerving to see my parents out of context like this, to realize that they're not only my parents, but real people who existed before me, outside me.

It was so quiet, all I could hear were the sounds of each of us chewing; the more I tried to tune it out, the more focused on it I became.

"Well, you made great time," Isobel offered, trying to break the walls of silence surrounding each of us. "Must not have hit any traffic."

Those were the longest ten and a half hours of my life. I considered saying it out loud, but instead stared down at my food.

"You know, Chris," Isobel continued, after no one answered. "I promise there really are things to do here. There's some stores, a few restaurants, a movie theater, even. You could drive into town; it's only about ten minutes or so. The theater only plays old stuff, but still." She paused and looked at me like I should be impressed, then added, "There are kids around who are your age. You might even make some new friends."

My mind rewound the list of small-town amenities, before it replayed the key words. "Wait, did you just say *I* could drive?"

"He *coulddrive?*" Dad echoed, the beer gently slurring his speech.

Mom dropped her fork abruptly and pushed her plate away. She rolled her eyes, which she did every time my dad referred to me as "he." I wondered if she even realized she was doing it, or if it had just become a reflex.

"Seriously?" Mom snapped, glaring across the table at Isobel.

"Why not?" Isobel's voice turned high and sharp, ready to challenge. "I have my old station wagon just sitting there out back."

"That rusted tin can piece of junk?" Mom said, shaking her head. "No way."

Isobel grinned at my mom like they were playing a game and it was just getting interesting. "Hey, it's what's on the inside that counts, little sister." Then she kicked my foot under the table and nodded discreetly, as if to say: *Don't worry. I got this.* "Besides, I just had it inspected the other day. Had to throw on some new brakes, is all. It's perfectly safe, I promise."

Dad nodded to himself and smiled slowly, absently moving the food around on his plate. When he looked up at Mom, her face was a stone—hard and cold and unyielding.

She narrowed her eyes at him, crossed her arms tightly over her stomach, and sat back in her chair. "I'm sorry, is that your way of asking what I think? Since when does that matter?" she asked him. Then suddenly the legs of her chair scraped against the floor, fingernails on a chalkboard, and she was on her feet. For a moment she looked like she wanted to knock my dad over in his chair. But instead she carried her plate to the sink and said, "Excuse me. I have a headache."

Dad watched her walk away, and for a second I thought he was considering going after her. But then he shifted his eyes to Isobel, and lowering his voice, mumbled, "Thanks a lot." And then they both started giggling like they really were still teenagers.

Isobel leaned into me so that I could smell the beer on her breath, and whispered loudly, "All right, I give up. What crawled up her ass?"

I shrugged, but I knew exactly what her problem was. She'd drawn a line between us, and she couldn't stand the fact that this time I wasn't going to cave in and cross back over to her side. I couldn't, even if I wanted to—Mom didn't get that.

"So?" I tried to refocus the conversation on the car subject. "Dad, can I?"

He gave me a long hard look, and sighed through the words. "I'll talk to your mother about it, all right?"

Isobel raised her arm out to me for a fist bump, and then went to the fridge for another round of beers for her and my dad. I finished my salad while they volleyed *remember when* stories across the table, swapping secrets they'd already told each other a million times, laughing while reliving the best moments of their youth—the time she crashed her father's car, the time he snuck out of the house to come see her and got caught, the time when they started a fire in their high school chemistry class, and of course, the inevitable, that time her little sister had a secret crush on her boyfriend and stole him out from under her.

When I left to go upstairs, they barely noticed.

The old floors creaked under my feet as I walked up to my room for the summer. My bags and boxes, mostly full of books—just the essentials—that had served as my friends this past year, were lined up against the wall. The room was furnished with a dresser, a nightstand, and a twin bed, all made of a dark, heavy, clunky wood that looked old yet indestructible. I sat down, and the mattress whimpered, buckling, then bouncing back up.

I grabbed my phone off the nightstand where it had been charging. Coleton had texted me hours ago with a video of a chimpanzee escaping from its enclosure at a zoo. I couldn't help smiling, even though smiling was pretty much the last thing I wanted to do right then.

I responded: Haha, very funny

He texted back immediately: thought you'd appreciate! :) Then, after a calculated pause: soooo . . . you doing ok?

Was I okay? I had no idea, but I couldn't deal with him worrying about me again.

I'm fine, just preparing to be bored to death for the next two months

I saw that he was typing a response—we still hadn't discussed what had happened the other day, or how angry he was, how scared I'd made him. I didn't want to have that conversation right now, so I cut him off before he could send it:

thanks for the video. I'm beat, though. Going to bed (the passive aggression of the day was exhausting)

Cole's typing stopped, then started back up again: OK, later.

I made my way over to the pile of things that were mine, but, like my parents downstairs, they seemed out of place, not really mine anymore. I sifted through until I found my telescope, its tripod, the eyepieces safely stored in their cases. It made me feel better knowing it was here. I'd bought it second-hand with my own money, saved from ten- and twenty-dollar bills stuffed in birthday cards from various relatives over the years. My parents would've bought it for me new, they said, but I wanted to make sure something this important was really all mine, something that they couldn't take away from me.

They can take a lot, and they have, but not my telescope. And they can't take away the feeling I get when I look up into the night sky at the stars I've come to know so well, all at various stages between being born and dying. "'We are made of star-stuff,'" I whispered to myself. Carl Sagan famously said it decades ago; I have a poster with that quote hanging on my bedroom wall back home. That's what I think about when I feel alone. That's what I see when I look out there into the universe. It means we're all connected. Everything we are and everything we know, everything we see and touch and feel, life, all of it came from out there. Except the real beauty of it is, when you get down to it, there is no *out there* or *in here*.

When a star goes supernova, expanding until it can no longer withstand its own gravitational force, it collapses and

explodes, and from its remains comes all of this. We exist—
everything we are—because a star died. Sometimes I wonder
if maybe this is what religion feels like. It does for me.

I stood in the center of my new bedroom for a moment,
not sure what to do. I thought of Mom downstairs in one
room, and Dad and Isobel in another, me up here, and
Coleton 687 miles away. I thought of this house sitting by
itself in the middle of nowhere, and I wasn't feeling very
connected, not feeling *one* with anything, not even myself.

I opened the narrow closet door and pulled on the string
that dangled down in front of my face. Attached to the end
of it was a rabbit's foot key chain, with tie-dye-colored fur.
A bare bulb flickered to life, illuminating the stash of empty
wire hangers swaying gently on the rod. I pulled on the rabbit's foot again, feeling the tiny claws press into my palm, and
the light went back out. For a second I wondered if maybe
this was my mom's bedroom when she was growing up here. I
wasn't sure if I could bring myself to ask her, though.

I shut the closet door, and when I spun around to face the
other side of the room, I realized that there was another door,
this one with a lock and an opaque, stained glass window in the
center. The setting sunlight was glowing dimly through its mot-
tled surface. I walked over, turned the dead bolt, and pulled
on the handle. The door stuck like it hadn't been opened in a
while, suctioned shut with moisture and wind and time. But
finally the seal cracked and the door popped open with a low
moan. It led outside to a small square deck suspended in the
air. I stepped out cautiously, taking mental note of the busted
railing on one side. Like everything else in this house, the deck

looked worn and tired. It was held up by what appeared to be flimsy wooden stilts, planted in the ground below. But as I took small steps toward the edge, I realized it was sturdier than it appeared. A ladder had been built in between the beams that supported it, and when I leaned over the edge, I saw that there were several rungs missing.

I looked across the field, and, to my surprise, there was another house. This one sat far back from the road and had a paved driveway instead of gravel and dirt. Landscaping and blue siding and shutters flanked each window. Even in the fading light I could tell it was a lot newer than Isobel's house. Though there was also an old barn sitting adjacent to the house that looked more like an antique: some odd choice of lawn decoration or house accessory. It was missing bits here and there, making me doubt there were any livestock residents.

I'm sure my mom would have an opinion about it, something to do with curb appeal.

Sitting down on the old planks of wood, I took a deep breath and looked up. Aside from Coleton and my books, the stars had been my friends too—probably my most reliable friends these past few years. They're constant, even when everything else is changing. Though I guess they're changing too, just more slowly. I lay down on my back and kicked off my sneakers, folding my arms behind my head as a pillow.

The sky out here was so clear, so wide open.

I could see Jupiter overhead, and Saturn rising up above the tree line in the southeast, Ursa Major, Ursa Minor, Polaris, each one exactly where it was supposed to be, each one telling me exactly where I was.

MAIA

A SLOW ACHE WAS BUILDING IN MY CHEST AS I RODE my bike away from Bargain Mart. Past the school, with its Spirit Rock that never ceased to make me feel like the shittiest sister on the face of the earth. Then past the gas station where that graffiti was still taunting me, even hidden around the back of the building where I couldn't see it. As I pedaled on, I wished hard that I had somewhere else to go but home.

I regretted not going to the beach with my friends. I was going to be feeling sad and crappy anyway; it would've been nice to at least feel that way in a different setting.

I rode my bike down all the familiar empty streets, alongside the fields and small farms and sparse houses where nothing was ever out of the ordinary. I pedaled out a steady pace—not too slow, not too fast—one that I knew would get me home right as it would become too dark to see.

Something was different when I approached my house. I

couldn't tell what it was at first, and then I realized: It wasn't my house that was different; it was my neighbor's. There was an extra car in the driveway, extra lights on in the house.

It's so pathetic that I know that.

Even more pathetic, it actually made me feel excited for a second, the thought of something, *anything*, being different.

I left my bike on the front lawn and tried not to make too much noise as I entered the house. Someone had left the kitchen light on for me. Mom, probably. It was barely even nine p.m., and they'd already sent themselves to bed.

I understood, in a way. It was still weird to be at home without Mallory, because when she was here, she was always doing something interesting, talking about something fascinating, keeping us entertained with her daily revelations, her quirky observations. When she was around, you could almost forget how screwed up our family was, even back then.

But there's nothing like a tragedy to shine a spotlight on all of our already-weak places, like fractures in a bone that never quite healed. Some families might pull together in their grief and become stronger, but with mine, it just seemed to strain all those places that wanted so badly to snap.

I opened the fridge, and there was the lunch I'd packed this morning. Sitting down at the kitchen table, I opened the crumpled brown bag, unwrapped my cheese sandwich, and ate it in silence, peeling the crusts away, as I always did. Mallory used to think I was weird for doing that. "Why don't you just cut the crusts off when you make it?" she would ask me every time I ate a sandwich.

I shrugged and whispered, out loud, "I don't know."

Just then, I thought I heard footsteps creaking up the basement stairs. I stopped chewing so I could listen. Nothing. I swallowed. Then I heard the sound again, only this time the steps were retreating. Dad. He was probably coming up to use the bathroom. I almost wanted to call out, let him know it was just me in here. But I didn't.

So, I sat alone in the kitchen, the crunching sound of the little goldfish crackers between my teeth amplified inside my head. The whole rest of the house was dark. Dad was down in the basement with his tiny TV. Mom was upstairs in her bedroom with her romance novels. Our dog, Roxie, was no doubt in Mallory's bedroom eternally waiting for her to come home each night.

We couldn't even blame our current state of affairs on Mallory. I still remember how my parents sat me and Mallory down and explained it, as if we were children. They said it was no one's fault. But we knew exactly what had happened: Dad had cheated on Mom. Whether it was a one-time thing, like he swore, or a relationship, as she insisted, it didn't matter. It was over. And everything that our lives had been before was over too.

They said they hadn't been happy in a long time, which was news to me—I'd thought they were really happy. I'd thought we were all happy. But Mallory wasn't surprised. She had seen something I hadn't. They said they were going to put our house up for sale; they were going to go their separate ways. They said we'd spend equal time with both of them. And they loved us.

Then they did all kinds of repairs and updates on the house that they'd been putting off for years. Replaced the leaky roof, updated the plumbing, redid the kitchen, and renovated the inside of the old barn. New vinyl siding on the house and professional landscaping. They dropped the price, and dropped the price again. But it never sold, and now neither of them could afford to move out without the money from the house. So, Dad moved into the newly finished basement, and Mom had the new master bedroom with the walk-in closet and the claw-foot tub she'd always wanted.

Mallory and I were supposed to share the barn, but it became hers. Her studio. Her sanctuary. She had her art. She had her dreams, her plans. Me, I never had much of a plan, didn't have dreams, at least not the kind you need extra space to make come true. My dreams were more nebulous, less concrete. Did I want to get out of this town someday? Of course.

But it's hard to figure out what you're supposed to be when you've never even really known who you were in the first place—that was something I'd realized only recently. Something I didn't think my friends would understand. After all, I looked the same and dressed the same and talked the same as I always had. But I wasn't the same.

I crumpled up my brown bag and threw it into the garbage can under the sink. I took my sneakers off so I wouldn't make any noise as I walked up the stairs to my bedroom. As I passed Mallory's room, Roxie looked up quickly, then set her head back down on the blanket at the foot of the bed and sighed.

I closed my bedroom door silently, peeled off my grimy Bargain Mart T-shirt, and got into my pajamas. I walked over to the window, like I did every night, even though the view never changed.

But that night it had.

It was too far to see clearly, but the door on the second floor was wide open; light from inside the room spilled out onto the wooden deck. There was someone out there. I watched for a while, but they didn't move.

I turned off my light, fell into bed, and stared at the ceiling, listening to the silence all around me. *I really should've gone to the beach*, I thought as I closed my eyes.

CHRIS

A DOOR SLAMMED SOMEWHERE. IT SHOOK ME AWAKE, my brain and body scrambling to remember where I was. I lifted my head and looked at the old clock radio on the nightstand, its neon-green numbers blinking 12:00, 12:00, 12:00.

The room came into focus in bits and pieces. The light was different here, slanting in through the slits in the blinds. And the morning sounds—they were different too. No garbage trucks rumbling or neighbors' dogs barking, or car alarms being set off. Just birds: a whole orchestra of whistling and whispering, knocking and tapping, the call and response of an indecipherable language.

I reached for the notebook I kept on the nightstand, the pen clipped to the cover, and I scribbled a note to myself to look up what kinds of birds live around here. Lots of the great scientists kept journals: Albert Einstein, Marie Curie, Thomas Edison, countless others. I had a whole stack of full notebooks at home, hidden in a shoe box at the back of my closet. I kept thinking maybe someday I'd look back on them and realize I had some brilliant idea, the missing piece to a problem I would be trying to solve years from now.

I wished I could've stayed in bed. But that would have been too much like surrendering. So I dragged myself up to my feet, opened the door, and stepped outside onto the deck. I heard voices down below, so I crept to the edge without the railing and leaned over to see. My mom stood there with her hands firmly planted on her hips, showered and dressed, as if she'd been up for hours and was ready to get this day over with. To get her time with me over with. Isobel hovered behind Dad, who was hunched under the open hood of her old station wagon. Then Dad moved around to the driver's side and leaned in to start it. The engine choked and sputtered, and for a second I worried it wasn't going to turn over, but then it roared to life.

They all stood there, watching for any signs of malfunction. But it stayed strong. Dad nodded in approval, then looked to Mom.

"Fine," she said.

"You're sure?" he asked.

"I said fine."

Isobel glanced over her shoulder at that moment, as if she had somehow known I was watching. We exchanged a quick smile before I raced back inside to shower and get dressed.

I went downstairs and I played the game. Acted surprised when Mom and Dad told me they'd let me use the car for the summer. Acted grateful when they said I could take it for a test drive by myself. Acted like they were being reasonable when they said if I wasn't back in five minutes, they'd change their minds about the whole thing.

Maybe I really was a flight risk. If I was, it was only because they'd kept me locked away like a prisoner for the last year. They thought they were protecting me—I got that. But what *they* didn't get was that they were suffocating me in the process.

The station wagon was a total piece of shit. But it was my piece of shit now. Turning the key in the ignition that first time, feeling the car rumble to life all around me, was freedom.

The car wasn't so much a color, as it was rust and patches of faded paint. The old leather seats were so worn and soft and holey that the foam was popping through in a million different places. I flipped the visor down, and it nearly fell off into my lap. The AC didn't work, and all I could smell was motor oil. I rolled all the windows down by hand, adjusted the mirrors, and had to really work the sticky gear to shift it into drive. My parents and Isobel all stood and watched as I eased the car down the gravel driveway and turned out onto the road.

Once I was out of their view, I spun the dial on the radio, but all I got was static. I reached over and popped open the glove box—it was jammed full of papers and an assortment of dusty old cassette tapes that had to have been sitting there since the nineties. Their plastic cases cascaded onto the floor of the passenger side. I reached over and grabbed one of the tapes, tried to read the faded handwritten words scrawled on the paper label.

I looked up just in time to swerve.

MAIA

I WOKE UP WITH THAT PICTURE IN MY HEAD. SO I threw on a hoodie and rode my bike out to the gas station again. I brought Mallory's camera with me again. Stared at the words again. Felt each one weighing down on me, again.

The longer I stood there contemplating them, the less sense they made.

"What do you want from me?" I said out loud.

I honestly didn't know if I was talking to Mallory or myself. I tried to take in a deep gulp of air, but it was laced with gasoline, and the smell went straight to my head. Suddenly a tidal wave of dizziness rolled through my whole body—it was either because of the gas fumes in the air or the fact that I was pretty sure I was developing an iron deficiency from trying to be vegetarian in a place that doesn't *do* vegetarian.

I looked at the wall again, the handwriting, the words, and I shook my head.

I wasn't sure what I actually believed about the whole life-and-death-spirit-world-afterlife thing. My parents' approach to religion was pretty progressive; they wanted us to choose for ourselves. Dad is Christian, but not the church-every-Sunday kind of Christian. Mom is Jewish, but like Dad, not the temple-every-Shabbat kind of Jew. Combine those with growing up in Carson, a *very* church-every-Sunday kind of Christian place, and Mallory and I were sort of left to our own devices.

Mallory had mixed and matched belief systems and had said recently that she felt more Buddhist than anything else. Me, I always thought of myself as a religious independent. I prayed. Sometimes, anyway. But it was always less *to* any specific entity and more of a just-putting-it-out-there sort of thing.

Our family traditions were as follows:

1. We had a small handcrafted wooden cross that always hung in the hallway, along with a mezuzah affixed to the doorframe outside on an angle.
2. We celebrated Christmas and Hanukkah every year with both a tree and a menorah.
3. Easter *and* Seder.
4. Eggnog *and* Manischewitz.

We kept things pretty basic. Focused on the holidays— light the candles, sing the songs, open the presents. It's not like we ever really talked about the big-picture stuff. *Like, hypothetically, if one of us were to die tomorrow, what do we all believe happens next?*

I breathed deep, in through my nose, out through my mouth. My dizzy spell was beginning to lift the way the sunlight had burned off the morning fog that clung to the road.

I left without any answers, only more questions.

On my way home the muscles in my thighs burned. I pedaled hard as I came up the hill. I knew I should've braked when I started to come down, but I pushed until the tires were spinning so fast, my legs were whipping around, feet flailing from the pedals. I squeezed the hand brakes too quickly, and for a moment I teetered back and forth, catching myself just in time.

After coasting to a stop in the middle of the road, I planted my feet firmly on the ground and stared down the straight, narrow, two-lane road, struggling to catch my breath. I tried not to think about my house sitting there just another mile away, or my neighbor's house, or the view from my window that never changed—this whole town that always stayed the same, save for my sister's absence. All this wide-open space, sometimes it felt like there was nothing but me for miles. Sometimes I loved that feeling; other times it was hell.

I focused on the breeze hitting my skin, the scent of rain on the air, the clouds collecting overhead. I watched as they moved faster: one dense gray fleet of clouds growing closer, eclipsing the soft white cottony ones that floated behind. Out of nowhere, a giant dark storm cloud was suddenly backlit by the sun, still hanging low in the sky. The silver lining shimmered around the edges, and I could feel it in my bones. Something was happening.

This was another one of her pictures. Almost exactly.

I reached around to pull Mallory's camera out of my bag. The clouds seemed to be holding still, waiting for me. I quickly looped the strap around my neck and positioned the camera, adjusting the lens—the long road fading in the distance, the trees like a tunnel, and then the open sky with its competing clouds and magical light—this was practically the same picture I had seen pinned up on the wall of the barn.

I lowered the camera for a second and closed my eyes. My hands went to their familiar spots on my handlebars, fingers fitting into the indentations imprinted in the foam. I steadied myself, filled my lungs with air, and tried to feel whatever it was she had felt.

It was like I could taste everything—the sun, the clouds, the trees, the coming rain, the road, my past, my future—on my tongue. Mallory had been here. Now I was here. But somehow I never even heard the car coming.

CHRIS

I SLAMMED ON THE BRAKES. THE TIRES SKIDDED AND spun and screeched. My body lurched forward against the seat belt before it slammed me back again. My heart was skipping beats, my hands sweating as they gripped the rubbery steering wheel.

No impact, no crash, no screams. Those were the important things.

But there, in the center of the road, inches from my front bumper, was a girl. She had one foot planted on either side of a bicycle that looked to be just about as old as this car, with a canvas bag strapped across her body and a big fancy-looking camera hanging from a strap around her neck.

Perfectly still, she stared at me through the dirty windshield. I held my breath, waiting for her to freak out or go off on me. But she didn't. There was something in her eyes I couldn't read, an emotion on her face I didn't know. Not surprise, and not fear. She was calm. I was the one who was scared—frozen scared.

She removed her hands from the handlebars and lifted the camera in front of her face—took a picture. Then she lowered the camera again, and when she looked at me, for just a second, I thought I saw the beginning of a smile get caught in the corner of her mouth. She kicked her foot against the ground and took off without so much as a word.

Shaking, I managed to turn the cumbersome vehicle around with something akin to a ten-point turn. Heading back the way I'd come, I left a wide margin of space between us as I approached her. I drifted alongside, watching her closely. She was sockless in a pair of grass-stained Converse, and I realized her pants were pajama bottoms. Underneath a faded hoodie that had "CHS" stamped across the back, her plain white tee was threadbare, like it had been washed a thousand times.

She had thick, dark hair, pulled back in a loose braid that was coming apart. Either she hadn't planned on being seen or she just simply didn't care. I always admired people like that; I wished I could get away with not worrying so much about what I looked like. Long dark strands of hair kept getting caught in the wind, whipping around her face and shoulders like ribbon, forcing me to notice the curve of her neck—it was long and slender. It made her look elegant, even in pajama pants.

I stuck my head out the window and opened my mouth. I was about to say sorry, to ask if she was okay, but she looked straight ahead as if I wasn't there. In profile, her jaw was set, determined in a way that made me not want to interrupt, even to apologize. It suddenly seemed like anything I could say wouldn't be enough anyway.

"Hey, I . . . I'm sorry. I didn't mean to—"

"It's fine!" she yelled, without even glancing over at me.

"You're okay?" I called out the window.

But she didn't answer. Instead, she stood up on the pedals and pressed forward even faster.

I slowed to a stop and pulled off into the dirt by the side of the road. She looked back once as I watched her speed away. Just as she disappeared from sight, a raindrop hit the windshield.

Part of me wanted to know where she was coming from, where she was going. But I turned the car off and took a deep breath. My neck ached, and it felt like the seat belt had cut right across my shoulder and torso. I pressed my hand against my chest; my heart was still racing and I could already feel the bruises blooming up under my skin, tender and sore. They weren't bad, not the kind that settle in your bones. The memory of those kinds of bruises stole my breath for a second, icing my skin and raising the fine hairs on my arms. With a shiver, I shoved that old thought right back where it had come from.

By the time I got back to Isobel's, it was pouring. The three of them were still waiting on the porch when I pulled up the driveway. When they asked how the drive went, I left out the part where I almost killed someone.

MAIA

I MADE IT TO MY HOUSE JUST BEFORE THE RAIN. I LEFT my bike on the lawn and ran up the steps, Mallory's camera slung over my shoulder. My heart was racing, but not because I was scared. It was because I was so alive. Right then. So there, so *in* it.

I wondered if that was how Mallory had felt all the time. I looked around, wanting to tell someone what had just happened. I could call Hayden. She'd think it was weird. Funny, maybe. But then I'd have to explain what I was doing standing in the middle of the road in my pajamas. And I couldn't explain that to her—I could barely even explain that to myself.

I pulled the camera off me quickly; I didn't want my parents to see. They wouldn't like me touching her things, especially something as important as her camera. As I held it in my hands, I realized what I had done. I had taken a picture—I mean, not a real picture, because there wasn't any film, but still—it wasn't a *Mallory* picture.

I don't know why. Or how. It was an accident, or maybe it wasn't. Maybe I had wanted to see what the scene would've looked like to Mallory. Or maybe Mallory was the one who'd done it. Maybe she'd showed up then, stepped into my skin, and pressed down on the shutter button. I never used to believe in stuff like that, but losing someone the way we lost Mallory—that will make you believe in things you never thought you would.

I don't know why I didn't hear the car coming, or why he didn't see me until it was almost too late. But if I hadn't stopped, if I hadn't waited, if I had moved even an inch in the other direction, he would've hit me.

I stood there, the rain pinging against the tin roof awning, breathing in huge lungfuls of air, and watched that same station wagon pull into my neighbor's driveway, extra slowly, overly cautious. As he got out of the car and jogged up to the house, I wondered who he was—I knew for sure I'd never seen him around before.

His slim, soccer-player-like frame wasn't a Carson look. In a meat-and-potatoes town where ketchup was still a vegetable and where boys were beefy and bred for football, I would've remembered seeing him.

I heard stirring inside the house and fumbled to stuff the camera into my bag. I kicked my shoes off in the doorway and tried to make my way through the kitchen and up the stairs to my room as quietly as possible.

"Morning, cupcake," my dad said. He was sitting at the

table with the paper open. He didn't ask where I'd been, and I didn't tell him. In some ways it was nice to have so much freedom—but in other ways it felt like they'd simply given up on parenting.

As I sat down across from him, the straight line of his mouth softened.

"Any good news today?" I asked.

"Nope." He sighed and folded the paper in half, looking up at me for the first time. "The world's still going to hell."

I nodded; he laughed. This used to be our morning bit. Back when laughter and easy conversation were still permitted in our house, before everything was ruined. For just a second, things almost felt the way they used to. But then Mom waltzed into the kitchen. She was on a mission, headed straight for the coffeepot. She jumped when she saw us sitting there together.

"Oh," she said. Then, to me, pointedly, "Good morning, Maia."

I said "Hi" and immediately felt guilty. I was now the only rope in their tug of war. It wasn't fair. Loving one automatically made me a traitor to the other. There was no way to be fair anymore.

"Well," Dad said, standing up and clutching his paper like it was all he had in the world. I waited to see if he'd say anything else, but that was it. He was careful not to make eye contact with Mom as he drifted out of the room like a ghost, his footsteps on the stairs to the basement echoing through the silence he left behind.

Mom cleared her throat, and proceeded to add her two

spoonfuls of stevia, pouring her fat-free half-and-half into her coffee. "So," she began, with a plastered-on smile, like she was playing the part of a mother rather than really being one. "What's on the docket for you today?"

"I don't know," I began. And now I felt like I was playing the role of a daughter rather than actually being one. "I'll probably go over to Hayden's for a while," I lied. Hayden was at the beach, where I should've been.

She nodded as she took a sip from her mug.

I started biting the edge of my fingernail absently.

"Stop that," she said, laughing in that hollow, forced way she did when she was nervous. Sometimes I think it made her nervous to be my mother, to be *a* mother, like she didn't want to let me get too close. Maybe losing one daughter had put her off parenting altogether.

I set my hands in my lap. Thankfully, right on cue, Roxie shuffled into the kitchen. She was like one of those dogs who can sense when a person's blood sugar is getting too low, except she always knew when the tension in the house was getting too high and one of us needed her to be a buffer.

In her failing eyesight, she held her nose to the air for a moment, then started toward my mother and stopped short when she bumped up against her legs. "Good girl," Mom whispered, bending over to run her hands through Roxie's shaggy mane, kissing the top of her head as she moved the long fur away from her eyes. Something tugged like a knot being tightened in my stomach as I watched them. My mom was closer to a half-blind, sometimes-incontinent, smelly old dog than she was to me. I'd had this realization many times over this past year, but it always affected me the same as if it was the first time.

"Oh, did I tell you I ran into Isobel at the grocery store the other day?" Mom began, straightening up quickly, as if she had exciting news. "She said her nephew's coming to stay with her for the summer. I never even heard they had another child. Chris, I think." She paused and looked at me as if I was supposed to say something. "Not sure what the story is there. I didn't ask, but I got the distinct feeling maybe he got into some kind of trouble back home."

"Mom . . . ," I said slowly, grinning, "are you gossiping?" She had always warned me and Mallory about busybodies and rumormongers, said they weren't to be trusted, said gossip was the lowest form of social interaction.

"No." She laughed at herself, though, because she knew I was right. "I'm just passing along news that could potentially be relevant."

"Uh-huh."

"I am!" she said, swatting her hand at me from across the room. "All I'm saying is, be friendly when you see him, of course, but maybe not too friendly."

For a second it felt like old times, but then we heard Dad's footsteps on the stairs, coming back up again, and that fleeting, wispy moment just slipped away.

Mom rushed out of the house, then Dad behind her, both of them careful not to cross paths again. Roxie walked over to me and lay down at my feet with a huff. I scratched her behind the ears before I stood up and made my way to the kitchen window. Across the field, through the sheets of rain, I could see the station wagon parked in my neighbor's driveway.

"Chris," I whispered, feeling myself smile as I rolled his name around in my head a few times. *Chris. Chris. Chris.*

CHRIS

MOM AND DAD LEFT THE NEXT MORNING, EARLIER
than they needed to. I helped put their bags back into the car,
and then we all congregated on the porch.

Dad hugged me tight, activating those seat belt bruises
that had indeed appeared hours after my near accident in
Isobel's station wagon. He kissed me on the cheek, and then
gave me one of those swift, firm guy pats on the back for good
measure. "Only a phone call away, Chris," he reminded me
yet again.

When it was Mom's turn to say good-bye, I honestly didn't
know what would happen. She opened her arms, uncertainly.
I moved in to give her a hug, but her body went rigid, as if she
was trying to keep space between us. When we parted, she
opened her mouth, but it was like she couldn't force herself
to say anything remotely kind or comforting or reassuring, so
she didn't. As Isobel and I stood there watching them drive

away, I felt a lump in my throat, bubbling up slowly from somewhere in my chest. I coughed out a quick laugh, only to keep it from choking me.

Isobel turned to me. "What's so funny?"

I shook my head, because of course nothing was funny at all.

"What?" Isobel repeated, smiling, waiting to be in on the joke.

"She hates me, doesn't she?" I asked, although it really wasn't a question so much as an observation.

Isobel's smile faded. She wrapped her arm around my shoulder and gave a little shake. "Come on, don't say that."

"Why not? It's true. She fucking hates me."

"Your mother does not hate you, I promise. She just—she needs more time, that's all."

I nodded, tried to believe she was right.

"And by the way," she added, an afterthought, "you really shouldn't say 'fucking' in front of your aunt. I mean, who the fuck raised you, anyway?"

I laughed. Hard. Isobel always seemed to know what to say to make me feel better.

She sat down on the top step, patting the spot next to her. "On the bright side," she continued as I sat down, "your dad seems to be handling it all really well."

It's true, he was. Or at least, he thought he was.

Yesterday he'd offered to help me set up my telescope, which he'd never shown any interest in before. And last night before it got dark, he took me to the garage and said I was going to help him fix the gutter falling off the side of Isobel's house. He handed me tools from my grandfather's workbench, one by one, telling me what each one was called—brackets and hangers and screws and drill bits. When he placed the power drill in my hands, it felt heavier than it looked. I wondered if he would have asked me for help last summer, back when my voice was still high and light.

We carried the tall, rickety ladder and set it up next to the side of the house. Dad climbed up one side of the ladder, and I climbed up the other. He seemed so confident in me when he told me to keep a firm hand underneath the gutter while he drilled the screws in place. He smiled like he was proud. I'm not sure if he was proud of *me*, per se. Maybe he was proud of himself for trying to get on board, in whatever way he knew how.

Then to top it off, he took me outside and popped the hood of the station wagon, started showing me where to check the oil and coolant, and demonstrated how to go about changing a tire. It was like he was trying to have some kind of odd medley of makeup, rite-of-passage, TV-father-son moments with me, all over the course of two days. When I casually told him how I would've gladly done stuff like this with him even before, he just said, "I know that," but I think he missed the point I was trying, gently, to make: My ability to use tools and fix things had nothing to do with whether I was a man or not.

"Yeah, I know," I finally told Isobel. "It's weird, though. I thought for sure it would end up being the other way around—just when I thought I had them figured out, they go and change things up on me."

"You know, that's probably what they're thinking about you too, kid."

She had me there. I tried to look at everything from their point of view. I really did. But I was still so confused about their reactions. Mom had always been the one who was cool about everything, so understanding, so supportive of anything I ever wanted to do or be.

In second grade when I wanted to quit Girl Scouts after the first meeting.

In third grade when I flipped out backstage at the school concert because of the dress, the tights, and the fucking bow in my hair that matched the rest of the girls in the chorus.

In fourth grade when I told them that I despised the name Christina and would only answer to Chris from then on, which is what most everyone called me anyway.

In fifth grade when I refused to try on anything but boy's clothes during our annual back-to-school shopping trip.

In sixth grade when she finally let me get the haircut I really wanted. I remember it so clearly, the way the hairdresser was beaming as she spun me around in the chair to face the mirror, how it felt to run my hands along the shaved sides of my head. That was the first time I'd ever looked at myself and thought, *This is me.*

In seventh grade when I told them I liked girls.

In eighth grade when things got really bad and I was getting bullied every day about my hair and clothes and liking girls.

And then in ninth grade, I really started to feel like a stranger in my body, the body that had served me so well up until then. The body that used to feel so light and free and unencumbered, the body that could run faster than any other kid in the neighborhood, the body that had always felt strong and lean, was suddenly weighed down with new softness and curves that more than embarrassed me; they made me want to hide away from the world, from myself. It wasn't that I felt ashamed, exactly, just wrong. And the worst part was that this new body seemed to come with a whole new set of rules, expectations of ways I was supposed to think and act and be. Maybe those rules had always been there, but they were now being ruthlessly enforced at every turn.

When I talked to Mom about it, she tried to tell me every girl feels what I felt. But I wondered if that could be true. Could it be possible that every girl could feel, in such excruciating exactness, the world rearranging itself around her, setting up all new borders and limits? Was every girl walking around in such pain, feeling the price of her body like I did? Maybe. But for me, that price was too high. I wasn't just losing myself; I was becoming someone I was not. And that scared me.

Anyway, Mom was the one who dealt with all of that.

Dad, he was good when it came to the fun stuff. It was easy to cheer me on at the track meets, and it was easy to say "good job" when I brought home straight As. But with everything else, he just sort of kept his distance, nodding along. He didn't have much of an opinion on anything, and was content to let Mom do the heavy lifting. I try not to think about a lot of the things that happened before.

Running helps. It always has. I took the gravel driveway down to the main road, and my feet immediately fell into an easy rhythm with my breathing. I was getting stronger every day. The sun was going down at my back, my shadow stretching out before me, measuring the pace, pulling me forward, keeping me company as I sped past the field and the blue house and the barn and the trees.

When I was driving this road the other day, I hadn't noticed the incline, but I felt it now, burning into my muscles, hurting in the best way. It was like my body could gauge when I'd reached one mile, two miles, three. It was then that my lungs started to ache, the pressure in my ribs becoming almost too much. But I ran harder, ran through it. I told myself to push just a little farther. Keep breathing. Keep moving.

Up ahead, I saw another gravel driveway spilling out onto the road, and I let myself slow down to a jog—I'd make it to the driveway and then circle back around and return the way I'd come. But as I reached it, I saw that the driveway quickly got lost beneath a thick cover of overgrown weeds and brush. There was a chain strung between two of the big trees alongside the driveway with a sign attached that read: PRIVATE PROPERTY. I tried to peer in, but it was just woods as far as I could see. Yet something caught my eye, a spark of metal glinting in the sunlight.

I looked both ways to make sure there was no one in sight before I stepped over the chain. A few feet in, I could see that it was a handlebar: a bike. I was sure it was her bike, the girl who I almost ran over. An image of her flashed through my mind like a photograph: the pajama pants and her neck and her hair flying through the wind.

I could make out the beginnings of a foot-trodden dirt

path. I took one step, and a wave of panic sliced through me. The familiar pinpricks in my chest, the uneven breaths I couldn't control, shallow then deep, my whole body flashing hot then cold, the sensation in my fingertips going tingly. It was that old fear working its way, slow and mean, through my body, because the last time I'd followed a dirt path leading into the woods, I'd almost died.

Usually I practiced after school on the track, but when the weather was nice like it was that day—the perfect end-of-September chill in the air—our coach would let us run on the trails that wove through the woods behind the school. Coleton had joined track that year. I think partially just to hang out with me, but mostly to appease his parents. They didn't like the fact that he sat around playing video games and reading comic books and watching sci-fi movies and getting into heated debates online about all of the above. His parents never really got him, and they hated that other kids thought he was a weirdo, but that's probably why we became friends in the first place.

When we started high school, his parents told him he needed to join something, expand his social circle. Which was code for: I made them *very* nervous. They thought it was my fault that he was constantly getting bullied, and I knew they blamed me for that time someone had written *HOMO* on his locker in giant red letters. I knew they called him names like that for hanging out with me, even though it didn't even make any sense because I was a girl. Well, sort of.

Anyway, he wasn't very fast and didn't have much stamina.

I tried to hold back that day, since it was just the two of us on the trail, but I left him behind pretty quickly.

Underneath the music from my headphones, I thought I heard someone call out my name. I thought maybe it was Cole, but when I turned, I saw it was another kid from school: Ben. He was off the path a ways, deeper in the woods, along with two other boys from my class, Tobey and Jake. That part wasn't too unusual; sometimes kids cut through the woods on their way home.

"Hey, wait up!" Ben shouted.

That was the part that was unusual. I glanced behind me again, not thinking much of it because he couldn't possibly be talking to me. We'd gone to the same school our entire lives, and I don't think Ben and I had ever exchanged even one word. But there he was, jogging up behind me. I slowed down and came to a stop too abruptly, messing up my rhythm.

"Huh?" I finally answered, pulling my earbuds out, music seeping into the air.

"Dude, you gotta come see this," he said to me in this relaxed way, like we talked all the time. "We got some fireworks," he continued, gesturing behind him to where Tobey and Jake were waiting. "We're about to go set 'em off. You wanna come?"

I shrugged, pretending to consider it before politely declining. "No, I don't think so," I said, trying to catch my breath. "I gotta keep moving." I took a couple of steps, about to sprint off before my heart rate went down too much.

"Fine," he said, holding up his hands like I'd insulted him. "Just trying to be friendly. Sorry. Won't happen again." This was another one of those unspoken rules I'd been getting more and more familiar with. When you're a girl, some boys will try to make you feel guilty for saying no, regardless of the circumstance. The truly terrible part is that sometimes they succeed.

I should've known better. But it felt so damn good to think, even for one misguided second, that maybe they really were just trying to be friendly. That maybe they saw me. Not the *tomboy*, not the *dyke*, not the *freak*. Just *me*. Wasn't Mom always saying I needed to give people a chance to see how great I really was on the inside?

"Wait," I said as he started walking away. "I guess I can come for a minute."

He twisted around and smiled, saying, "Cool," in that casual way. "Come on."

As I followed the three of them deeper into the woods, getting farther off the path, I kept looking behind me to see if maybe Coleton had caught up after all. But there was no one in sight.

A small voice inside me whispered just one word: *Run.*

But I had gotten pretty good at ignoring the voices in my head.

MAIA

SOME PLACES ARE HAUNTED BY THE THINGS THAT happened there, but I believe there are other places that are haunted by ideas. I think the Bowman House is haunted in both ways. Only a few miles down the road from where I live, the Bowmans would've been my next closest neighbor after Isobel, if the house were still standing.

There were a lot of stories about what happened, whether it was arson or simply old electrical work, and whether Mr. and Mrs. Bowman and their teenage son died in the house, or later at the hospital. It was back sometime in the 1940s, and I don't think anyone's ever bothered checking the facts. Kids have always used it as a hangout on the weekends, throwing parties, doing séances and stuff like that—my parents said that's how it was even when they were my age.

I've been coming here a lot lately too, but not for that reason.

The Bowman House had always been scary to me, but I came here right after Mallory died because this was one of her favorite spots. She said it was because something intense and important had happened here, and that means something. The whole house burned. Only the foundation remained, along with portions of stone walls and the brick fireplace and hearth that leads up to the chimney and stretches all the way past what would've been the second story, standing still amid the rubble.

She had taken endless pictures here. The house had a story to tell, she said, and she wanted to help give it a voice. The Bowman House photos were the series of photographs she submitted to the magazine in DC to get the job she would never start.

She thought it was magical; I thought she was morbid.

I had her camera with me now, wishing I could see things through her eyes, see what made this place so beautiful to her. I was sitting cross-legged on the crumbling concrete slab, gazing up at the chimney, trying to listen to that story Mallory said the house had to tell, but my mind kept drifting back to my own near-death experience out on the road.

I heard something behind me, rustling through the leaves. I figured it was just a bird or squirrel, but then a stick snapped too close. I twisted around quickly and saw that it was him—*Chris*.

"Oh, sorry," he said, once he realized he'd startled me. "I was just—"

"God, creepy much?" I muttered. My cheeks flushed, embarrassed that I'd been caught doing something weird—listening to the house—embarrassed that I'd just said something really rude, and finally embarrassed for *being* embarrassed. Mallory never got embarrassed, never felt ashamed or awkward.

I pushed myself off the ground and wiped the dirt from my knees and the palms of my hands, hoping he hadn't heard.

"Out for a run," he finished uncertainly. But after a pause, he asked, "Wait. Do you mean me or *that?*"

"Well, I was talking about you, but"—I turned to look at the house again—"I guess you're right, it could apply to either."

He looked down at his feet and laughed, like he was the one who was embarrassed now. "I promise I wasn't trying to be a creeper, or anything."

"Sorry," I offered. "You just surprised me."

He took a step closer, and I watched him survey the scene, squinting as he tracked the height of the chimney with his eyes. "Do you live here?" he asked.

"No . . . ," I said slowly, trying not to laugh, but I could feel the corner of my mouth twitching. "Nobody lives here."

"Well, not *here*, here. I mean, I saw the private property sign out by the road. I thought maybe you lived somewhere else, like on the property somewhere." He looked around, as if he was searching for evidence of other structures nearby, but finding none. "I only ask because I saw you the other day. Right near here."

We toss the awkwardness back and forth at each other, neither of us wanting to be caught holding on to it for too long.

"You mean when you almost turned me into roadkill?"
I said, hoping he could tell I was joking—I realized after I
said it, this was the first time in I don't even know how long
that I'd talked to someone who hadn't already known me my
entire life. He laughed, which made me relax a little bit.

"Yeah, sorry about that. I guess I wasn't really paying
attention." He took one giant step onto the foundation where
I stood, so we were on equal ground. Eye to eye, we were the
exact same height, which made me really look at him. He
had one of those faces that was exactly symmetrical. In profile the slant of his cheekbones was in line with the slope of
his nose, the same parallel angle, like they'd been carved that
way, his features striking a perfect balance of soft and strong.
And then there was the edgy cut of his hair—more stylish
and purposefully messy, nothing like the traditional "Carson
Crafty Clips" clean crew cuts that are standard here.

Perfect faces are boring, I remembered Mallory once saying.

I was about to look away, concluding his face was boringly
attractive. But then he took a step closer and I noticed a small,
hook-shaped scar under his right eye; and as I scanned his face
again, he smiled, and my gaze got caught on this one dimple he
had at the corner of his mouth on one side and not the other.

I started gathering my things—Mallory's camera, my
phone, my bag—if only to force myself to stop staring at his
mouth. "It's okay, I wasn't paying attention either."

"So, what happened to the house?" he asked.

"Time," I answered right away, not taking into account
how odd it might sound, only because I'd been thinking about
that same question a lot lately. "Well, a fire. And then time."

He nodded, considering this. "So you . . . take pictures?" he asked, gesturing to the camera. I looked down at this thing that still felt so unfamiliar in my hands—this thing that was not mine at all, and I suddenly worried he was going to say something about what must've looked like me taking his picture the other day, so I blurted out the first stupid, defensive thing that came to mind.

"So, you . . . like small talk?" I countered, amending with another "sorry."

"I take it you're not a fan?" he said, politely sidestepping my rudeness. He shrugged and shook his head, saying, "Me neither."

I thought back to what my mom had told me. But standing across from him, he didn't *look* like trouble. I glanced down at my dingy Bargain Mart T-shirt—I had no right to judge anyone, especially while wearing this.

"I'm Maia."

"I know," he said, pointing at my chest. "Name tag."

"Right," I mumbled. I felt the need to break the silence that was ramping up, so I added, "I'm your next-door neighbor. I live in the blue house, across the field from your aunt—the one with the really old barn."

He narrowed his eyes at me and said, "Now who's the creeper?" He was almost smiling, but not quite, like maybe he was only half joking. When I didn't answer, he looked around at the solid barrier of trees surrounding us, and asked, "Is it even possible to have neighbors out here? To me, neighbors are the people whose windows you can see into from yours and are constantly in each other's business."

"You'd be surprised," I told him, thinking of all the rumors that flew around after Mom and Dad's divorce, although I suppose some of those were technically true. "Proximity has nothing to do with nosing into other people's business."

"So, how do you know where I live?" he finally asked.

"You're new here."

He furrowed his brow, seeming confused about the correlation. "So?"

"So, everybody's already all up in your business."

He waited a beat before asking, "What have you heard?"

"Not much. Except you might be somewhat of a *troubled teen*." I air-quoted with my fingers for effect.

"Troubled teen." He raised his eyebrows and rubbed the back of his neck, looking around uncomfortably. "What does that mean?"

"Drinking, drugs, vandalism, general problems with authority," I mused.

Something relaxed in his stance then; a smile crept along the edges of his mouth. "And reckless driving?" he asked, that dimple forming like a punctuation mark to his words.

I felt my face mirroring his smile.

He continued, "I'll own up to the reckless driving part, but the rest—I promise it's nothing that exciting."

He started to walk toward me, and instantly my heart began to beat faster, a thrilling yet slightly terrifying flutter being activated in my stomach. I looked down at the camera, pretending to mess with the dials. It was an unfamiliar brand of nervousness vibrating along my skin, and I hoped he couldn't see it.

"I gotta get going," I told him, trying to channel some of Mallory's bravado as I walked past him, stowing her camera in my bag. He followed me out of the brush and back onto the pathway that was patched in clumps of weeds and damp bare earth, where my bike was waiting.

"It was nice meeting you," he said. "Officially."

"Yeah," I agreed as I started to wheel my bike out toward the road.

When I began to take off slowly, he jogged up next to me and said, "Wait. I forgot to tell you my name." I pedaled faster. "It's Chris!" he called out, slowing to a walk.

"I know!" I yelled as I sped off, leaving him behind.

CHRIS

I WALKED BACK TO ISOBEL'S HOUSE. FOR ONCE I didn't feel like running.

I was trying to think of whether or not I'd ever known anyone named Maia. I was trying to remember everything I knew about cameras and photography. I was trying to commit the sound of her voice to my memory—the way her southern accent only came out on certain words.

It was nearly dark by the time I got there, and Isobel was sitting on the porch steps.

"I was about to send out a search party," she said as I strolled up the driveway. "Good run?"

"Yeah, actually. Really good." I sat down next to her, and she handed me a bottled water that she must've brought out a while ago because the condensation had turned the label soggy.

"Just make sure you're pacing yourself," she warned.

"I know." I sighed, feeling my good mood already slipping away. "Really. Can you please not look at me like that?"

"Like what?"

"Like . . . the way *they* look at me," I answered. *Like all you see when you look at me is that day*, I thought. Like all you can think is that if Coleton hadn't stepped in when he did, it could've been worse. Coleton never looked at me the same after that day. He started to look at me like my parents did, like they were afraid for me, like maybe they were a little afraid *of* me. But I didn't say any of that to Isobel. I shook my head, didn't want to get into it. "Never mind," I mumbled.

She made this weird growling sound in the back of her throat and rolled her eyes. "Don't do that. Your mother always does that. It drives me crazy. Just say it."

"You know what I mean," I told her, not quite raising my voice, like my father. "Like I'm all fragile and defenseless."

"Who said that? I know you're not fragile and defenseless! You're the strongest person I know. I'm speaking from a strictly medical standpoint—you have to be careful of your ankle, and especially your back. Just don't push yourself too hard." She paused, staring at me, unflinching. "All right?"

"Yeah, all right," I relented. "I know."

She leaned into my side and knocked my shoulder. "I'm glad you're here, by the way," she told me, and I could feel the storm cloud that had been quickly closing in on me retreating again.

"Me too."

"I think this'll be good for you. And your mom and dad,

too. You just need to relax, have some fun. You know, be a kid. And *they* need . . . I don't know, some perspective on the whole situation."

I laughed. "Tell me about it."

"Life goes by fast. A year from now you'll be heading off to college, then after that you're in the real world. You'll never get this time back."

"Why can't my parents see it that way?"

"Because they're your parents."

We sat in silence, listening to the chorus of croaking frogs and buzzing insects that were congregating in the shadows all around us. Every few seconds a firefly would light up, then disappear. We didn't have fireflies where I lived. We didn't have this strange chirping of nocturnal creatures. We didn't have the wide-open skies. We didn't have old abandoned burned-out houses. And we didn't have people like Maia. I decided right then that these differences were good things; they meant that I was living, not wasting any more time.

I cleared my throat so I'd sound more casual when I asked, "Hey, what's Bargain Mart?"

"A store in town. Sort of a one-stop shop; they have a little bit of everything." I could feel her side-eyeing me, her speech slowing down slightly, dragging out the word, "Why?"

I shrugged like it was nothing. "Just wondering." But when I turned and saw her smiling at me, I knew she wasn't going to let me off the hook. "What?" I asked.

"You met Maia."

I opened my mouth, about to deny it, but she'd see right through me. "Okay, how could you possibly know that?"

"I could just tell—I know you better than you think." It was true how well she knew me. She knew me better than anyone else, even Coleton. "Well, that and I happen to know that Maia works at Bargain Mart. That, and I saw her riding by on her bike right before you got home." She laughed, then added, pointing at me, "And then there's that goofy grin on your face."

"We had one conversation."

"Okay, fine," she said, holding her hands up in a gesture of surrender.

"She just seems . . . different," I added voluntarily. "I don't know, interesting."

Isobel didn't say anything for a few seconds; she was looking off to the side like she was considering something. "You know, I think you two might get along if you can actually get to know each other."

"Okay," was all I said. And I tried really hard not to smile in my goofy, telltale way that apparently lets everyone know what I'm thinking.

"Okay," she repeated. And with that, she stood up and went inside.

I walked around to the back of the house. I was pretending to stretch, while I looked out across the field at the blue house. There weren't any lights on, except for the barn. Its double doors were open halfway, and yellow light spilled out like paint onto the grass. I lunged into the shadows when I saw the shape of her walk past the door.

Maybe I really was a creep.

. . .

I had been standing outside Bargain Mart for several minutes, trying to work up the nerve to go in, when this guy exited through the sliding glass doors that kept sending blasts of cold air in my direction every time they opened and closed. He glanced at me as he passed, and immediately did a double take.

He backed up, reversing his steps so he was in front of me. I stood up straighter, wiped the sweat from my hands on my shorts. I could feel my mind churning, trying to anticipate which way this was about to go. He was really tall, like basketball-player tall, and appeared to be around my age, with his hair all slicked back with too much gel.

"Matt, right?" he said slowly, squinting at me.

I cleared my throat, stalling to assess the situation. "What?"

"Your name's Matt, isn't it?" he said, but before I could answer, he asked, "Did anyone tell you about Bowman's Friday night?"

Matt. He mistook me for someone named Matt.

"No," I managed, through the desert in my mouth.

"This Friday. Bowman's," he said, nodding and grinning.

"No, I mean my name's not Matt."

He looked at me more closely, like he was sizing me up. I waited for that glimmer of recognition—it's something that happens in the eyes first, something that can't be hidden. But there was none. He simply shrugged and continued, "Well, anyway, come if you want."

"Cool," I said, this wave of relief washing over me. "It's Chris, by the way," I added, though he hadn't asked.

"Right, Chris," he said, as if he had suddenly remembered who I was. "Later," he mumbled, before continuing toward the parking lot. I stood there for another minute and watched him toss his plastic bag into the back of an old pickup truck. The windows had been left rolled down, the doors unlocked—I guess this is one of those small towns where people can do that sort of thing.

I took a deep breath, blew it out slowly.

Isobel was right, I needed to relax, and maybe even have fun. That's why I came to Carson. And that's why I was standing outside this store.

"Fuck it," I whispered to myself, and finally stepped through the sliding glass doors.

The store was lit with a fluorescent glow, the kind that always makes my head hurt, and it smelled like floor cleaner. It was set up like your typical big box department store. There were signs hanging from the ceiling with arrows pointing in every direction—Household Goods, Furniture, Shoes, Health & Beauty. The store hummed with a mix of dated music coming from aged speakers and the constant beeping of items being scanned at the registers.

I always hated these kinds of places; they made me feel claustrophobic. But I was on a mission. *Be brave,* I told myself as I wandered the mazelike aisles.

I'd circled the store twice and still hadn't seen her— every time an employee looked at me suspiciously, I picked up an item I didn't need. I was about to give up when I finally spotted her. She was standing at a table, folding girls' T-shirts very slowly and unenthusiastically, not even bothering to separate out the various colors. She didn't see me as I approached her. She didn't even notice when I was standing directly next to her.

"Maia?" She looked up at me like I'd just woken her from a dream.

"Oh" was all she said as she stared at me.

"It's Chris," I offered.

"No, I—I remember."

When she didn't say anything else, I stupidly volunteered, "I just had to pick up a few things I forgot to bring with me." But then we both looked down at what I was holding in my hand.

"So, you had an urgent need for erasers, shoelaces . . . and lobster claw oven mitts?" she asked, the shape of her mouth quivering slightly, like she was having trouble keeping a straight face.

I felt my cheeks getting hot as I looked down at these ridiculous items. I wondered if I was wearing one of those goofy grins again. But I decided to just go with it.

"Yeah, it was kind of an emergency," I finally said.

She let a breath escape, not quite an actual laugh, but more like a *Ha*. There was something in her smile that made me wonder, for just a second, if she could tell that I'd made the trip just to see her. Because, of course, nobody *forgets* to pack erasers and shoelaces and oven mitts; nobody actually *needs* erasers and shoelaces and oven mitts.

As we stood there in the girls' clothing department—a scene like so many of my terrible childhood moments—I saw an opportunity.

"Hey, so I just ran into some guy outside—he actually never told me his name, now that I think about it—but he invited me to a party on Friday. At Bowman's, whoever that is?" I paused, and then asked, "You wanna go?"

"Was he about this tall?" She held her hand up above her head, exaggeratingly high. "Slicked-back hair, stupid look on his face?"

"I . . . guess so."

"That's Neil." She said his name like the word tasted bad in her mouth. "Pass." She balled up the shirt she had been folding and refolding. "I have no desire to party with helmet head Neil and the pretty people."

"Helmet Head Neil and the Pretty People?" I repeated. "That sounds like a really bad band name."

She did another one of those *Ha* laughs.

"So I take it you're not friends with Neil?" I asked.

"'Not friends' would be an understatement."

"Okay," I relented, hoping I didn't look too deflated by her decline. "Well, you're working, so . . . I just saw you over here and wanted to say hi. So, hi."

"Hi," she replied, holding her hand up to wave good-bye.

I started taking small steps away from her, and as soon as I turned my back, she said "Wait. Chris?" I turned around so quickly, the sound of my name in her voice echoing in my mind. "Bowman's isn't a *who*. It's a *where*. That old burned-down house. You know, where we were the other day? That's Bowman's."

"Oh. Okay, thanks." I waved again, and I knew I was smiling too much, but I couldn't help it. Once I was far enough away from her, I ditched the erasers, shoelaces, and oven mitts in some random spot in the snack aisle on my way out of the store.

Back in the station wagon, I turned up the music and took the long way home.

MAIA

I WAS STANDING AT THE STOVE, MAKING MYSELF A box of mac and cheese—the orange-powdered kind—when Dad came up from the basement holding his sad microwave dinner.

"She gone?" he asked me, lurking in the doorway of the kitchen.

Mom had just left for her weekly Friday night dinner and drinks with the women's group she had met online. It was supposed to be some kind of support group, either for losing a child or for cheating husbands, I was never sure.

"Coast is clear," I called over my shoulder, doubting he heard the sarcasm behind my words, doubting he got that I thought he was being ridiculous, hiding from his ex-wife, sneaking around his own house, trying to make me his lookout.

With his back to me, he stood in front of the microwave,

carefully ripping open the cardboard box, pulling back the corner of the plastic. I turned back around as he hit the start button. I could feel him looking at me, wanting me to turn toward him and say something, anything. He needed me to constantly assuage his guilt, every moment of every day.

Sometimes I could do it; other times it made me resent him almost as much as Mom did. Because he gets to have his basement purgatory where he can be both victim and villain, and get away with feeling shitty all the time. And Mom gets her women's group and her alcohol and self-righteous indignation, and she's also allowed to feel shitty all the time. Me, I get to supervise them both, sitting here in the kitchen so they can talk at me and not each other, so their cold war can continue into eternity. Didn't they think I'd like to have permission to feel shitty all the time too? Couldn't they give me a day where I could sulk around and behave like a child and let go in front of them, and they both would be stuck mediating my mess?

I focused all my attention on stirring macaroni noodles—*I'm not open for business, Dad.* So we stood in silence for the full four minutes and thirty seconds it took for his dinner to cook. He used the bottom of his shirt to bring his steaming plastic tray to the table and sat down, the odor of artificially processed Salisbury steak, and mashed potatoes and gravy, wafting through the kitchen while I drained my pasta and stirred in the cheese mix and butter, along with a splash of Mom's fat-free half-and-half.

I knew he was waiting for me to sit down with him at the table, so I took my bowl to the living room and turned on the

TV. I only got in a few bites before I realized that the whole encounter with Dad had made me lose my appetite.

I looked at the wooden clock on the mantel. It was one of those vintage mechanical clocks that you have to wind up once a week—that's been my "job" for as long as I could remember. I wondered what would happen if I just stopped doing it, if Mom and Dad would even notice, or if they would just let time stand still forever.

It was just after seven thirty.

I ran back into the kitchen and dumped my mac and cheese into a plastic container and stashed it in the fridge. I glanced at my dad and said, already walking away, "I'm heading out."

The gray wooden barn sat in the shade of the tree line like a secret. I made my way along the side of the house, stepping on the circular paver stones Mom put in because Mallory had kept tracking a path from the house to the barn that was killing the grass.

The door creaked as it opened easily beneath my hands, the wooden handle worn and soft from a century of oily fingers and palms. I flipped the light switch, and one by one the grid of fluorescent lights that hung down from the ceiling flickered to life, illuminating the giant, open room. Her old wooden worktable in the center was just the way she'd left it—papers and pencils and markers and erasers and sticky notes and even a ceramic mug whose contents had long dried up scattering the surface. I walked the walls lined with photos pinned up like haphazard, chaotic wallpaper.

I was looking for one photo in particular—I'd seen it

before, but I couldn't remember where it was. After three laps around the barn, I finally saw it—the corner of it was tucked right under the graffiti picture, directly in the center of the wall.

I knew exactly when and where she'd taken it.

I got there first. I hid my bike farther down the road, buried under the cover of leaves and branches, where it wouldn't be seen. I knew everyone would be arriving soon, so I hurried down the familiar overgrown path. I stepped up onto the concrete foundation, walked over to the chimney, and pressed my palms against the soot-stained bricks. I swore I felt a pulse, like a heartbeat, under my hands. But I guess that had to have just been mine rebounding off the old masonry.

A car door slammed. Then another. Voices. Footsteps.

I hopped down and quickly tried to guess which tree Mallory must've been in when she took that picture. Then I carefully climbed the rungs of low branches, up into one of the nearby trees, and waited. I looked down at the lot. The first partygoers had begun to assemble with supplies: wood and cardboard for the fire, cases of beer, ice, coolers full of probably more beer, and plastic Bargain Mart bags full of snacks.

The sun was going down, and from up here I could hear so clearly, as more and more cars pulled off into the grass along the side of the road. Suddenly I wasn't sure what the hell I was doing, but then I imagined Mallory sitting with me, waiting, and I remembered how she'd once said that the most important thing about being a photographer isn't the camera or skill or genius ideas; sometimes it is just being there at the right time.

How would I know the right time when it came?

All the people from my school I never talk to and who never talk to me filed into what was left of the Bowman House in droves. Someone started building a fire near the fireplace, dousing the logs and crumpled newspaper with lighter fluid. They cheered as it roared to life.

I smelled the weed before I saw who had it—that unmistakable sticky, sweet, earthy scent I had come to know so well. I closed my eyes and pictured Mallory in her bedroom, kneeling in a nest of pillows on the floor by the window, her elbows perched on the ledge of her windowsill, blowing a long, thin stream of smoke outside.

Mallory still had a spell on me back then—I was only thirteen, fourteen, maybe. She seemed so much older than me, so much wiser. So when she'd drag me into her bedroom, and tell me to talk to her, tell me she didn't like to be alone while she smoked, I was more than happy to oblige. Except she knew I never had anything worthwhile to say, so I was her perfect captive audience.

I could close my eyes now and see her face so clearly, the way the drug would relax her into this lazy way of speaking. She'd tell me all kinds of deep thoughts and dark secrets I'm sure she'd never have shared otherwise, like her philosophies about art and how she couldn't wait to get out into the real world and leave this all behind. I felt special when she would let me in, like I was worth something. But then we would always fall asleep, and in the morning she'd kick me out of her bedroom and it was like those conversations never happened.

Eventually I wised up and realized she didn't actually need *me*. I could've been anyone. And I finally stopped coming when she called—that was the most radical thing I'd ever done in my life. Up until now, anyway. I guess that's when she replaced me with Neil, whom she'd always referred to as "helmet head Neil" before they became real friends, back when he was just the guy who supplied her with pot. Neil was someone who could keep up with Mallory, offer her the unwavering adoration she craved, someone who would come every time she called and constantly remind her how much of a fucking genius she was.

He managed to stick around long enough to become her best friend, despite the fact that everyone knew he wanted it to be something more. I think she liked leaving people wanting more. Maybe that's why she stopped liking me—I didn't want anything from her. Except that wasn't the whole truth. I did want something from her: I wanted her to go back to the way she was when we were younger, when *we* were best friends, when our parents were just our parents and hadn't become flawed, broken, angry, sad people.

Almost as if he could tell I'd been thinking about her, Neil arrived onto the scene—we had never been friends, real or fake.

The last time we spoke was at a party over spring break, the one I'd only been invited to out of pity. He sidled up to me, brought me a drink—something real and strong, not the cheapo beer everyone around us had. He said we were drinking to Mallory and that deserved the good stuff. We tapped our red plastic cups, and the brown liquid sloshed around, the toxic smell burning my nostrils and the back of my throat as I brought the cup to my lips. He said "To Mallory," and I repeated "To Mallory" and took a sip.

I coughed and choked as I tried to swallow it down, and he laughed but told me everyone does that at first. We sat down on a couch that I sank into like quicksand and pretended to make small talk—people had been wanting to talk to me so much after Mallory died, I was starting to get the hang of it: Keep things on the surface, never say anything you mean. I took tiny sips at first—this stuff was floor cleaner, I was convinced. But the warmth that was spreading through me was unlike anything I'd ever felt, like butterflies in my stomach, except it was butterflies everywhere. Butterflies in every cell of my body.

He built up to it in stages, working up the nerve to speak the question he had been waiting to ask for the three months since she'd died. First he just said he wanted to come over sometime—he kept it casual, innocent. My sips grew longer, and the butterflies stopped batting their wings so fast.

"To the barn," he added.

I took another and another, and thought, hey, maybe these people were onto something with the whole getting wasted thing, because I was starting to feel pretty good.

"To look through Mallory's photographs."

I finished off my drink. He wanted to take some of them—he knew which ones were her favorites; he knew the most important ones. And as he refilled the empty cup between my hands, I was feeling both powerless and powerful all at the same time. That was when he said the words that twisted into my heart like a corkscrew and flipped some kind of switch inside me:

"It's what Mallory would've wanted."

Now I looked down from my spot high above the party-goers and molded my back into the crook of the tree—its branches and trunk cradling me. I let my legs dangle on either side as I sat, watching, listening. The sound of the bonfire hissed and crackled like whispered secrets, its sweet smoke rising up into the canopy of trees. The laughter and shouting and pounding music was somehow amplified as it rose above all the sound-absorbing things on the ground.

I had to stop thinking about that night. I brought the camera up and looked through it. I was here to do what Mallory had done, to find the hidden stories between the lines—at least, that seemed like something Mallory would say—but all I saw was that the kids from my school were the same as they'd always been. Last year's party was nearly interchangeable with this year's. The same faces, the same fire, but the picture wasn't the same. Mallory's picture had mystery, like it was something ritualistic and meaningful, and not just a bunch of drunk kids from Bumfuck Nowhere with nothing better to do on a Friday night.

There were no hidden stories to see; I already knew all of theirs, just like they knew mine.

But then I saw Chris. I watched his face as he stood there in the crowd. From here I couldn't really see the crooked smile or the dimple at the corner of his mouth that hadn't fully let go of me for days. Neil offered Chris the little glass pipe that he was holding between his fingers, and I couldn't hear what Chris said, but he smiled and looked down, shaking his head. And just like that, he was absorbed by the crowd.

After the first hour, the party was in full force and everyone was deteriorating, getting rowdier and sloppier. That's when I began to watch Chris more closely—that's when he began to stand out; he had slowly become the calm point in all the chaos.

I knew everyone's stories except for his. And then I thought about the three-pack of erasers and the shoelaces and the lobster claw oven mitts. How I'd found them in a pile, hiding in the cookies and crackers, when I was straightening at the end of my shift earlier this week.

He sat with the others around the fire, not drinking or smoking, seeming neither interested nor bored. He did a lot of polite smiling and nodding, a lot of gazing into the fire. He didn't say much to anyone. I was beginning to think maybe he was watching too, like I was, but in a different way.

After a while, he stood and picked up a broken tree branch that was on the ground. He kept stoking the fire with it, moving the logs and random tinder, sending the sparks flying upward. I was scared the glowing embers would catch the leaves on the low branches or that someone might look up and follow the embers' path as they ascended toward me.

If things were different, maybe I'd climb down and go talk to him, do a little flirting, or maybe we'd even have a drink together, share a laugh—all those normal, sweet little moments. But things weren't different.

I brought Mallory's camera to my eye, twisting the lens so I could see him more clearly, look at him more closely. "Hold still." I breathed the words my sister was always saying, to people, to objects, to animals, to places. I moved my whole body, shifted just half an inch to the right, cropping everyone else out of the frame. Sure to keep my arms and hands and fingers exactly as they were. I could imagine her in this very spot, doing all of these same things. The tip of my index finger slid against the button, wanting to press down.

Looking through the camera made me dizzy, like I was that night at the party over spring break. I moved my left hand cautiously, my fingers against the tree bark, and I tried to brace myself as I lowered the camera from my face, its weight tugging at the strap around my neck like an anchor trying to drag me down.

My left foot was all pins and needles. I shifted my leg, and the branch beneath me winced and swayed gently, shedding a few stray scales of bark. They fell to the ground soundlessly, unnoticed. But I'd lost my balance. I had to think fast. I reached for the branch above me to steady myself, but it cracked, then snapped.

My hands grabbed for anything to hold on to, getting scraped as the branches slid right through them, leaves slicing my palms, like paper cuts. I caught myself before falling all the way down, but in the commotion I'd been spotted.

"Hey, who's up there?" someone yelled.

I could see the shadows of several people on the ground, coming closer, heard someone else saying, "What the hell?"

One of them shined a flashlight on me. "I see you," he

said, and there was no mistaking that voice, no getting out of this now. Clumsily, I used my arms and legs to maneuver from branch to branch—the rough, jagged tree bark opening up my knees and elbows along the way.

When I jumped down, I stumbled, unsteady on my feet, and was face-to-face with Neil. He turned the light off and just stared at me, silently. But somehow I still heard those words echoing through my head as if he was saying them again, right now: *It's what Mallory would've wanted, what Mallory would've wanted, Mallory would've wanted.*

As more and more people crowded around us, I was transported back to that moment again, standing up in the middle of Neil's cousin's living room, shouting over the music, gesturing wildly with my drink. It had all been too absurd, all the pretending, all the tears and solemn words, the sham of mourning. If anyone had had a right to be sad, it was me. If anyone was going to proclaim what it was Mallory would've wanted in the case of her dropping dead in the middle of gym class at the age of seventeen, shouldn't *I* have been the one telling them, and not the other way around? People were gathering—their faces were serious, I remember that—and I thought, *Wow, maybe people really want to hear what I have to say.*

And with my first-ever audience, I had told Neil exactly how stupid and pathetic he was for loving Mallory. "Because everyone knows she was only ever using you, Neil," I had said, looking around at all the faces with their eyes glued to me. "She was just stringing you along. Don't you know, even if she'd lived a hundred years, she'd never have loved you back?"

I don't know what I thought would happen. In my mind I was expecting people to cheer me on, realize how wise I was, commend me for telling such hard truths.

"Mallory wasn't some angel," I continued. "She was the most utterly self-centered, self-involved person on the planet. She cared more about her precious art than people!" I shouted, laughing, crying, spilling my drink.

Not that I actually remember much of what I said, but I was able to watch it later when someone posted a video of it online. It was titled "DRUNK GIRL LOOOSES HER SHIIIIT AT PARTY."

I thought I had been so eloquent, but I was just screaming, barely intelligible. I stuttered and slurred through the words. And in the final seconds of the video it showed me taking a few steps toward Neil. I said something as I stumbled into him.

You can't hear what it was because I was talking too low, but I remember that part. I said: "There are no more photos—I burned them. They're all gone, okay?"

I still don't know why I lied. In the video, Neil's face went blank and pale—he looked like I had just told him Mallory died all over again. But then his face changed quickly, turning red and hard and clenched in places you wouldn't think a face could clench. A part of me wanted to immediately backpedal, to tell him it was just a bad, mean, drunken joke. But I knew right away, there was no taking it back. The video ended then, and I don't know what happened next. I don't remember how I got home, how I ended up in my bed that night.

That look on Neil's face, the hard, angry, clenched one

from the video, that was exactly the way he was looking at me right now.

"What the fuck is that?" he said, not looking at my face but at the camera around my neck. "Give it to me," he demanded, reaching toward me with both hands.

I backed away from him, and I tried to sound strong when I said "No!" but my voice was shaking.

"Give it to me before you destroy that too!"

People were already surrounding us, just like they had that night all those months ago. Except this time, Neil was the one who was wasted—likely a combination of weed and alcohol and grief. This time *he* was the one who stepped in close to me and said, so low that no one else could hear:

"Mallory hated you. Did you know that?"

It was like a snakebite—I was too stunned by the initial strike to feel the poison in those words at first. Maybe he could see that it didn't quite hurt enough, so he added, "She fucking *hated* you." Yes, there was the sting. I could feel the burn of the venom working through my veins. And while I stood there, incapacitated, my back up against the tree, Neil grabbed on to the strap of the camera, nearly choking me as he wrestled it from around my neck.

CHRIS

I DIDN'T KNOW WHAT HAPPENED AT FIRST. I HEARD some shouting coming from outside the circle of firelight. Then I thought I heard another voice, a girl's voice, not quite yelling, but on edge somehow. That's when I saw Maia standing in the shadows, surrounded by a group of people, including helmet head Neil. She was standing too still, like she was rooted to the ground. Her eyes were looking at Neil, but in this far-off way, like she wasn't really *seeing*.

I was on my feet before I knew what I was doing.

As I approached Maia and Neil, I got the sensation that I wasn't so much walking of my own volition as I was being pulled into their orbit. I fell into formation with the others, as more and more people took notice. It didn't take long for me to catch up on what had transpired: Maia had been hiding in the tree, spying and taking pictures. Some of the boys were laughing at her; some of the girls were calling her names. Neil was leaning into her, way too close, saying something, threatening her, maybe—I couldn't make it out.

My heart was starting to beat faster, the way it did before a race, my body preparing for something. He was grabbing at her, pulling at the camera around her neck, jerking her back and forth, until he got the strap loose from her hands and pulled it over her head, sending her hair whipping across her face.

This is bad, that old voice whispered in my ear. *Run.*

Neil was holding her camera like he was daring her to try to come get it. When Maia lunged, Neil grabbed her wrist to keep her away.

Run, I wanted to shout at her.

But before I knew it, I had snatched the camera out of Neil's hand.

Somehow, I had stepped between the two of them. Everyone stopped their chattering. All eyes were on us, the whole world telescoping in, then expanding back quickly.

"Give that to me," Neil said, breathless.

"Just take it easy, all right?" I said, attempting but failing to employ my dad's even keel voice of reason.

"Take it easy—are you kidding me?" he repeated under his breath, laughing in that scary way people do when they're about to lose it. "Who *are* you, even?" he shouted. "You don't know anything about what's going on here, so why don't you do yourself a favor and stay out of it!"

"Well, I know it's not cool to beat up on someone who's half your size," I said, trying way too hard to keep calm. I glanced behind me to look at Maia, who still had her eyes locked on Neil.

"I wasn't beating up on her—did anyone see me beating up on her?" Neil spun around to face the crowd and stumbled for a second, losing his balance. "But if you want me to be the bad guy, that's fine," he continued, turning toward me again. "You're half my size too, or didn't you notice that, tough guy?" he yelled, getting in my face, backing me up so that I was tripping over Maia's feet.

Then, right before I thought he'd actually hit me, someone put a hand on Neil's shoulder.

"Come on, just let it go," the guy said. "This is supposed to be a party, right?" Then to me, "That'd be your cue to leave."

"Yeah, okay," I said, but I was having trouble moving.

"Just get her the fuck away from me, man. I'm serious," Neil shouted, pointing at Maia over my shoulder. "Before I fucking kill her!"

"Like, *now*," the other guy told me.

"Okay, okay," I said. "We're leaving. All right? Everyone relax." I started walking, but Maia was standing still.

"Maia, let's go." I was grabbing her arm, and I knew that was also not cool, but I didn't know what else to do. "Come on!" I said, and finally her feet began to follow. I ushered us out of the woods, past the burned-out house and onto the dirt path, ignoring the taunts now being thrown at both of us.

When we made it out to the gravel driveway, we stood there for a second, neither of us saying anything.

There was music and shouting and laughter again. When I turned to look at Maia, she was staring behind us into the woods, as if she wasn't sure how we'd gotten out here.

"Are you okay?" I finally asked.

She whipped around to face me, her eyes stabbing into me like daggers. Instead of answering, she held her hands out, wiggling her fingers, reaching for the camera. "Do you mind?" she snapped. I handed it to her, and she started turning it over and over, examining it like she could see invisible fingerprints Neil had left behind. She was breathing heavily as she pulled the camera strap over her head and across her chest. Then she started walking down the road.

"Hey, where are you going?" I asked, but again she didn't answer. She ducked back into the woods for a second, before popping back out, now wheeling her bike alongside her.

"Look, it's really dark out. Why don't I just drive you? We're going to the same place, anyway."

She turned away from me, swung her leg over her bike, and kicked her foot off the ground, ignoring me like she had that first day I met her. She was leaving. I stood there in the middle of the road, between the cars lined up on both sides, like I was trapped in some kind of dream where nothing was making any sense.

"You're welcome!" I called after her.

She stopped abruptly. Got off her bike. Let it collapse right to the ground, and then marched up to me, until we were only inches apart from each other.

"Oh, thank you!" she said, clasping her hands together. "Thank you for inserting yourself into something that was none of your business in the first place. Thank you, *hero*— there, is that good enough for you?" She bowed forward

and bent her knees into something that looked like it was supposed to be a curtsy.

"Okay, so I'm supposed to apologize for helping you?"

"Who asked for your help?" she snapped, looking around with wild eyes.

"You looked scared. I was just—"

"I was *not* scared!" she interrupted. She started walking away, but then twisted back around immediately to face me again. "And if I somehow gave you the impression that I needed rescuing—sorry to disappoint you, but I don't."

Something knotted in my stomach. I could feel the blood rushing out to my extremities, a tingling in my fingertips. I saw right through her. I've *been* her. It's not that she didn't know that whole situation could've turned very bad, very quickly. She's a girl. She knows about all of those fucked-up, unfair rules.

"Look, I get it," I said, watching as she picked her bike off the ground. "But you don't have to take it out on me."

"Oh, please. You don't get anything." She looked up at me and smiled, except I realized she was not actually smiling and she was not really looking at me; she was looking through me. "Another thing. We're not friends, if that's what you're thinking, so from now on how about you just leave me alone." Then she swung her leg over her bike and started pedaling down the road before I could even respond.

"Whatever," I mumbled. Except my body felt anything but *whatever*. It felt like taking off after her and telling her exactly what I know, exactly where I've been, exactly *who* I am. I wanted to tell her that she might think she's being strong and tough, but she has to be careful and she should try to blend in more, not make herself such a target.

I started running. Someone needed to tell her these things. But she shrank into the distance. I had to bend over to catch my breath, an old pain pinching in my rib cage as I coughed. Next, a stinging in my left ankle. Then my spine.

MAIA

I WANTED TO GO FASTER, BUT MY ARMS AND LEGS HAD turned to gelatin, like my bones had softened inside me and were now useless. The tree and fire, the camera and Neil, me yelling at Chris—those words still echoing through the air, still pounding through my body—had washed out all my thoughts and used up everything I had in me.

It was almost eleven by the time I got home. Everyone was in bed, the house dark, as usual. I was hungry and tired. All I wanted was to keep my mind exactly as it was: not thinking, not feeling. I wanted to take my leftover mac and cheese up to my room and eat it in bed, and then fall asleep without even brushing my teeth.

I trudged up the stairs, each step a chore. As I walked by Mallory's room, Roxie lifted her head, like she did every night. I brought my microwaved container, along with a fork and a glass of water, and set it down on Mallory's nightstand, then silently closed the door behind me.

I didn't turn on the light as I sat down on her bed. The moon shone through the window, offering just enough light to see. Roxie sniffed at the air and watched closely as I speared the individual noodles with the tines of my fork and proceeded to eat them four parallel noodles at a time. As the food settled into my stomach, the blankness in my mind began populating with thoughts again. I looked down at the palms of my hands, scraped and stinging.

Mallory hated me—she *fucking hated me.*

I had the urge to call Hayden. I wanted to tell her everything, but I wasn't sure where to start. I didn't know how to explain the handful of tiny things that had happened in the few days she'd been gone. I didn't know how to explain the way those things had changed everything. She was probably busy having fun, and besides, she wasn't going to be able to tell me what I wanted to hear. I wanted her to tell me I'd done nothing wrong, that everything was okay and things would go back to normal soon, that I was a good person, that my sister didn't really hate me.

I leaned back onto Mallory's bed, let myself sink into her pillows. Roxie rested her chin on my foot, and sighed.

So, I had yelled at Chris.

I'd yelled at him for being the kind of guy who thinks he's the answer to some girl's problems, a girl he doesn't know the first thing about. I knew I'd been harsh with him, but what was more important was this insipid, nagging thought in the back of my mind. If Mallory truly hated me, nothing I could do now would ever be able to change that.

CHRIS

I SLAMMED THE DOOR BEHIND ME. I DIDN'T MEAN TO.

"Chris?" Isobel called from the living room. I tossed my keys onto the kitchen table, just as she came into the room. "You're home early."

"Yeah," was all I could say, my voice tight and strained. I'd driven around for at least an hour, trying to calm myself down, but I still had all of this adrenaline racing through my body and my brain. I felt like I'd have to run a damn marathon to get it all out of me.

"What's wrong?" she asked.

"Nothing."

"Did someone do something to you?"

"No, god!" I was pacing, but the kitchen was too small for pacing so it felt more like I was trapped in a cage, so I tried to stand still. "I just—I don't know why I even bothered. People are assholes everywhere."

I started pacing again, but no, that was worse. "Forget it. I'm just—I'm going upstairs."

"Wait, wait, wait," she said, and she was holding her arms out toward me. "Come on, talk to me."

I backed away from her and held my hands up so she wouldn't try to touch me. I could not handle being touched right now, and I hated myself for that.

"I really, really just want to be alone, Aunt Isobel. Okay? Please."

"Okay," she relented. "But I'm here. All right?"

I nodded and started walking away.

"I love you, kid," she said to my back. I couldn't bring myself to respond.

I made it up to my bedroom, and even though I wanted to slam that door too, I didn't. I toed my sneakers off and kicked them across the room. I threw my jacket on the floor. Didn't even bother unbuttoning my shirt, just tore it over my head, balled it up, and chucked it into the corner—my undershirt is always the last article of clothing to go. I was taking off my jeans when my phone vibrated in my pocket—it was Coleton.

How's the party going?

I regretted telling him about the party, regretted getting excited about it in the first place. I regretted all the extra time I took getting ready, all that stupid optimism. I regretted how proud I was for a minute when I thought about how I no longer had to double and triple up on sports bras and spandex tops because Dad had willingly—no, happily—let me use his credit card to buy real binders. I regretted how confident I felt as I looked in the mirror and smoothed my hands over my chest. But the thing I really fucking regretted was thinking that maybe I'd actually made a couple of friends here, or that life really could be different, that I could just feel normal for once, whatever the hell "normal" even meant.

I looked at the screen for a moment, considering a response, but set my phone facedown on the nightstand. *Later*, I told myself, *I'll talk to him later.*

I tried to go outside to the deck, but the clouds were thick, the moon bright and hazy, drowning out the stars. I went back inside and turned off all the lights before I finished undressing. I had to fumble through the dark for my pajamas. I couldn't risk catching a glimpse of my body in the mirror—not tonight, not when I was already hating everyone and everything, not when Coleton was clueless and the stars were hiding and Aunt Isobel was *not* the one person I really wished I could talk to, though sometimes, at the right angles, she looks a lot like her.

I lay down in bed and stared at the ceiling. I pulled the covers over me, then threw them off again. I sat up and repositioned my pillow, lay back down, closed my eyes, opened them. I had messed everything up with Maia, just when it had seemed like maybe things were going somewhere with her. But I couldn't even think about that. This whole night had scrambled my brain—pushing things around, rearranging my thoughts like furniture, making my mind a maze of old memories bumping up against the new ones, confusing me. I closed my eyes and there it was, the inevitable, moving forward from the place in the back of my mind: That day. Everything that happened next.

My parents had pressed charges against all three of the boys who beat me up. They were expelled from school for the rest of the year. Their parents had to pay my medical bills. They'd be on probation until they each turned eighteen. But big fucking deal—they had already finished with their stupid community service while I was still laid up in bed.

My two broken ribs were pretty much better by then, though those first weeks of breathing exercises with Isobel had been excruciating—I'd have just as soon stopped breathing altogether if that had been an option. The surgery for my broken nose and the orbital fracture of my right eye socket had gone well, and I had recovered from my bruised liver and sprained left ankle all within a few weeks. But I'd still had to wear that back brace for the spinal fracture and go through weeks and weeks of physical therapy before it fully healed.

Coleton was the one who kept me from going over the edge. He was my only real connection to the outside world, especially after Isobel left to go back home. Most days were spent sitting or lying in bed, finishing my online classes in no time at all because they were so fucking easy. After my eye was better, I read like a fiend. A book a day, sometimes more.

Then at night, after my parents were in bed, I watched all the videos on the Internet—every last one I could find. About being trans. About transitioning. I didn't need to watch them all, though, because within the first thirty seconds of the first video, this guy was sitting there already telling my whole life story. Someone on the other side of the world, whom I didn't know and whom I would never meet, knew me at my core. I always believed there was an infinite universe out there, and somehow, I was supposed to be a part of it. At least, I tried very hard to believe that. And for maybe the first time in my entire life, I was finally beginning to see a way to make that happen.

The voice in my head started changing then—no longer telling me I was unacceptable. It was a different voice, but one I'd heard before. It was the voice that had told me to run that day in the woods, the one that had been whispering to me in a million different languages every day, telling me all the ways that this was not the life I was supposed to be living. The only thing that was right was my mind. My mind wasn't confused. It had always known itself. All alone in my bedroom, day in, day out, that voice got louder and stronger, until I couldn't ignore it anymore.

Isobel was the first person I told. She didn't even pause a beat before she let me know she was behind me forever, no matter what—those were her exact words: *Forever*, she told me. *No matter what.*

The day I finally told Coleton, he had come over after school as he did most afternoons. He dropped off my new library books and talked about how much everything sucked at school without me, which I appreciated hearing, even if I knew he was the only one who felt that way. We played video games like we always did.

But after hours of running through the same battle and

losing horribly, he finally said, "I probably really need to get home after this try."

I knew it had to be now or I'd never work up the courage again. I paused the game. I took a deep breath—I'd gotten so good at breathing deep that it barely hurt anymore. He looked over at me like he knew it was something big.

"What?" he asked.

"I just—I wanna talk to you about something."

He set the controller down on the floor and turned toward me. "Okay."

"So you know how there are some people who are born one way and then, they like, change their bodies?" I began.

"Okay," he repeated, squinting at me.

"Well, it's like their bodies don't match their minds."

"Oh-kay," he said again, less certain this time.

I paused, took another full, deep breath. I wasn't explaining it right, I knew that—I was just having trouble saying the word, like getting the actual word out of my mouth: *transgender.* It felt like a forbidden word, a word from a language nobody ever spoke out loud, or at least nobody I'd ever known.

"Like someone who has the body of a boy when they're supposed to be a girl. Or you have the body of a girl when everything else about you is like a boy—I mean, not *like* a boy, is a boy. You *are* a boy. And these people, they end up changing their bodies."

"Okay," he said, nodding again, understanding, getting it, at last. "And?"

"Well, that's—me," I said.

He stared at the carpet, in the space between us, for what felt like forever. "That seems pretty extreme, don't you think?"

My heart started pounding. I couldn't tell if it was out of anger or sadness or fear. This was not the reaction I'd been expecting from him. "Why are you saying that?" I asked, hearing the edge in my voice.

"Listen, you already look like a guy. I mean, no offense or anything, but most people wouldn't even know. You remember those girls we met at the mall that one time?" he asked, in that tone he often used back then, like he was trying to cheer me up.

"Yeah, that *one* time. That one time I got a girl's number." He was always bringing that up whenever I needed a boost, except it wasn't going to cut it this time. "But then I was too afraid to ever call her, because what would be the point? God, it's not about girls, Coleton!"

"Well, I don't know!" He threw his hands up. "I don't know what to say, okay?"

"And besides, I *don't* look like a guy. When we were kids, maybe I used to, but—it's not about just *looking* like a guy, anyway."

"Well, what's it about, then?"

"It's not about looking like anything. It's about . . . *being*. Being who I really am, a whole person. Not just someone who confuses people and gets weird looks all the time."

He considered this for a moment before responding. "You know I've never thought of you as, like, a *girl*-girl, right?" Three months earlier I might've believed him. Then again, three months earlier he might've meant it.

"Even after what happened?"

He looked down at the spot on the carpet again. "Is that what this is about?" he asked. "Because you can't let them—"

"No!" I interrupted. "*That*, and all of this"—I gestured around my room, at my back brace, my books, our game, at everything my life had become—"it just made me realize I can't wait any longer to start living or my world is just going to keep getting smaller and smaller. I can't be afraid anymore. This is who I've always been. I can't keep lying to myself and everyone else."

He sat there, quietly, for what felt like minutes but had to have only been seconds. "I'm not trying to argue with you. I just want to make sure you've really thought about it."

"Believe me, I pretty much think about nothing else."

"All right," he concluded with a shrug.

"All right," I repeated. "Is it, though?"

"Yeah, of course it is," he said, picking his controller up off the floor and nodding toward mine, still held tight between my hands. "Come on, one more?" he asked.

As we sat there playing, I was surprised things felt a lot like they always did, except a lot lighter. A few minutes in, he started laughing and paused the game again, turned to look at me with wide eyes. "Holy shit, what are Joe and Sheila gonna say?"

And even though my parents' reaction to what I'd just told him was definitely not going to be a laughing matter, I laughed so hard that my lungs and ribs and back ached. If things could've stayed like that between me and Coleton, then I think we'd have been fine.

But they didn't.

So, at 2:43 in the morning I sat up, the smell of wood-smoke still stuck to my skin and hair, and I picked my phone up off the nightstand. I tapped out the only response that felt possible, even if it was a lie: It was awesome.

PART TWO

july

MAIA

I WAS STUCK WITH FITTING ROOM DUTY: HANDING people plastic tags with numbers printed on them and unlocking doors and picking clothes up off the floor. Clothes weren't the only refuse of the changing rooms. Old sodas, iced-coffee cups, chunks of gum whose flavor had run out, receipts, the occasional petrified french fry or well-aged Cheerio that had been dislodged from a stroller . . . they all found a temporary resting place in the Bargain Mart fitting room. Someone even decided it was an appropriate place to dispose of their child's dirty diaper.

In between all of those fun tasks, I had to answer the phones and talk over the loudspeaker, telling different departments to pick up the call on line one, line two, line three, and then I had to talk to the person again when they called back, angry, because no one ever picked up in the department I transferred them to in the first place.

Hour after hour passed the same as the one before.

I'm friendly enough to not get fired, but not so friendly that people want to stand around and have whole conversations with me. It's a delicate balance.

My phone kept vibrating in my back pocket, but I didn't look for two reasons:

1. I wasn't supposed to have my phone out on the sales floor.
2. I already knew who it was.

Hayden and our friend, Gabby, had returned from the beach a couple days earlier, and they'd been texting me practically on the hour, every hour, since.

The phone at the fitting room rang. I picked up, reciting the same lame greeting we were forced to say each time: "Thank you for calling your friendly Carson Bargain Mart. How may I direct your call?"

I had my next line all prepared—"Hold, please"—when Hayden's voice broke the static on the other end of the line. "What's the deal, did your phone stop working?"

"Oh, hey," I said, doing my best to sound happy to hear from her. "Sorry, I was planning on calling you later today."

"I'm just getting off work now." I heard a sequence of beeping sounds I immediately recognized. She was getting into her car; they were the alarms that go off when you've turned the key but haven't buckled your seat belt. "Can you take a break?"

"It might be tough to get away right now," I lied.

"Well, try. It's been so long, I'm not gonna remember what you look like! I'll be there in five."

She hung up without giving me a chance to make up another excuse.

I walked out into the forest of bras and underwear to find Donna, the older woman who just last week had hugged me in the break room and cried on my shoulder over Mallory. Her pity was as oppressive as her smothering hugs. But it meant I could count on her for favors.

"Hey, Donna, can you cover the fitting room while I go on lunch?"

She squeezed my hand and said in the most solemn voice, "Of course."

"Thanks," I mumbled.

By the time I made it outside to the cluster of old rusty metal picnic benches that have no doubt been sitting behind Bargain Mart since Donna started here in the 1970s, Hayden was already waiting for me there. As I approached I saw that she had two Styrofoam DairyLand cups sitting on the table. I already knew mine was a strawberry milkshake, and hers was vanilla with mini peanut butter cups.

The sun was blazing, the humidity ratcheting up by the minute. It felt like the inside of a dog's mouth: sticky and stinky and wet. Welcome to July in the South, also known as hell on earth.

"Hey," I said as I scooted into the bench.

"Oh! Sorry, but"—Hayden tore off her DairyLand hat

and placed it on top of the table—"I'm saving this spot for my friend who I haven't seen in forever 'cause she's been avoiding me."

I smiled as I sat down.

She clutched my milkshake, like she was protecting it.

"Wait, Maia?" She reached across the table and took my face between her hands, smushing my cheeks and poking at my forehead and chin. "Is that really you?"

I batted her hands away and whined, "Stop!"

"Fine," she said, pushing the strawberry milkshake back to its spot in front of me. "So?"

"Yeah?"

"So . . . ," she repeated as she unbuttoned and wriggled out of her DairyLand shirt, which bore the DairyLand Fairy mascot emblazoned across the back. I always thought it looked more like an evil ice-cream swirl-haired demon with insect wings than a fairy. "Why are you avoiding me?"

"I'm not avoiding you."

"Liar," she said as she moved the strap of her tank top aside to examine the sunburn line on her shoulder, wincing.

"No, I've just been kinda busy." Lie, lie, lie. "Working and everything. The usual." I didn't know how to tell Hayden that lately being around her, or anyone, only made me feel completely alone.

"Well, how about you come over tonight? Just the two of us? I need to show you our pictures, so you can see all the fun you missed."

"Gee, thanks, Hayden."

"Well, then you're gonna wanna come next time."

"I already do." I sipped on my milkshake, but it did little to cool me down. "Can we do it sometime next week instead?"

"I guess." She paused, then added, "You're still coming with us to the Fourth, right?" I studied her face as we sat across from each other, but I couldn't tell if she actually wanted me to say yes or no. I looked down into the now-melted, soupy milkshake and gave it a stir with my straw, uncertain if I could bear attending the Fourth of July town celebration this year.

"Earth to Maia," Hayden said, waving her hand in the space between us.

"Of course I'm coming. It's practically mandatory, isn't it?" I tried to joke, but like all the words that seemed to pass my lips lately, it came out wrong.

"You make it sound like community service or something." She slurped her milkshake and gave one of her polite, tight-lipped smiles. Then she squinted out at the baking parking lot, the sun bright against her burned cheeks, and looked back at me with that pity face she'd learned since Mallory died. If she could quit doing that, then just maybe we could get back to some sort of normal.

"Are you okay?" she finally asked.

I shrugged. "I'm fine."

She raised her eyebrows, and I counted the seconds she stared, not believing me—one, two, three—"Look, I heard about what happened at Bowman's."

"Oh, *that*?"

"Yeah, that—the party you went to while we were at the beach, even though you vowed to never again attend another party without me."

"It's been a week." I spooned a soggy lump of milkshake into my mouth. "Hasn't someone else done something stupid or embarrassing in this goddamn town by now?"

"Why didn't you tell me about it?"

"I don't know, probably to avoid the are-you-okay conversation." That got me a laugh, but she was still watching me too closely. "It really wasn't a big deal, Hayden. Neil hates me. I don't care for him either. That's all. End of story. No one even took a video this time, so it couldn't have been that bad, right?"

She laughed again, but this time it was faked; she wasn't letting me off that easy. "No one said it was that bad, but . . ." Her voice trailed off in that way she often does when she'd rather the other person finish her sentence for her, like a song that fades out because it doesn't know how to end.

"But what?" I asked.

"Is it true that you were hiding and watching them?" She scrunched her face up like this conversation was putting her in actual physical discomfort. "Did you really have Mallory's camera?"

Part of me wanted to tell her about everything—the gas station wall and the quote and the pictures and Chris. Especially Chris. I wanted to know what she thought of Chris trying to step in and help me with Neil. *Was that chivalrous or sexist, Hayden?* I wanted to ask her because I'd replayed it in my head so many times and I still wasn't sure. But I couldn't.

So instead I said, "I should really get back in there."

"Yeah, okay. But—"

"Thanks for the shake," I told her as I stood and threw my empty cup into the garbage.

"See you on the Fourth?" she called after me.

I smiled my big fake Bargain Mart smile. "Can't wait."

When I got back to the fitting room, Donna was there with a whole shopping cart full of socks and underwear that needed to be repackaged. Why people felt the need to rip open the plastic and touch the socks or underwear prior to deciding whether or not they were going to buy them, I would never know.

Every once in while a customer would stop by, talking about the weather—it was getting dark and cloudy. Another person told us that the National Weather Service had issued a flash flood warning. People were not buying clothes; they were stocking up on batteries and bottled water and milk and bread. I understood the need for batteries and water, but why they all planned on making milk sandwiches was beyond me. Granola bars and beef jerky seemed more logical.

Donna talked my ears off about living through Hurricane Hugo in 1989, which she would tell me about every time we had some kind of weather going on. "Trees uprooted, no power for two weeks, flooding, windows blown out of buildings." She went on and on. "I thought it was the end."

I sensed she meant The End, as in biblically, the end of days.

In her next breath, she said, "Why don't you go ahead and get home," adding morbidly, "while you still can."

As soon as I walked through the sliding glass doors, I was thankful for Donna's early dismissal because the wind was already blowing hard, thunder was rumbling miles away, and the clouds were dark and full. I hurried around to the side of the building where my bike was waiting.

When I pulled it out of the metal bike rack, it was hard to move. I kneeled down to get a closer look, and that's when I realized they weren't just deflated; there were two ugly puncture wounds, one on the wall of each tire. I knew right away it was no accident. It was Neil. He wasn't going to let what happened at Bowman's go that easily. I stood back up and looked around, half expecting to see him somewhere watching me, but no one was in sight.

A drop of rain hit my forehead. They splattered one by one, cold against my skin, falling faster and faster, pockmarking the dusty gravel.

I had several choices:

1. I could wait it out inside.
2. I could wait for one of my parents to give me a ride on their way home from work.
3. I could call Hayden and ask her to pick me up . . . that is, if I hadn't been so weird with her earlier.
4. Or, I could walk.

In case Neil really was watching, I chose option four. I wheeled my bike out of the parking lot and onto the road— those deflated lumps of rubber flapping against the pavement like slabs of raw meat. I would trudge through the goddamn apocalypse in spite of him.

CHRIS

I WAS STARTING TO GET THE HANG OF SMALL TOWNS, but only after I realized there was really, truly nothing to do.

Not that it wasn't fun hanging out with Isobel. It just wasn't exactly as I'd imagined it would be. We'd talk and laugh and do puzzles and play games and eat microwave popcorn and watch movies. But it wasn't like when she stayed with us for that month and a half, helping me get better. Here, she had her regular life. She had to go to work, and sometimes she worked crazy double shifts at the hospital that was already over an hour away in Charlotte. I'd never admit this to my parents, or even to Coleton, but it was starting to feel a little too much like home: me, stuck in a room, alone, reading, planning, and thinking, thinking, thinking.

I'd traded one prison for another.

I hopped into the station wagon—I didn't know where I was going. The car bounced and rocked back and forth as

I carefully drove over the railroad tracks and past Bargain Mart, and the brick cube that was the post office, and a corner store that boasted in its window that it sold both "Live Bait!" and "Custom Headstones," a sampling of which were proudly displayed in the patch of weedy grass next the crumbling parking lot.

There was one stoplight. And then nothing, as far as I could see.

I liked the car windows down and the music blaring, even if it was only Isobel's old cassette tapes from the nineties. They were full of songs from bands I'd never heard of, music that sounded like it was from another planet—tinny and off-key and imperfect, singers who couldn't really sing but made their voices raw and open. There was something so real about it. Something that made me lose my sense of time and place, sort of like the feeling I get when I look at the stars. When I was driving, I could lose *myself*.

I was in the middle of getting lost when a wave of thunder rumbled in the distance. I turned the volume low on the radio. I took my foot off the accelerator and slowed down, watching the speedometer decelerate—55-50-45-35-15— before I pulled off onto the shoulder of whatever no-name road I was on. I stopped for a moment, checking my mirrors before I made a U-turn.

By the time I got to Carson, the rain was already there, the sky darkening by the minute. I went over the railroad tracks and past the Bargain Mart, and through the podunk "downtown," my body feeling heavier with each mile.

Through the screen of rain I saw something on the side of

the road. *Someone.* The windshield wipers swished back and forth as fast as they would go, leaving streaks of water that made it hard to see, but I could tell right away who it was: Maia. She was wheeling her bike alongside her.

As I slowed down next to her, she looked up quickly, her hair dripping in strands, and waved me on with one arm. I lined the words up carefully in my mind before I even rolled down the window because I already had one strike against me and I didn't want to say the wrong thing again. I had to shout over the pounding rain: "Hey, you want a ride?"

"No," she yelled back over the noise.

I stopped the car completely, and she stopped walking too. Squared off her feet like she was ready for a fight, but the effect was weakened when her voice—strained and splintered—fought for enough volume to yell, "I said I don't need help!"

"I know. That's why I said *want* a ride, not *need* a ride."

She pushed her hair out of her face and opened her mouth, but before she could say anything else, another crack of thunder roared—it vibrated through the car, rattling the windows. She looked around, and reluctantly nodded. I braced myself against the rain as I ran to the back of the station wagon to open the trunk. It was coming down sharp like needles. She wheeled her bike over, and I grabbed on to the handlebar while she took the rear tire, our hands touching for a moment as we both reached for the crossbar at the same time. In that second it felt like lightning had touched us both.

"Go, get in," I said, adjusting the bike's position.

She ran over to the passenger side, and I scrambled into

the driver's seat, which was now soaked from the rain falling into the car.

"Shit," she breathed as she slid in and quickly slammed the door behind her.

We looked at each other, dripping and soaked, and both started laughing.

I could feel her watching me as I shifted the car into drive and pulled back onto the road, but when I glanced over, she looked away.

"This weather's no joke," I said.

She didn't respond, so I turned the volume on the music back up just a little, anything to cover the silence.

Finally she cleared her throat and said, "Thank you," as if they were the most difficult pair of words she'd ever had to utter.

"You're welcome."

I didn't know what to say next, so I didn't say anything.

It seemed like minutes passed before she broke the silence again. "You know, I knew what I was doing back there." She paused. "I mean the other night—I knew what I was doing."

"All right." I tried so hard to stop myself from saying anything else, but I couldn't quite exercise that much restraint. "You know I was only trying to help, though, right?"

"I know, but I didn't want help—I didn't want to *need* help."

"I get it."

She just stared at me, squinting, and I could tell she didn't believe me.

"No, I really do. I mean, I know better than you'd think. I know what it feels like to be targeted. Someone once had to help me out in a situation, and I didn't want to need help either."

"Oh," she whispered.

"I guess I just couldn't stand by and do nothing. But not because I thought you were some damsel in distress—I would've done the same thing for anyone." I was worried I'd said too much, but something in the space between us loosened in that moment.

"So maybe"—she paused—"maybe you were partially right. Maybe I was taking it out on you," she said, her voice softer. "But Neil doesn't *scare* me, okay?" she added. "We just—we have history." I couldn't tell what the expression on my face looked like, but it clearly must have given away exactly what I was thinking, because she quickly added, "I mean, not *that* kind of history."

It was still raining when I turned into her driveway, but not quite as violently as it had been only minutes earlier.

"Well, thanks," she said, unbuckling her seat belt as we approached the house.

"No problem." I got out of the car and helped her get the bike. It was only then, as we began maneuvering it back out of the trunk, that I noticed both tires were completely flat.

We stood there next to each other, her bike in between us, and right then, the rain slowed down to a drizzle.

"Okay, well—" I started, but she interrupted me.

"So are you going to the thing on Sunday?"

"What thing?"

"The Fourth of July thing—it's just this stupid town picnic fireworks thing."

"I don't know, are you?"

She laughed, that *ha* laugh again. "Yeah, I'll be there. I
mean, it's not like I have much choice."

"Why not?"

She looked at me for a second, then took a deep breath
like she was preparing to say something long-winded, but she
just shrugged and mumbled, "I don't know."

"I might check it out," I said.

"Maybe I'll see you, then."

"Yeah," I agreed, while biting down on the inside of my
cheek to keep my grin in check. "Maybe."

I watched as she wheeled her bike toward the house and
leaned it up against the railing of the porch. As I pulled out
of the driveway and back onto the road, I let the smile I was
holding in take over my face. I'd told her maybe, but I knew
there was nothing that could prevent me from being there.

MAIA

I WAS WAITING FOR HAYDEN AND GABBY ON THE blanket we'd laid out by the lake, picking through the macaroni salad on my paper plate with my plastic fork, separating out the mushy, green, formerly frozen peas from the mayonnaise-coated macaroni and cubes of cheese. Someone had gotten edgy this year and used sharp cheddar. Hayden and Gabby were waiting in line for barbeque.

I'd never been a huge meat eater—I couldn't quite get past imagining the faces of the animals—but the switch happened all at once. We had a bunch of people at the house after Mallory's funeral, and there was a ton of food. I remember Mom and Dad hadn't eaten for days, and I felt like I should've lost my appetite too, but I was starving—it was all I could think about during the service.

I went into the kitchen, and when I realized I was alone, no witnesses, I grabbed for the first thing I could find: the plate of pigs in a blanket I suspected one of the mothers had brought. I swiped a whole napkin full of them and smuggled it to the bathroom, where I could eat without judgment. I locked the door behind me and laid the napkin out on the bathroom sink. They smelled so delicious—the warm buttery dough, the salty sweetness of the meat—I ate five of them in a row, devouring them as if I'd never eaten anything before in my entire life.

Someone knocked on the door, I remember, and I swallowed one last huge mouthful and yelled, "Just a minute." I flushed the toilet and ran the water, and as I looked up into the mirror, I remember being struck by this overwhelming sense that I didn't quite recognize myself. It was something subtle, but unmistakably altered.

I leaned in closer. Was it my hair, something around my eyes?

No. It wasn't either of those things.

It was Mallory. Or *not* Mallory. Her absence from my life made me look physically different to myself, made me into a stranger. Then suddenly that full, warm, satisfied place in my stomach opened up like a hole inside me, and started churning faster and faster, like the slushie machine at the gas station. It had been days since she'd died, but this was the moment it first hit me that she was gone. Not just gone for the weekend or staying at a friend's house or off on some photography expedition with Neil. But gone. Forever.

And the person I was when she was here was gone too.

Losing control over my own body, I stumbled through the two short steps it took to get from the sink to the toilet, barely making it in time. On my hands and knees, I leaned over and I threw up everything inside me—I threw up my heart, my lungs, and all of the vital organs I imagined had been swimming around within me—purging the last remnants of my life as I knew it. Then I lowered myself the rest of the way down onto the floor and closed my eyes, all those people on the other side of the door taking turns knocking and calling, "Are you okay?"

No. I was not okay.

I gave up meat in that very moment, with my cheek pressed against the icy tiles, the bitter, acrid taste of my insides still on my tongue.

Hayden and Gabby were holding on to each other's arms and squealing, each precariously balancing a flimsy paper plate in her free hand, as they made their way back to our blanket. Gabby kicked her sandals off in the grass and plopped down next to me. She was wearing these short-shorts and a bikini top. She had found all these yoga videos online and had been doing them every day for the past year. Now she took any chance to show off her flat stomach and sculpted arms and thighs—at school, she had taken to walking around the locker room in only a bra and underwear.

"What?" I asked. "What's so funny?"

"Oh, nothing," Hayden said, waving her hand.

"Yeah, you kinda had to be there," Gabby added.

The weirdest part of suddenly being the third wheel in our friendship was that they were both *my* friends first. They hadn't even liked each other—I'd practically had to force them to start hanging out together, and now, when I wasn't looking, they had somehow become best friends, rendering me useless.

"I'm sure you could catch me up." I smiled and tried to laugh, as if I was merely joking, but I don't think it was very convincing.

"It was just this stupid thing someone said," Hayden insisted.

"Who?"

"Maia, dude." Gabby called everyone dude. "Why does it matter?"

"I just want to know." I don't know why I couldn't let it go. Maybe part of me thought they were laughing at me. Or maybe I was trying to pick a fight. "Why don't you want to tell me?"

"It was something stupid Gabby's little sister said—she didn't realize she was saying something sexual," Hayden finally told me.

"Really?" Even I could tell it wasn't a question; it was a dare. "Well, what was it?"

Hayden and Gabby exchanged a loaded glance.

Gabby sighed, and then said, "Is this 'cause we went to the beach without you?" Adding, before I could answer her, "Even though we asked you—no, begged you—to come a million times?"

"What's 'this' supposed to mean?" I set my plate down and air-quoted with my fingers for effect. "There is no *this*. I'm just trying to get you guys to fill me in on the funny story. Why can't you just tell me what she said?" I insisted again. "Why is it such a big deal?"

"She said 'beating off,' okay!" Hayden yelled, her eyes growing all wide and dark the way they do when she's really passionate or angry about something. "But it's not funny without the rest of the whole situation, and . . ." Hayden looked at Gabby, to finish.

Gabby rolled her eyes. "And we didn't think we should be going on and on telling you some pointless story about my sister that wasn't even really all that funny to begin with."

"You can talk about your sister. What do you guys think, I'm gonna fall apart at the mention of the word? Sister!" I yelled. "Sister!" I cupped my hands around my mouth, and shouted it: "Sisterrrrr!"

"Jesus," Gabby mumbled.

"Fine," Hayden said, talking over me. "It'll never happen again. Will you stop yelling?"

"No problem, I'll stop embarrassing you." I stood and picked up my plate and my bag.

"Maia, come on," Gabby whined as I started walking away from them.

"Let her go," Hayden countered.

Raw, formless anger coursed through my body as I made my way over to the edge of the lake where the ducks and geese were waiting; they immediately began to close in on me, sensing I had food to spare. All I'd been able to eat was a handful of greasy, salty potato chips and half a hamburger bun that I'd filled with condiments only—lettuce, tomato, ketchup, relish, mustard, onion—but without the burger part, there wasn't much of a point. So I started ripping pieces of plain bread off and tossing them to the smaller ducks. I tore at the bread until all that was left on my plate was a pile of soggy, discolored, condiment mush and pale green-gray peas.

"You know, that's really bad for the birds," a voice said. It took me a minute to realize the words were directed at me.

I looked over my shoulder to see that Chris was walking up behind me.

"Oh, hi." I was surprised at how relieved I was to see him standing there and not Hayden or Gabby. "Wait, what?"

"The bread," he clarified. "It's not good for them."

"Oh," I said again, looking down at my plate. "Why not?"

"It causes all kinds of problems. Malnutrition and deformities and things like that. It can even kill them," he told me. "I read an article about it a while ago. They have these little pouches in their beaks where they store food, and if the bread gets stuck in there, it can get moldy and poison them."

I thought about it for a second as I watched the geese pecking through the grass for crumbs. "Everyone feeds them bread, though."

"Yeah, I know. Exactly." He stuck his hands in his pockets and rocked back on his heels and said, as if just realizing the strangeness of this conversation, "So, spread the word."

"I will."

We looked out at the lake for a second before he said, "How's your bike? Still out of commission?"

I nodded.

"That sucks," he sighed. "Well, let me know if you want help with the tires," he offered.

"You know how to do that?"

His gaze drifted off and he grinned in this shy way, like

he'd only just realized that might be helpful. "Well, no," he admitted. "But I know how to look up videos that will show us how."

"Thanks," I told him. "I might take you up on the offer."

"Cool." He nodded and looked around uncomfortably. "Well, I just wanted to say hi. Again." He smiled and said, "So hi," as he started backing up.

"Hi," I echoed. "And thanks for the PSA." I gestured toward the ducks and geese.

He glanced over his shoulder as he walked away, and waved, calling out, "Anytime!"

I looked back at my friends, and they appeared so small in the distance, sitting there together, probably discussing me and my outburst, deciding if keeping our trio intact was still worth all the effort it took to be my friend lately.

I started walking, and without having a clear idea in my mind of what I was doing, I walked right past my friends.

I followed Chris.

CHRIS

I WOVE BETWEEN THE GROUPS OF PEOPLE STANDING around talking, sitting in circles of lawn chairs, spread out on blankets, the smells of food swirling in the air. Then I heard my name being called.

"Chris? Chris!" I turned around and saw Maia jogging up behind me. "Wait up," she said.

I shoved my hands into the pockets of my jeans as I stood there, unsure of what she was going to say. I prepared myself for something insignificant, like *Oh, you dropped this*, and she'd be holding out an old receipt. But I really hoped it was going to be something more meaningful, like *I'm glad you're here. Do you wanna hang out?*

"Hey, so I was just wondering—" she began, but stopped short, slightly out of breath.

"Yeah?"

"Did you really have your heart set on staying to watch the fireworks?" she finished.

"I kind of hate fireworks, actually," I admitted, feeling something light and fuzzy bouncing around inside my chest. "So not really, no."

"Hatred of fireworks—you really aren't from around here, are you?"

A tiny spark of shame flickered in my chest. Was there something inherently manly about watching things explode in the air that I just didn't get? "Do *you* want to stay for them?" I asked.

She made a face like I had missed the entire joke. "It's either going to be the same bang-pop show the fire department has been knocking off for the past decade, or boys from my school with their pop rockets and shells smuggled over from South Carolina, just waiting to see who will be the first to lose a finger."

"So, no fireworks?"

"No," she said, and then cocked her head as if she was thinking about something. "I guess I grew out of fireworks. What if I took you up on the bike offer instead?" she asked.

"Now?"

"Yeah. I mean, unless you don't want—"

"No, I do!" I cringed at how excited I sounded, but then she smiled and it lit up the air around her.

We walked toward the huge field behind the church parking lot, and I was so damn happy that the hospital had called Isobel into work. When she told me she couldn't come along tonight, I almost didn't leave the house. Part of me worried about running into Neil. Part of me also worried about running into Maia, and an even bigger part worried about not running into her.

Walking next to her now, I was glad I'd taken the risk. I was glad I'd come alone. And I was really glad I had clicked on that stupid article about bread and waterfowl.

We sat in my car outside Bargain Mart and watched exactly three videos on how to replace a bike tire.

"Well, it *looks* pretty easy," I offered, refocusing on the video instead of the way I could feel the heat coming off her body.

"Yeah, but everything looks easy when you watch it online."

"True," I agreed. I thought about all those videos I'd watched when I was laid up in my bedroom back home. It did look easy, the solution so clear, right there in front of my face. When I was watching those videos of all those people who had become who they were meant to be, it looked like the only obstacle I had to overcome in order to be myself was me.

Yeah right.

She picked her bag up off the floor and began rooting around inside it, clearly searching for something in particular. Finally she pulled out a pen—one of those felt-tip-marker type pens—explaining as she did so, "I like lists."

She uncapped the pen with her teeth, and wrote the supplies we'd need on the palm of her hand, numbering them as she wrote:

1. bike levers
2. tubes
3. air pump
4. extra patches

She whispered each item as she pressed the pen against her skin. Something about that made my heart pound, made my mind run away with this crazy fantasy of her writing those words on my hand instead. And the second I thought it, I couldn't stop wishing it was actually happening. I redirected my gaze out the window.

I'd lived so much of my life in a constant state of wishing and waiting; sometimes it was hard to stop these thoughts in my head from running wild.

She took a deep breath, looking over at the building, and said, "It's weird. I used to come to Bargain Mart all the time before I worked there. It was sort of the thing to do around here, believe it or not. Now I can't stand it."

"Let's be quick, then. We'll just get what we need and go." I opened my door, prepared to get out, but she still sat there with her seat belt fastened.

"Okay," she agreed, but she kept her fingers clutched around the door handle for a moment before she opened it.

"Hey, I just thought of something." I closed my door, and she looked over at me. "I remember seeing this little bicycle shop the other day when I was driving through New Pines."

"New Pines?" she repeated. "That's an hour away."

I nodded as I stuck the key back into the ignition. "You game?"

She was quiet for a second, and then a slow smile tugged at the corners of her mouth. "Really, though," she said. "You don't mind driving all the way out there?"

"Are you kidding?" I started the car up. "I love driving."

She closed her door. "Okay. Yeah, let's do it."

I pulled out of the parking lot and headed toward the edge of town. Once we crossed over the train tracks and passed the stoplight, I accelerated. Maia rolled her window down all the way and let her arm fly out, catching the wind. I allowed myself tiny glances, just enough so I could still watch the road, but I managed to see the way she fanned her fingertips in the oncoming breeze, like she was caressing the air, how her eyes half closed, how she fell into the comfort of a drive much in the same way I did.

We drove for a while and it was quiet, but unlike before, it didn't feel uncomfortable. As we passed a sign on the side of the road that said COUNTY LINE, she finally spoke.

"Do you know I can't even remember the last time I crossed the county line?"

"Seriously?" I asked, suddenly realizing how confining it must be to live in Carson, not just visiting for a couple of months, but to be there for years on end. And then I found myself thinking about my parents, about Isobel. "Have you always lived in Carson?"

"Most people who live in Carson have always lived in Carson."

"I don't know how you do it," I said, but then I quickly added, "I mean, no offense."

"None taken." She laughed. "It sucks."

"It doesn't suck. It's just—I don't know. It's nice in some ways, but I've only been here two weeks, and I feel like if I didn't get out of there every couple of days, I would go crazy."

"I know the feeling. I could've gone to the beach with my friends a couple of weeks ago, but—" She stopped in the middle of her sentence, and right as I was about to ask her to finish, she continued. "Things have been kinda weird with us lately."

"How come?"

She waited before answering—I'd never met anyone who would actually think before speaking. Her thoughtfulness was intriguing, fresh. "I don't really know." She looked at me and stifled another laugh. "I also don't know why I just told you that."

"If it makes you feel any better, the same thing is happening with me and my best friend."

"Why?"

I thought about it. I had lots of theories that mostly revolved around me changing, but it seemed too complicated to explain out loud, in words that would make sense. "I guess I don't really know either," I told her instead.

She nodded.

A few minutes passed before she spoke again. "Can I ask you something?"

"Okay," I replied.

"So what are you really doing in Carson? Is it punishment or something?"

"No," I told her, laughing. "I actually wanted to come here."

"*What?*" she shouted, her face twisting in confusion.

"See, my parents have kinda had me on house arrest for a while now," I explained. "Like seriously, home school and everything. So, it's just nice to be away."

"Why?" she asked, drawing out the word, her voice still tinged with shock. "What did you do?"

I debated what I could actually tell her. Not much. So I settled on, "It's complicated."

She narrowed her eyes for a moment, studying me, and I was sure she was going to ask more questions, but then she nodded and said, "Understood."

"I just needed some freedom, even if I had to exile myself to the middle of nowhere to get it," I told her, adding once again, "No offense."

"No, I know what you mean." She repositioned herself in the seat, tucking one of her legs under the other, facing me slightly. "It's sort of like my bike is my only freedom. I can't really go any farther than my legs and daylight will take me, but at least it's something. It's not really the same thing, I guess."

"No, it is," I said.

"Maybe that's why these last few days without my bike have been such torture," she mused. She inhaled sharply, like a tiny gasp, as if just realizing. "I guess that was the point."

"So what happened to your bike, anyway?"

She smiled in this nonsmile, ironic way. "If I had to guess," she began, looking up into the sky, "I'd say Neil happened."

"Helmet head Neil. Right." That was what I had suspected,

but I hadn't wanted to come out and ask. "'Cause of the whole history thing?"

"Yep, the history."

"Can I ask, why did he freak out on you anyway?"

"Ugh," she groaned, shaking her head slowly back and forth. "Also complicated."

"Understood," I said, echoing her previous response to me. Only, she didn't actually understand, and neither did I, any further than understanding the fact that neither of us wanted to explain what the real deal was with our situations. I waited to say anything else because I didn't want to push it, but I had a legitimate concern I needed to lay to rest, one way or another. "One last question, and then I'll never bring him up again."

"Oh-*kay*."

"Is it complicated, as in he's a giant, jealous ex-boyfriend who's going to beat me up for hanging out with you kind of complicated?"

"No," she said, laughing. "Just plain, nonjealous, non-ex-boyfriend complicated."

"Got it." I made like I was zipping my mouth shut, and she laughed again.

Okay, I could admit it: I liked her.

Liked her, because even though we had not been on speaking terms for nearly half of the short time we'd known each other, and we didn't even really know each other to begin with, it felt like we were starting over. Some people won't let you start over—like my mom, the way she couldn't let go of the past. I respected Maia for that. I enjoyed being this close to her. I liked that she wrote stuff on her hand, that I could make her laugh. I even liked that she seemed a little defensive sometimes. But the thing I really liked was that she treated me like I was just a regular person, that I was just me.

The silence that followed was all right, but a subject change was in order. My dad was always big on subject changes whenever things got even slightly uncomfortable. I think it was because he was shy but didn't want people to know. He'd been taught that men aren't supposed to be shy, but that was always one of the things I liked about my dad.

"Are you still in school?" I asked. There, that was a good topic.

"One more year," she said with a sigh.

"Me too."

"Yeah? Then what, college?" she asked. "You look like the college type."

"Ouch. Why did that feel a little like an insult? Yes, college. Is that not cool?"

"No, it is. I just—I don't know. . . ." She trailed off, and right as I was about to ask her to finish, she started talking. "It just seems like lately everyone has it all figured out except for me."

"Believe me, the college part is the *only* thing I have figured out."

I glanced over at her. She was squinting, studying me like she was trying to decide whether or not she believed me.

"Well, what about you?" I asked, because I didn't know how I could ever begin to describe all the things I didn't have figured out. "What do you want? Isn't there some dream you have?"

I was beginning to recognize the way she would stare out the window and get quiet. She was thinking. I waited, biting down on the inside of my cheek to stop myself from speaking again until she answered.

MAIA

I COULD ALMOST SEE A LINE DRAWING ITSELF between us. But it was a different kind of line than the one that stood between me and my parents, me and my friends, me and Mallory, even. This line was curving, closing in on me, stretching at the ends like arms reaching around. It was trying to become a circle instead of a line, a circle without ends and limits, a circle that was making my world smaller and smaller, crushing me with each breath I took.

Somehow, I knew if I let that line close around me, I'd never be able to escape its boundaries. As I looked out across it, there he was, looking at me, waiting for an answer. And so the words just spilled out of my mouth, smooth like butter, one after another, as if I'd rehearsed them a million times, as if they were really mine:

"I want to take pictures," I lied.

If only I could've stopped myself there.

"I want to travel the world and take photos on every continent," my voice said. "I want to work for *National Geographic* someday. I want to see my work in art galleries. I want to do something special. I want to be someone." I could hear the passion in the words, feel the emotion like a lump in my throat, heat simmering in my chest.

Except all that fire—it didn't belong to me.

These were Mallory's words. I'd heard them before, me sitting in our barn, her standing there emoting, dreaming, sermonizing, that vinegar-floral-sulfur scent of her makeshift closet darkroom chemicals still disintegrating into the air, making my head fuzzy. I would sit and listen as the photographs dried out, the breeze whipping them against the strings they were pinned to, *thwap thwaping* like the beat that underpinned her future. I knew the tune so well, it was easy to repeat.

When I glanced over at him, he was looking at me the way people always looked at Mallory, like they were in awe, under a spell, so I quickly added, "I mean, I just want to get outta here. Like everyone else."

"No, that's—that's not like everyone else at all. That's a real dream."

"I don't know." I shrugged, the relief and guilt tugging at me with even force, rocking my mind back and forth. I tried to convince myself that Mallory might actually be okay with me borrowing her dream for a little while. "All right, well, now you have to tell me yours. What's your college dream?"

"It's going to seem so bland in comparison."

"No, it won't," I assured him. "Tell me."

"Okay," he began. "Well, I've always loved space. Ever

since I was a little kid, I've wanted to know everything I could about astronomy and the universe and stars and planets and black holes. I've never wanted to do anything else. So that's what I'm going to go to school for."

"What are you talking about? You want to be, like, an astronaut or something; that's way cooler than what I said."

He started laughing. "I'm not sure I'd ever want to actually leave Earth, but something in astrophysics or aerospace would be pretty cool. Sometimes I think I'd like to teach. Be a professor."

"Wow, you must be really smart, then."

"I don't know about that." He looked straight ahead at the road, but I could tell he was trying hard not to smile, which was pretty irresistible. He cleared his throat and added, "I'm just a geek."

Mile by mile, the endless fields began to give way, houses popping up sparsely at first, then with more volume. A few businesses entered the mix, until the ratio flipped and it was more businesses than houses. When we entered New Pines proper, Chris slowed the car down to precisely thirty-five miles per hour, like the speed limit sign demanded.

And just like that, I felt something of Mallory stirring in the space around me. I glanced over my shoulder into the backseat. So did Chris, although he didn't know what we were looking for. Had she been sitting there, right in the middle grinning at us, one arm hanging over each of our seats, it wouldn't have surprised me in the least. I wished even for a flicker of a second she had been there. But, of course, the backseat was empty.

"You know, I've driven through New Pines a lot," I said, because he was expecting me to say something. "But I've only ever stopped here once before. When we were kids. We were on our way to the beach—I think that was the first and last family vacation we ever took."

New Pines is halfway between Carson and the coast. It's probably the size of Carson, but it's one of those small towns that has somehow been able to turn its history of decline around and transform itself into a funky, hip, crunchy little touristy place where people stop on their way out to the beach, whereas Carson just slowly fizzled out.

"Who's 'we'?" he asked.

Had I said "we" out loud? I wondered.

"My family and I," I said, deliberately omitting the specifics. It was years ago when we came here, back when our parents were still together. I was nine, so Mallory was maybe ten or eleven.

A montage of images flooded my brain: *pink ice cream—*strawberry—dripping down the side of a giant waffle cone onto her arm, her tongue licking the trail it left behind; her arm reaching across the table, tipping my ice cream cone into my face, mashing it into my nostrils. It was birthday-cake flavored, I remember that, with swirls of sky-blue frosting and specks of multicolored sprinkles mixed in. That used to be my favorite, although now I can barely remember what it tasted like.

She laughed.

My parents laughed.

And finally I laughed too.

Looking back, I wished we had a picture, because the memory was so blurry around the edges that I wasn't sure it could be trusted. I wished Mallory's older self had been there in that moment, like she had managed to be present at all the right moments, ready to capture it. But she wasn't her yet. I wasn't me yet. *Me. Am I even me right now, or am I like Mallory was back then, still trying to find her camera—the way she would see the world through ground glass and technology, the medium by which she would record it all?* I hadn't found my version of that yet, and I sometimes wondered if I ever would.

Chris continued driving down the street, but I wished I could put the world on pause. Because it all happened in that ice cream parlor, right there—we were passing it.

Then on the other side of the street, I could see her on the sidewalk, hear her footsteps skipping ahead of me. That sidewalk, right there. She was running, so excited, her shadow bouncing beneath her.

I closed my eyes; her laughter echoed in my head.

I was running too, but I was way behind, in the background, like I always was.

A camera shutter snapped. At least, that's what my mind told me it was. In reality, it was probably a test firework being set off in the distance.

I twisted around in my seat, already unclicking the seat belt and flinging it off my body.

"Hey, can you pull over up here?"

"Yeah. What is it?" he said, slowing to a stop at the side of the road as I opened the car door. I heard him say something else through the open window, but I was speed walking, practically jogging, my sandals tripping me. I ran back along the wrought iron fence, the black parallel lines moving the scenery in the background like an animation—a cartoon graveyard. It made me feel like I was running in place and the cemetery was moving rather than the other way around.

Somehow, in spite of all of this, I made it back to the gate. I knew this gate. I knew this spot.

I couldn't remember the feel of cold metal on my fingertips.

It was her hands I remembered, trailing along the wrought iron. I was following her like a shadow, mimicking her every move, because that's what little sisters do. All except her hands on the gates. I was afraid to touch it, afraid of getting too close to death. She walked right up to it, though, stood face-to-face with it.

But that wasn't my only memory of these gates.

There was another.

This one was static, not a lived memory. This was one of Mallory's pictures. I closed my eyes. I could see its exact location on the wall in the barn where Mallory had pinned it up.

Which meant she had come back here. To the place where we stopped once and behaved like a functional, loving family. And now I was here again too.

I sensed Chris standing behind me. "Soooo . . . ," he said, drawing out the word. "What are we doing?"

"I have to come back here," I said, still looking out at the cemetery, my hands wrapped around the bars, the weight of the cold, rough metal finally under my own fingers.

Chris made a sound like a *hum*—a questioning, uncertain syllable.

"With the camera, I mean." I turned around quickly, and added, in as normal a tone as I could, "I have to come back with the camera. To take pictures."

We stood opposite each other on the sidewalk where Mallory had once been, where even a different version of me had once been, and he exhaled like he'd been holding his breath. His eyes went from narrowed and focused to soft and open, his mouth curving into a smile.

As he let out that breath of air, it was almost like he was making the *phew* sound. "I am so glad you just said that."

"Why?" I asked, and as he had me wondering what about this situation was so amusing, I felt my face inadvertently mirroring his smile.

"'Cause this whole thing just had a very beginning-of-a-horror-movie kind of vibe going on for a minute there." He stepped up to the gate and stood next to me, looking into the distance at the massive cemetery that stood beyond the wrought iron bars.

I looked into the distance too, and said, "Oh."

"I mean, I think you're cool and all," he continued, a light-heartedness in his voice. "But I'm not ready to die some kind of bloody zombie death for you." He laughed, and added, "Not quite yet, anyway."

He took a few steps, letting his hand trail along the fence the way Mallory's had. He was following along behind my memories of her skipping, light on her toes, and for some reason I felt light too, like my feet were barely touching the ground.

It had taken several minutes for his words to fully sink in, but as they did I laughed.

He turned around and asked, "What?"

"So, bloody zombie death. That's one of your tests of a relationship?" I asked, realizing too late I'd used the word "relationship." I held my breath as I watched for signs of freak-out, wondering if I should quickly swap out "friendship" instead, or clarify that I didn't think this was a relationship.

His eyes widened, and his voice was laced with faux shock as he gasped and said, "You mean it's *not* one of yours?"

I exhaled a laugh, relieved that maybe he hadn't noticed.

"Isn't a willingness to die a bloody zombie death a little more reliable a test than"—he paused, looking in the distance like he was searching for the rest of his sentence—"a dozen roses?" he finished.

The sound of his laugh was like a tiny volt of electricity zapping my confidence. Something nudged me in the side, like a poke under the ribs. I turned to look, again half expecting to see Mallory right there next to me.

Nudge. Nudge. Nudge.

She nudged at me until I said the words she had carefully lined up on my tongue: "Fine," I sighed in that playful way she used to do when she wanted to be extra melodramatic. "I'll take it under consideration."

"Hey, that's all I'm saying," he replied, not missing a beat.

And just like that, this whole thing—the witty banter, the back-and-forth—became so easy, so navigable.

He pointed up ahead. "There it is."

I could see the sign: PED-X CYCLE SHOP

The scent of incense and candles and lavender wafted out onto the street from a new-age-type store we passed. It snapped me back into the present like a rubber band against my wrist. I recognized those smells from Mallory's room. They hovered around the building like an invisible fog, the way it used to cling to her clothes and hair, following her wherever she went. We walked by a little storefront gallery that seemed to specialize in seascape paintings and pottery, and then there was the soda shop where Mallory's ice cream cone had melted, the place where my mom and dad had laughed together.

I slowed down as we passed the window, trying to find the booth where we'd sat as a family. I caught a glimpse of my reflection in the window, but then as my eyes adjusted to the interior, I saw something in the corner that was familiar, but again, not familiar from my memories.

It was a shiny jukebox, all lit up in neon.

I didn't remember seeing it there when I was a kid. No, I remembered it from another picture on the wall. I'd had no idea where it was even taken until this moment. I pulled up short and peered through the window with my hands cupped around my eyes. My reflection stood in front of me, and for a split second I swear I thought it was Mallory. I flinched like it was one of those jump-scare movie moments.

Chris stepped up beside me and looked through the glass too, craning his neck to see. "What?" he asked.

"I thought I . . . ," I began, but by the time I got the words out, my eyes had settled back on my own reflection again. "Nothing. Never mind," I said, and as I turned back to look at him, I had this overwhelming sense that I was exactly where

I was supposed to be—because Mallory was everywhere I turned. She had spent time here, and now I was discovering all of these pieces of her that she had left behind like a trail of bread crumbs.

When we got to the bike shop, I pulled on the door handle, but it wouldn't budge.

"Oh shit," Chris said, pointing to the window.

CLOSED, the handwritten sign said. Then underneath: HAPPY INDEPENDENCE DAY.

CHRIS

JUST AS WE WERE ABOUT TO WALK AWAY, A MAN came to the door and unlocked it. He appeared to be around my dad's age, a little less gray maybe. He was wearing a polo shirt that said "PED-X CYCLE."

Pushing the door open, he looked at me and said, "Come on in."

"You're not closed?" Maia asked.

"Not if y'all can find what you need in the next five minutes." He looked at me again and smiled, even though Maia was the one who'd asked the question. "So, what can I help you find today?"

I gestured to Maia, who glanced at the words on her hand and told him, "Both of my tires are flat, so I need to get two new inner tubes. And I need an air pump, too. And bike levers," she added, sounding so sure of herself, like we hadn't just sat in the car watching the same videos for the first time.

I watched the man's face as he listened to her—or rather, *didn't* listen to her—and I understood why she suddenly sounded like someone else. He was fidgeting as she spoke, kept opening his mouth like he was about to interrupt her, squinting his eyes hard and scrunching up his face, like she wasn't making sense, even though she was.

"First thing's first." He looked to me. *Again.* "Do you know what size her tires are?"

I knew this routine well. This guy was a jackass. I'd been treated like this plenty of times.

"Who, me?" I responded. "No."

"*I* know my tire size, though," she replied firmly.

"You know all the numbers that are printed on the side-wall of the tire?" He looked at me again, then back to her, like he'd just challenged her with some sort of a dare rather than an answerable question.

Maia pulled her phone out of her pocket and said, "Yes. I even took a picture."

She was putting misogynistic bike guy in his place.

I said to her, "Hey, I'll let you do your thing—I'm gonna look over there."

She nodded, and when she met my eyes, I felt like we had a silent moment of understanding.

"All right," he said as I drifted away from them. "Let's see what you got there."

I was checking out the cycling apparel, all the Lycra and technological fabrics, and I wondered if I could use something like this for running. As I walked by a floor-length mirror, I couldn't help myself. I pulled the bottom of my T-shirt down, making sure my chest was smooth and flat. Just then, Maia appeared next to me in my reflection.

"Hey," she said. "Ready?"

The man locked the door behind us, and we stood there, Maia with her bag of supplies, me hoping she hadn't caught me checking myself out in the mirror.

"Well," I said, looking around, "what should we do now?"

Almost like it was an answer to my question, a firework sounded in the distance. We both looked up, searching for the explosion in the sky, but it was still too light to see where it had come from.

She shrugged, and looked around, as I had. "It'll be getting dark soon," she began. "I don't know. Maybe we should just go back?"

"Really?"

"Yeah." Her voice wavered, though. I suddenly got the feeling I had missed something. "I mean, nothing's going to be open now anyway, with the holiday and all."

"We could walk a little farther?" I looked down the road, at the line of shops that seemed to hold so much potential, so much possibility—we were out here living, not asking anyone for permission. I wanted so badly to stay.

There was a definite tension pulling at the space between us, and when I turned back toward her, I recognized something in her expression, in the tone of her voice when she said, "No, I just want to go. I mean, I didn't even really tell my friends I was leaving."

I felt like an idiot, the realization hitting me at once. I was a guy. I was just some guy she didn't really know, in a place that was far away from home, where there weren't a lot of people around, and it was about to be getting dark, and no one knew where she was or who she was with. Of course I got it.

"Okay, that's fine. Yeah, let's go."

As we walked back to the car, I didn't know the right thing to say. I had so many different thoughts swirling around in my head. It was a strange feeling—a good but strange feeling—to really be passing. Not as a girl who was really a boy, or a boy who was really a girl, but to be seen as just a boy.

But then I had to remind myself of how boys could be—how men are *taught* to be. Not just rude and condescending like the shop guy, but how they could turn scary and mean and dangerous. It wasn't something I could ever really forget about; it was always there in the back of my mind. I had a whole list of scenarios tucked away in my memory of things that had happened, and it was not made up of the really terrible stuff, like what happened that day in the woods. It was filled with smaller things—a particular look a boy gave me while passing in the hallway at school, or some guy walking too close behind me on the street, or a man sitting down next to me on the bus and taking up too much space, letting his thigh knock against mine. All of those seemingly innocuous things men do every day that can be threatening as hell. Meanwhile, they're completely oblivious.

I would never be that type of man.

Which meant that if Maia said she wanted to leave, the

only thing I was supposed to do was take her home. Not try to persuade her to change her mind or make a point or suggestion, however well meaning. The only thing I was supposed to say, immediately, was, *Okay, let's go.*

I was starting to understand that there's also a price that comes with being a boy, one that's different from being a girl. Maybe the price is more one of a responsibility—to not only be a decent person, like everyone else, and not only to *not* turn scary or mean or dangerous, but to never forget.

I found myself wondering, as I had once wondered if other girls felt the consequences of their bodies the way I did, if other boys felt consequences too, like the one I was suddenly coming face-to-face with, as I walked down an unfamiliar street with an unfamiliar girl.

When we made it back to the car and started driving, I wished that I could tell her I wasn't thinking anything about her. Not really, anyway. At least, nothing mean or perverted or dangerous. That I really did just want to hang out. I wanted to know her. I wasn't looking for anything else, not expecting anything.

Ten minutes had passed before she said, "Who is this?" looking at the radio, as if she just realized music had been playing the entire time.

"I don't know, it came with the car," I said, laughing. She drew her eyebrows together, like she was trying to understand what the hell I meant or why it was a joke. "It's like an actual cassette tape my aunt had in the car. There's a whole bunch of them in there." I gestured to the glove box.

She paused and looked around, like she was only just now

seeing the car for the first time, realizing it was as old as dirt. She opened the glove box and peered inside.

"Full disclosure," I began, hoping to lighten the mood. "That's why I almost hit you that day on the road."

"What do you mean?"

"I was messing around with the tapes. That's why I wasn't paying attention."

She laughed. "Nice to know I'd have gone out for a good reason. I like it, I think—the music."

"Yeah," I agreed. I wanted to say something else, though, about the bike shop guy. I wanted to acknowledge that I realized he was being a douche, to ask if that's why she wanted to leave, if it bothered her. But I probably already knew those answers.

The sky was darkening. The sun had just set. It was a new moon tonight. The sky was so clear. Too bad the firework were about to obliterate it all with their smoke and chemical Venus was rising in the west. I wanted to hear her talk aga hear her voice, so I went with the one subject that was alw easy for me to talk about.

"Hey, check out the moon, Maia."

She looked up through the windshield. "Where?"

"West."

"Where?" she repeated, this laugh in her voice. "Y give me right or left."

"There." I pointed to her right. "Can you see it?

"No. . . ," she said.

Careful to keep the car centered in the lan slightly toward her and looked up, pointing m

in the direction I was looking. "See? It's a new moon, so it's dark, but with the light right now, you can see the complete outline of it."

"Oh wow," she breathed. "Yeah, I see."

"I love when it's like that," I told her.

"That's really beautiful."

"Yeah, plus when the moon is dark, it's easier to see everything else—the stars and planets, I mean."

"It looks fake," she mused. "Like a cutout or something someone just stuck up there."

I liked the way she saw things; I guess it was because she was an artist.

"See that one bright star near the moon, kind of below it and to the right?" I asked her. "You know what that is?"

She squinted at the point of light. "Is that really a star? It's so bright."

"No, it's Venus."

She smiled as she looked at the sky. "It's so crazy to think about," she said, and I waited for her to finish. I counted silently: *one, two, three, four.*

"What?" I finally asked. "What's crazy?"

"Just thinking about being on Earth, the way it's just sitting there in space, in the middle of nothing."

I was physically biting my tongue, repressing the urge to correct her or explain all the ways that Earth is not just sitting there in the middle of nothing. Where would I even begin? Kepler's laws of planetary motion? Galileo? Newton? General relativity? The entire timeline of the history of physics was running through my mind on a loop.

"Okay, don't look so horrified," she said with a snort. "I know it's not really like that."

"Sorry," I said. I felt embarrassed; I could be a snob when it comes to this stuff.

"I know you people just love to think southerners are stupid, but I'm not a total moron, believe it or not. I fully understand it all has to do with gravity and orbits, or whatever else. I just mean . . ." She paused, searching for the words, but this time I couldn't stop myself from interrupting her.

"I don't think southerners are stupid."

She said, "Okay," but I could tell from the way the curve of her mouth was set that she didn't believe me.

"Hey, my parents grew up here, just like you—I don't think they're stupid."

"But *you* didn't." She squinted at me, like she was trying to see me better. I felt the beat of my heart pumping faster. "Let me guess—you grew up in . . . Connecticut?"

"Connecticut? No."

She looked at me even harder, this smile playing at the corners of her mouth. "Massachusetts?"

I smiled back. *"No,"* I replied, wondering what kind of criteria I was fulfilling in her mind about the kinds of people who grew up in places like Connecticut and Massachusetts.

"I know," she finally said. "New York."

I hesitated, but then gave in. "Okay, yeah. So?"

"Nothing." She shrugged. "I could just tell."

"How?"

"Maybe it's the way you talk."

Suddenly I really wanted to know what I sounded like

to her. I wished I didn't care so much, wished I wasn't so self-conscious about it. I'd been purposely talking lower for years, before the hormones, even before I consciously understood what I was doing, but I cleared my throat before speaking again just to be sure.

"I grew up in New York State, not New York City, which is what everyone thinks when you say 'New York.'" I lived on the complete opposite side of the state in a suburb of Buffalo that was pretty much like any other suburb in America. "Where I grew up and New York City—it's like two different worlds."

She nodded like she was really considering this. "It's sort of the same here, in a way. I mean, Western North Carolina is totally different from Eastern North Carolina. We have the mountains on one side, the ocean on the other—two completely different landscapes, different weather, different ways of doing things. Then you have places like Charlotte and Raleigh and Winston-Salem dotted throughout, all this nice metropolitan culture. But between, it's all hog farms and tobacco fields and soy crops and a bunch of land waiting to become the next big thing. But really, we're just another part of that big line of fields between where you want to be and the emptiness in between. Carson is just another spot of nothing."

"Whoa. That's big stuff," I said. "Yeah, I didn't think about that. You're right."

As I reviewed our conversation, I realized I'd never let her finish what she was saying. "I interrupted you before. What were you going to say?"

"Before you called me stupid?"

"I did not call you stupid!"

"Relax, I'm kidding!" She laughed at me again, in this way that made me laugh at myself.

I breathed in deeply. The air was cooling off outside, and it calmed me. "You were saying how it was crazy to think about—"

"Oh, right," she said. "I just meant, like, I remember when I was a little kid, before I knew about the science of it, I used to stay awake at night actually worrying about Earth, thinking one day it would just stop spinning and fall and fall and just keep falling forever."

A firework soared up into the sky at that moment and burst above us, casting a rainbow across the car, over Maia's face.

"I don't know," she said, quieter. "Sometimes I still think about that, I guess."

I opened my mouth to respond, but watching her, I couldn't tell whether what she was saying made her sad or worried or something else. I got the feeling she wasn't really talking about the planet anymore.

"When I was a kid," I offered, "it was the opposite for me. I used to have this theory about the universe and everything that helped me to not be afraid, when I thought about Earth and the planets and the stars and the Sun and all of it."

"What was it?"

"Well, everything is perfect. It's all orchestrated in this total balance of creation and destruction. I mean, the scale of the cosmos is so vast that we're not even evolved enough to comprehend it. But when you think about the beginning, and how much has had to happen for us to be here—how the universe had to evolve, and how our galaxy is just one tiny part, and our solar system is an even smaller part, and Earth is miniscule in comparison—it's incredible that somehow life evolved on this planet. All the comets and asteroids that had to collide with Earth to give us the oceans and gases and metals and everything we would need. It seems like chaos, but it's not at all. Us sitting here in this car having this conversation has been like thirteen billion years in the making." I stopped to catch my breath; I was getting carried away. But she was looking right at me, waiting for me to finish. "And when things are working like that, then it makes me feel like everything else in my life is going to work out too."

She was quiet, and I could feel the creep of embarrassment crawling up my neck. I'd given her too much of myself, way too much.

"You said you *used* to have this theory, but you still believe that," she said. "Don't you?"

It was like the opposite of being caught in a lie, except it was the same vulnerable kind of naked feeling. She had caught me in a truth. "Maybe," I admitted. "Is that a bad thing?"

She shook her head. "No, it's nice."

As we drove, fireworks exploded on either side of the car, some in the distance, others closer. All different colors. We had both windows rolled all the way down, the wind blowing in. She had her head resting against the frame of the car door, her hair blowing all across her face. I had to force myself to stop watching her.

MAIA

THE HEADLIGHTS SHONE ON MY HOUSE LIKE A SPOT-light. I knew I was supposed to say good night and thanks and this was fun and let's do it again and all of those normal things you say to people, but when I looked over at Chris and his smile, I couldn't think of any words to say. I wanted to lean into the space between us, something like gravity pulling me toward him. But I looked down at my hands in my lap, and said, "Well."

And then he laughed and said, "Yeah."

"Okay," I tried to begin again, but words were failing me.

"Bike tires part two another day, then?" he asked.

"I'd like that."

We were stuck looking at each other, except this time he looked away first. He ran his hand over his hair, and drummed his fingers along the edge of the steering wheel. I opened the door, and when the light inside the car turned on, it seemed to crush whatever the awkwardness was that had just taken place.

As I got out of the car, he raised his hand in a small wave. "Good night."

"Night," I said through the open window.

I went inside, but I stood there in the dark entryway and watched as his headlights faded down the driveway. The light was on in the kitchen for me. Mom's way of saying she still cared about whether I made it home each night.

No way was I going to fall asleep. Between Chris and finding those Mallory spots and the fireworks still going off in the distance, the air around me was vibrating. I immediately started filling the coffeepot with water. I scooped in the coffee grounds—huge, heaping spoonfuls, until the white paper filter was nearly overflowing.

The coffeemaker began its gurgling and hissing routine, and I pulled a mug out of the cupboard. While I waited for the coffee, my thoughts drifted out the kitchen window and across the field up to the second story of the gray house, where a light was on. Tomorrow suddenly seemed like a really long time to have to wait to see him again.

"Mallory, what are you doing?"

I spun around. Mom was standing there in her bathrobe, her eyes half open.

"Mom," I said. "You just called me Mallory."

She flinched at the sound of my sister's name. Her eyes opened all the way then, and she shook her head, her face getting all scrunched up. "No, I didn't."

"Yes, you did."

"I know what I said, Maia." She argued in that tone she usually reserved for my father, and I had the distinct suspicion that she threw my name in there just to prove she still knew it.

Just then, the basement door creaked open.

Dad shuffled into the kitchen, his hair disheveled, and he was now standing right next to Mom. "What's going on?" he mumbled.

Mom rolled her eyes—how dare he speak in her presence. Next I heard Roxie padding down the stairs. Her nails clicked against the linoleum as she walked up between Mom and Dad, yet another set of eyes on me.

"Nothing's going on," I said. "It's not even ten o'clock."

Mom crossed her arms and firmed up her stance for just a moment before she sank back into her tiredness and unfolded her arms again. "Who was that dropping you off just now?" she asked.

"Hayden," I lied, for some reason.

If she knew that wasn't the truth, she didn't give herself away. She looked at my dad and pulled her robe tighter across her chest, as if he was just some random man, a stranger, someone simply renting a room from her, and with whom it was inappropriate to be standing around in the kitchen while wearing pajamas. She started walking away, and I heard her say "Good night" from the living room.

Then it was just Dad and me, with Roxie standing in between us now, looking back and forth, probably trying to decipher which of us needed her more.

"Coffee at this hour?" he asked.

"I'm not tired," I explained, and I knew I was taking a

tone with him—that's how he used to describe it, back when he had the wherewithal to stand his ground. "Is that a problem?" I added, like an extra test. Maybe if I copped enough attitude, it would snap him back into parent mode. But I was wrong. Because the way he looked at me, all hurt, like an injured animal, you'd have thought I'd said, *Why don't you go fuck off and die?*

"No" was all he said. And then he walked away too.

Guilt trip. Squared.

The coffeemaker gave one last gurgle.

"Great," I muttered.

I bent down and scratched Roxie in that spot behind the ears that she loved, and whispered, "You're the only sane one left in this family."

Roxie followed me outside the way she used to follow Mallory when she'd stay up late in the barn drinking coffee on one of her work binges.

I'd filled my cup too high and spilled the hot coffee on myself at least three times as I made my way outside in the dark. I didn't really like coffee all that much, but I remembered how Mallory would make big pots of it, alternating with her weed, so she could stay awake to work. She'd said it helped her think straight, that it was natural and it wasn't like she was some kind of meth-head, which is what happened to a lot of the kids around here after graduating from CHS. But I always thought that was just Mallory-bullshit.

I pulled open the barn door and turned on the lights.

I walked along the wall of endless pictures, searching for

the places I'd seen today with Chris. There was the gas station graffiti that had been residing in the back of my mind ever since I found it. There was Bowman's—Bowman's bare and stark, and then Bowman's full of people in party mode. There was the empty road with the clouds.

There was the cemetery gate. And now, following in succession, a picture of a stone statue, worn and weathered; it looked like a saint or angel or something, with this halo of sunlight all around it. If I didn't know better, I would think Mallory had edited the photo that way. But she never did that. She'd said that if there was something in there you wanted out, then that was all the more reason it should stay in, and if there was something missing that should be there, then that's why you keep doing it, why she would always go back out the next day and do it all over again.

I would go back to the cemetery in New Pines.

I would do it over again.

I sat down at Mallory's table and rifled through the drawer until I found a sketchbook. When I opened it, there was nothing in it, although there had been pages ripped out, indentations on the blank paper underneath. I grabbed the red, waxy tipped pencil that was sitting out, and I made a list of all the pictures I'd found in real life so far.

As I sat there, surrounded by Mallory's things, I was brought back to a night we shared out here. It was barely a year ago, on one of those caffeine- and marijuana-fueled nights—the last night we were friends. She was pacing back and forth in front of me, ranting and elated at the same time: "The world's a mess, right?" she exclaimed.

"Yeah," I agreed, half-heartedly.

"Nothing makes sense. Everything's so chaotic and out of control. But when you're taking a photo"—she paused for emphasis (she was always doing that)—"it's like the only thing in the entire world that has to make sense is what's inside the frame. This little rectangle of space. And all the rest of it can fall away." She held her hands out as if she were letting something invisible fall from between her fingers.

I yawned. I had been reaching my breaking point with her for months, probably for my entire life, and this was the night when I'd finally had enough. I told her I was tired and wanted to go back to the house and get into bed.

When I stood up, she pulled on my arm and said, "Come on, we're having secret sister time, Mai."

"No we're not," I snapped. Maybe it was a little bit of a contact high that made me stand up to her that night. Regardless of why I did it, I did. And I'd never be able to take it back. "You're just using me," I told her, my voice full of needles. "You don't care that it's me here. You just talk *at* me while you get more and more obliterated and make less and less sense. You try to make me feel like it's some special sister bonding thing, when really you just keep me here so I don't tell Mom and Dad you're a pothead."

"Whoa-ho." Her voice lilted, and she took a step back, clapping her hands together like I'd just finished a performance. "Where did that come from?"

"From me!" I had to yell to get her to hear me, and that made me even angrier.

"I don't know if I should be hurt or impressed."

"Neither," I said through gritted teeth.

"Or both," she added, and turned her back to me.

She picked up a photograph that was lying on the table along with a handful of thumbtacks and brought them over to the wall, not so much ignoring me but pretending I had disappeared.

"I'm serious, Mallory!" I said, following along behind her.

She arranged the four thumbtacks in a row, holding the heads of the tacks between her lips as she centered the photo on the wall with both hands. "So get out," she mumbled through the hardware in her mouth.

I stood there for a moment and watched as she steadied the photo and then took each tack one by one and speared the corners with precision, never looking back at me, not saying another word.

I closed my eyes now as I sat in her chair, trying hard to remember what the photograph was. I remember looking at it right before I walked out, and thinking how she cared more about this stupid picture than being my sister. I stood, retracing the steps I had taken as I followed her that night, the sequence of events so ingrained in my mind that they led me directly to it.

The photo was of a stained glass window.

I touched the corner where one of the tacks was positioned on a tilt, not flush with the wall like the other three. Was that the tack she'd pressed in as she told me to get out?

The window was a square in the center of a rectangle of paper—the white space around it made it stand out. As I looked at all the surrounding photos, this was the only one cropped in that way. Maybe that's what she was talking about when I couldn't be bothered to pay attention. About how it's only what's inside the frame that needs to make sense.

That was the key to figuring out where this window was. It *had* been cropped. Cropped from something else, a bigger picture. I raced back over to Mallory's desk. I flung open the drawers. She had hundreds of multicolored file folders jammed in each drawer, only the colors didn't seem to indicate any particular organizational system.

In each folder, there were hundreds of plastic sleeves filled with even more negatives, row after row after row. Black-and-white ghostly images, all turned inside out.

I removed the file folders by the armful and splayed them out on the floor.

I took a deep breath, then a sip of coffee, and opened the first one. I grasped the first sleeve at the corners, between my thumb and forefinger, and held it up to the light. My eyes scanned each tiny image, one after another. Sheet after sheet. I'd made it through only three folders, and I'd barely even started to make the beginning of a dent in what was still left to go through.

I wished I hadn't messed things up with Neil so badly, because he could have probably told me in one glance where this window lived. I leaned forward over my thighs and let my forehead rest against a pile of slippery plastic sleeves. "Mallory," I groaned. I hesitated to talk to her outright, to ask a real question of her. Because not getting an answer would be too hard. This was stupid. Impossible.

I began collecting the folders again, stacking them one on

top of the other. I carried them in my arms and set them down on the edge of the desk. I went and got another stack, and another. And as I set down the very last pile, one of the folders at the bottom slid out of place, like a house slipping off its foundation. I reached out to try to catch it, but it was too late.

The entire collection, stack upon stack of thousands of plastic sleeves, cascaded to the floor. If they had been in any order, I would never be able to put them back the way they'd been.

"Goddammit," I muttered.

Roxie ambled to the edge of the mess and stood over the sleeve that was farthest away, almost reaching the wall. She sniffed at it and then looked at me. Defeated, I walked over to where she was standing and sat down on the cold, hard floor. She leaned in and touched her nose to mine, and then lay down.

I curled up into a ball around her, and she snuggled into me. My cheek was resting against one of those zillion plastic sleeves. I picked it up, preparing to toss it toward the larger pile, but, almost as a reflex, I held it above my head instead.

My eyes were tired and unfocused, but there it was. The negative I had been searching for. This was the one. I was sure of it. I stumbled to my feet and brought it over to the picture on the wall to compare.

It wasn't a window; I could see that now. Or it wasn't *just* a window. It was a door, a window inside a door.

"We actually found it." I wasn't sure whether the "we" I was referring to was Roxie and me or Mallory and me, but either way, we had done it. I was feeling closer to Mallory with every passing second.

Except now there was the next step, figuring out where the door was.

Instead of daunting, it felt exciting. Like I was finally onto something. Like this whole night meant something. Like I was *supposed* to leave the picnic, *supposed* to drive away with Chris, *supposed* to find the cemetery gate and the soda shop with the jukebox, and even the new age store with the incense.

I wanted to tell Chris, but then I'd have to tell him everything. Like one of those fireworks exploding on the side of the road, the realization jolted me: For the first time in my life I was doing something that had a purpose. I wished I knew how to share it with him.

CHRIS

I TOOK MY SNEAKERS OFF AT THE DOOR AND LAID my keys down in the little dish on the kitchen counter. The volume on the TV was turned up in the other room.

"Hey you," Isobel said as I entered the living room.

"Hey." I plopped down onto the sofa next to her. "I was trying to be quiet in case you were sleeping."

Subtext: I wasn't trying to sneak in. But she was already side-eyeing me.

I tried to focus on the commercial that was playing; some late-night fast-food chain that made my stomach growl. Isobel pointed the remote at the TV, and I watched the volume bar lower until it was almost down to zero.

"So, how was your evening?" she asked.

"Okay. How about you? Busy night at the hospital?"

"Usually the Fourth is a lot worse. Only about a half dozen idiots with some second- and third-degree burns this year. And a middle-aged man fell off his roof—broke a couple things. A guy with a bullet hole in his thigh . . . I'll never understand why people think it's a good idea to celebrate by shooting guns into the air. What goes up must come down. But all in all, not too bad." She paused, watching me nod along. "So, your night was just okay, huh?"

This was a game we played. I'd pretend I didn't want to tell her what was going on, and she'd pretend to drag it out of me, when really we both wanted the same thing.

"Yeah, it was okay," I repeated. "Just hung out."

Isobel clicked her tongue three times, and breathed in deeply. I finally met her eyes. She was all grins, and then she shook her head and said, "Uhn, uhn, uhn." As she exhaled, she sighed through the word "Kid . . ."

"What?"

She said only one word: "Trouble."

"Why?"

"*Why?*" she mimicked. "Trouble," she repeated, more firmly, pointing her finger at me.

I shook my head and laughed, and so did she. Then I stood up and gave her a hug and a kiss on the cheek. "Good night, Aunt Isobel."

"Good night, Trouble."

I'd started to walk away, when she called behind me, "Hey, Chris?" I turned to look at her again. "You know a little trouble is good for the soul, don't you?"

"I don't know what you're talking about," I said, taking the first step up the stairs.

"Oh, sure," she sang, and I heard the volume on the TV going back up. "Love you!"

"Love you," I called back.

When I lay down in bed, it was almost as if I could still feel my body moving. A phantom car ride. The scent of firework gunpowder lingered in the air. I felt light-headed and dizzy and perfectly warm and perfectly cool. Part of me wanted to ignore the sparkly feeling lighting up my chest, because I damn well knew what those sparkly feelings were all about.

They *were* trouble.

They were terrifying. But they felt so good too.

MAIA

I WOKE UP THE NEXT DAY, AND MY HEAD FELT LIKE A giant brass bell someone had been gonging at all night. I wondered if it was possible to have a coffee hangover.

I opened my eyes slowly, reaching for my phone that was still in my pocket because I hadn't even changed out of yesterday's clothes before I fell into bed. I hadn't bothered to brush my teeth or take off my shoes. I had no idea what time it was, as I waited for my phone to power on. I looked out the window. It was bright and sunny; birds were chirping, insects humming.

My phone turned on, telling me it was almost two o'clock in the afternoon.

As I looked at the screen, a whole series of messages from both Hayden and Gabby lit up. The headline was: They were pissed that I'd bailed on them.

There was a knock at the door downstairs.

I stumbled out of bed, and as I passed my mirror I saw

that my hair was mushed up on one side of my head.

Roxie was barking as the knocking persisted. I hoped it was Chris; Roxie didn't usually bark at people she knew. My heart felt light and wispy, like that drunken-butterfly feeling. I quickly ducked into the bathroom and tried to smooth my hair down.

KnockKnockKnockKnockKnock.

I ran my fingers through, breaking strands of hair as I twisted it into an only slightly more tidy disaster. As I rounded the corner, I finally saw that it was not Chris who was standing on my porch.

It was Hayden.

Those butterflies that had been holding on to my heart dropped it like a cannonball, its weight slowing me down as I took those last few steps to the door, dreading whatever was about to follow.

Hayden had her hand on one hip and her phone in the other. As I approached, she raised her sunglasses to her forehead and looked at me, pressing her lips together as she pocketed her phone. "Good," she said, her voice tight. "Now that I know you're alive, I can kill you."

I pushed open the screen door, and she walked in, like she had countless other times throughout our lifetime of friendship.

"I'm sorry," I said as I followed her into my kitchen.

"No." She shook her head. "You're not." She immediately made a beeline to the cupboard where we kept our glasses, pulled two down, and set them next to each other on the counter.

"Yes, I am."

I tried to put myself in her line of vision, but she wouldn't look at me.

She moved across the floor like she was dancing choreographed steps, opening the refrigerator door and pulling out the pitcher of Daddy's Famous Sweet Tea (as we grew up calling it), which was eternally stocked in this house. She reached into the freezer, pulled out a handful of ice, and dropped four cubes into each glass.

I remembered that Hayden and I used to watch my dad, mouths watering, while he boiled the water in a big metal pot on the stove, the giant red box of Luzianne tea bags sitting out on the counter. He'd stand there throwing in a handful of tea bags, stirring it with a wooden spoon, letting it all come to a rolling boil before adding in heaping scoops of white sugar, letting them disintegrate into the tea. He always said if your sugar fell to the bottom of the glass when you poured it, that was just plain lazy. While the tea cooled, he sliced up one lemon. It was always the same: He'd cut the ends off, stand the lemon on one end, and slice it vertically into quarters. Next, he took each quarter and cut it on an angle to get rid of the seeds. Then he would cut that wedge in half lengthwise so he ended up with eight equal lemon wedges. Last, he'd add a slit in the center of each, so they would sit perfectly on the edge of a glass.

Then he'd pour the tea off into two plastic pitchers, and stow them in the fridge, tossing the lemon wedges into a plastic container that lived there next to the pitchers.

Hayden knew this ritual well.

She brought the half-full pitcher to the counter, poured it over the ice cubes in each glass until it was nearly overflowing, popped the lid off the lemon container, and finally secured one wedge to the rim of each glass. Still steering clear of eye contact with me, she held one glass in each hand as she walked out of the kitchen.

"Where are you going?" I asked, following her as she made her way through the living room and up the stairs and down the hall to my bedroom. I watched her set the glasses down on my nightstand; then she walked back to my door and waited while Roxie made her way down the hall and into my room, before closing it behind her.

She sat on my bed, crossed her legs, and stared at me, still wordless.

I sat down on the other end, opposite her.

"You're not acting like yourself," she finally said.

I laughed.

"Something funny?" she asked, not nicely.

"You'd have to be there to get it," I said, turning Hayden's new catchphrase around on her. "In my head."

She nodded, then reached for one of the glasses of tea and handed it to me. She took the other for herself and held it out, clinking hers against mine, nearly making them both spill all over my bed.

"Cheers," she said, taking a sip. "While we're on the subject, just what the hell is going on inside that head of yours lately?" she asked. The shape of her mouth softened, and I knew she'd stop being mad at me any minute.

I shrugged. "I don't know."

"Bzzz!" She made a sound like a game show buzzer. "Wrong answer. Try again."

"Fine." I took a deep breath and let it out, deflating my lungs until I had no choice but to breathe again. "Where to begin?" I said, more to myself than to her.

"You tell me."

"You know how they say time heals all wounds, or something like that?"

"Uh-huh," she answered.

"Well, I don't think that's right. Or at least not with me, anyway. Because it just seems like the more time that passes, the harder things get."

"You mean with Mallory?" she asked.

"Mallory, yeah. But my parents, too. And me," I added, hoping she wouldn't ask for clarity on that last part. "I mean, shouldn't it be the other way around?"

She shook her head. "I don't know. I wish I did. I've never lost anyone. I wish I knew how you were feeling."

"I don't," I told her. "I don't wish for anyone to feel like this."

"You know I love you, right?" she said.

I nodded. I knew. I really did.

"Gabby too," she added.

"I know," I said out loud.

"Maybe we don't always have the right thing to say, but we're here. You don't need to keep everything inside all the time and deal with it all by yourself."

"Don't I, though? I mean, that's what it feels like to me." I sniffed back the tears that were playing on my vocal chords, warbling my voice. "It's like you guys are suddenly best friends and I'm just by myself."

"Are you kidding?" But there was something in her voice, the way she was being so emphatic about it. "Maia, don't be crazy—you will always be my best friend forever, okay? That's never gonna change."

But I knew I wasn't wrong. And suddenly I knew it wasn't anything she had done. Or anything I had done, or even anything Gabby had done. It wasn't only that we were changing; we were changing in different ways, heading in different directions. We were on opposite sides of this life-altering experience now, and there was no way either of us could cross back over.

I think she knew it too. Because she smiled, but it was a frowning smile, one of those smiles that is really just covering up sadness. I smiled back, I'm sure in the same exact way. I dabbed at my eyes with the bottom of my shirt. She pressed the corners of her eyes with her fingers and blinked hard against the tears that were getting caught in her eyelashes.

"Ugh," she moaned, fanning her face with her hands. "All right. We good? Can we move on to something more important now?"

"Yes, please," I agreed.

She took another sip of her tea, and I did too. The sweetness washed away that bitter taste that had been in my mouth for months.

"Inquiring minds, and all," she began, this mischievous smirk twisting her lips as she raised one eyebrow.

"Yeah?" I prompted, taking another big sip of the tea.

"What's up with you and the new kid?"

I gasped, and the sugar got caught in my throat, which launched me into a coughing fit. Hayden's eyes widened for just a moment before she crossed her arms and lowered her chin, looking up at me from under her raised eyebrows.

"Nothing!" I finally managed.

"Oh yeah, clearly. Nothing at all," she said, grinning as she waved her hand over me. She narrowed her eyes and shook her head slowly. "We saw you leaving with him yesterday." It was framed like a statement, but I knew it was a question in disguise.

"Come on, really," I insisted. "Nothing. I swear."

She shook her head, saying, "Nah-uh. Spill."

"He gave me a ride," I said, realizing only after it was out of my mouth that it was a poor choice of words in this particular context.

Hayden erupted with laughter and then howled, "That's what she said!"

"Shut up!" I reached for my pillow and whacked her with it.

"Hey, he's pretty cute," she said.

"Stop," I told her, even though I definitely agreed.

Then she started in with that song from *Grease*: *"Summah lovin,"* she screeched. *"Had me a bla-hast . . ."*

"My ears!" I yelled, although, in my mind I was recounting the million times we had watched that movie over the years, dancing and singing along to the entire soundtrack.

"Hey! I'm just sayin' go for it." She held her hands facing the ceiling, her arms and torso in the shape of a W, and added, "I mean, why not?"

"I'm not going for anything, Hayden." But even as the words hit the air, I knew I wasn't telling the whole truth. "We're barely friends," I added. And maybe before yesterday that part would've been true, but in my bones I knew that wasn't quite right either.

We hugged it out on the front porch, and as I watched her drive away in her mom's loud little car, a wave of relief washed over me, as if something had been repaired in our friendship. Or maybe it was that whatever had been coming undone was now a clean break, not jagged and messy anymore, but clear and crisp, and maybe healable.

I put away the pitcher of tea and the lemon wedges, and rinsed out our glasses. If my mom got home from work and saw the kitchen dirty and me all disheveled with my hair a mess, it would make it harder for her to pretend things were all right. As much as I sometimes wished we could rip away this veil of make-believe like a bandage, let the fresh air get at all the wounds underneath, I wasn't sure she could handle it.

I thought about how just last night she called me Mallory. I wasn't sure if she'd ever be able to let the air in. No, I'd play my part today.

I got into the shower, and had to try hard to not think about Chris as I ran the sponge across my skin. *Damn you, Hayden*, I thought. But she hadn't planted the idea in my head; I knew the seed of it was already there, waiting. A sharp knock on the bathroom door startled me right out of that little fantasy.

"Yeah?" I yelled, sticking my head out from behind the shower curtain.

The door opened and Mom stepped inside, saying, "Hurry up, because that boy is downstairs and your father's out there talking to him."

"He's what?" I said, turning the water off.

"I don't know. I got home and they were outside talking."

I murmured, "Oh god."

"Yep." Mom picked up the towel I had set out on the sink and handed it to me. "I'm sure that's a riveting conversation."

She left before I could decipher whom she was insulting, my dad or Chris. I got dressed in record time. I dragged a comb through my hair, detangling it by force and letting it fall across my shoulders, rather than the usual ponytail. I rummaged through the drawers under the sink until I found my strawberry lip balm, the one that made my lips shimmery and red and sweet-tasting.

I picked it up with two fingers and centered myself in front of the mirror again. After removing the cap, I pressed the waxy tip against my upper lip and glided it along the right side, then the left. I kneaded my lips together and stood back, examining the way they looked, all polished and shining, like they were separate from my face. I flashed myself a smile.

I leaned in closer, paused, considering for a moment.

Then I dragged the back of my hand across my mouth, rubbing back and forth until my lips went dry and matte once again.

"Idiot," I muttered, pulling my hair back into a sloppy bun.

CHRIS

I WAITED UNTIL MAIA'S FRIEND LEFT BEFORE I WENT over. My timing was impeccable because just as I finished walking across the field, carrying the bag full of bike supplies that Maia had left in my backseat, a truck pulled up the driveway.

He was waiting at the front porch by the time I got there, wearing a hat that looked like he'd been wearing it every day for the last decade. His boots and jeans and button-down shirt rolled up to his elbows were all covered in paint stains or plaster. I thought he must work in construction. He examined my appearance too. I could see that he was trying to figure me out, but if he made any conclusions, I wasn't sure what they were.

As I approached, I waved with my free hand and said "Hi." I told him I was Isobel's nephew. *Nephew.* The word sat heavy on my tongue. I told him I was there to see Maia. I had something of hers.

He regarded the bag I was holding with suspicion, as if it contained something dangerous that might detonate at any moment, so I volunteered, "Some stuff to fix her bike."

"What's wrong with her bike?" he asked, turning to look at it, perched against the railing of the porch.

"The tires are flat," I told him.

He set down the insulated lunch bag he'd been holding and walked over to her bike. He leaned in and examined each tire, running his hands along the rubber.

Another car pulled up the driveway and parked next to the truck. And as the woman stepped out and started walking toward us, I could see a little bit of Maia in her. The same dark hair, dark eyes, the same walk. As she came up the pathway, she looked me right in the eye.

"Hi," I offered first.

Her smile was tired, but pretty. The way my mom would smile after a long day. "You must be Chris," she said, and just when I felt a little flutter of excitement—the idea that Maia had been talking about me to her mother—she added, "Isobel told me you were staying with her for the summer."

"Yes," I said, and then, as an afterthought, "Ma'am."

She did one of Maia's *ha* laughs. "I'll let Maia know you're here. Nice to finally meet you."

"You too," I called after her.

It was not lost on me that her father and mother did not exchange so much as a nod.

"Here, why don't you help me turn this over," her father said.

I set the bag down on the ground and grabbed one end of the bike, following his lead. With only a small amount of awkwardness, we set it on the ground upside down—so the wheels were in the air and the bike was balanced on the handlebars and the seat.

"You've done this before?" he asked as I stood there staring at the tires as they spun gently with the air. "You know how to do this?" he clarified.

I nodded, but then added, "Well, sort of." I was thankful I'd decided to watch another video online last night before bed, but the truth was that even if I had a modicum of knowledge, I had no practice. He nodded back, but I wondered if he could tell by looking at my smooth hands that I'd never done this sort of thing before.

"Here, hold this steady for a minute," he said, with his hand firmly on the rear tire. I placed my hands where his were. And then he unclamped a lever, slid the chain aside, and smoothly popped the entire wheel off the bike just like I had seen in the videos.

"You have some tire irons in there?" he asked, hitching his chin in the direction of the bag.

I rifled through until I found the package of the little tools that the person in the video had called bike levers. "You mean these?" I asked, just to be sure.

"Yep," he said, nodding again.

As he waited for me to remove the paper backing and pop them out of the plastic case, I was positive he thought I was the biggest wuss on the planet. But then I thought about

Coleton: He's a boy, no debate about that, and he wouldn't have a clue how to do any of this either. It didn't make him less of a man, just a different kind, and I was actually okay with the idea of being a different kind of man too.

"You take this end"—he held up the flat side of the instrument—"and pry it in under the tire casing like this."

"Okay," I said, leaning in. I wanted him to know I was paying attention.

"Then you take another, do the same thing. Then you can just take it right off with your hands." I watched as he moved around the whole circumference of the tire, gently prying it right off the rim.

He proceeded to change that bike tire, exactly as I had seen it done in the video. Only, he didn't need to watch any video to know how to do it. It was like he had this innate, institutional knowledge. I wondered if I'd ever be at the point where I had that, or if I even wanted that—if it even mattered.

"Hey."

We both looked up at the same time to see Maia standing there.

As she got closer, there was this scent coming off her. I didn't know if it was her hair or her skin, but it was a clean, citrus fragrance that made me think of oranges. For once in my life, I was actually thankful for what was *not* in my pants, because right at that moment, the way my insides were stirring, I was pretty sure I'd have to hide a really embarrassing boner.

"What are y'all doing?" she asked.

"Your tires need fixing, don't they?" her dad said.

"Yeah," she responded.

"Well," was all he said.

He detached the front tire, and then murmured, "You wanna try this one?"

I took the tool that he was handing to me. I pried the tire off the rim, the way he had showed me.

"So, how'd they get flat anyway?" he asked. When I looked up at Maia, she shook her head in this discreet, almost microscopic way; I knew it meant I was not to say anything.

"I don't know," she answered, extremely convincingly. "I just came out of work and found 'em like that."

"What's happening to this damn town?" he said to no one in particular.

As he walked past Maia, he put his hand on her shoulder.

"Hey, thanks, Dad," she told him.

He didn't say anything back, but he did nod—he seemed to be big on the nonverbal communication, like a lot of dads are, I suppose.

"Yeah, thanks for showing me how to do all this," I said, and he waved in acknowledgment.

Maia crouched down next to me and made a face. "I hope that wasn't too weird."

I shook my head. "It was okay, really."

The crack of their front door closing was followed quickly by a series of clicking sounds and a scuffle. There was a dog headed straight for us. As it approached, already barking, I asked Maia, in the bravest way possible, "It doesn't bite, does it?"

She looked at the dog advancing on us and said, "Maybe if she had more teeth left."

"That doesn't make me feel better!" I said, scrambling to stand before the dog got to me.

"I'm kidding!" she wailed, grabbing my hand to pull me back down to the ground—and now I was scared for an entirely different reason. Her hand was touching mine, and I liked it. "Sit."

"Me or the dog?"

"Both of you, sit."

The dog maneuvered next to Maia and stopped barking.

"Roxie," Maia began, as if she was speaking to a human child. "This is Chris. Don't bite him." Then she turned to me and said, in the exact same tone, "Chris, this is Roxie. She will not bite you."

Roxie stood up and sniffed all over my arms and legs, then sat in front of me and stared, her face right in my face, her dog breath hot as she panted.

"If you just pet her, she'll leave you alone." Maia reached out and started stroking behind the dog's ears and down its back. "She can't see very well. I don't think she quite understands personal space anymore."

I let the dog sniff my hand and then followed what Maia was doing.

"See?" Maia said softly. "He's not so bad."

"Yeah, this is a lot less scary now," I told her.

"I was actually talking to Roxie."

I laughed. "Thanks."

Maia stopped petting the dog, and said, "Okay, Roxie. Go

lie down." The dog moved about three inches to the right, and then plopped down.

We took way longer to finish the second tire than her dad took to do the first, but it meant Maia was close to me longer, so I wasn't in much of a hurry. We stood the bike upright, both tires fixed and reinflated, and admired our work.

"Thanks, Chris."

"No problem."

I was preparing to leave when she sat back down and started petting the dog again. The dog woke up and looked at me like I should be sitting down too. So I did.

"Really," Maia continued. "I was thinking I'd be without my bike for the whole summer."

I nodded, only because I didn't really understand what she meant by that. Her dad was there the whole time; he could've fixed everything days ago, in five minutes flat. Instead of saying that, I tried to work around it by asking, "So, you didn't want your parents knowing about the stuff with Neil, I take it?"

"No way." She cringed, adding, "There are certain things I would rather keep completely separate from them. For their own good."

I didn't know what she meant by that either, but I could understand the sentiment—hadn't I kept huge secrets from my parents too? For their own good.

She glanced back toward the house and sighed, saying, "Parents are so . . ." She trailed off, never finishing. She didn't have to, though.

"Yeah," I agreed. "If it means anything, they were pretty nice to me."

"Oh sure, they *are* nice," she agreed. "They're just not nice to each other."

"Right," I said.

"Then again, it's probably not the best idea to live with someone after you divorce them."

"Seriously?" I looked toward the house too. "They're— wow, that is—"

"Fucked up?" she finished for me. "Yeah. I don't ever wanna end up like that."

I thought about all the tension and the fighting between my parents this past year, how I was driving a wedge between them, how I was scared they were going to end up like that too—just two strangers who share the same house but can barely stand to look at each other.

"Me neither." The guilt twisted into my stomach like a knife.

"What about your parents?" she asked. "They still together?"

"For now, anyway." I debated saying what was on my mind. But the silence seemed to open up just the right space for it. "Part of the reason I'm here wasn't just to get a break from them. It was to give them a break from me too."

"Why?"

"They don't really agree on much when it comes to me. If they ended up getting a divorce over it, I guess it really wouldn't be a surprise."

Sitting on the ground, with the day's heat beginning to fade around us, Maia looked at me in this thoughtful way.

"If they do," she started, "it wouldn't be because of you. You know that, right?"

"I don't know." I shrugged. "Maybe."

It was quiet, and I didn't want her to think I was feeling sorry for myself, so I started talking again, trying to be a little more upbeat. "Have you ever heard of binary star systems?" I asked her. "It's where there are two stars that orbit each other?"

She shook her head.

"Well, like four-fifths of all stars are binaries. But the two are so close together, they look like one point of light. Most of the stars in our galaxy that are like our Sun are in these binary star systems."

I was boring her, I was sure.

I cleared my throat. *Rein it in, Chris.* "Binary stars orbit each other, and they're so close sometimes that they can transfer mass, one to the other. Like one starts feeding off the other, and sometimes it just keeps gaining more and more mass until it basically consumes the companion star altogether."

She was tilting her head slightly as she listened, her brows knitted together like I was telling a joke and she couldn't decide what the punch line was.

I shrugged and added, "It's just something I've thought about before, when it comes to my parents. Although, maybe it's all parents. Or all couples, anyway. I don't know."

Her expression flickered like a light blinking in and out, bright one second, dark the next. Before I could interpret what it all meant, she let her head drop down, her chin to her chest, and I watched as she brought her hands up to cover her face. She didn't make a sound, but her shoulders were shaking. I thought she was crying, but then she tossed her head back and her laughter became audible. Not her *ha* laugh, but real, loud, hard laughter.

The dog jumped up and waddled toward the house.

"What?" I finally asked. "Why are you laughing?"

She drew in a sharp breath and held her hand to her side as she struggled to get the words out. "Sorry," she wheezed, breathless. "You just—I—"

"What?"

"That was—"

"*What?*"

"It's just—that was very cheerful, Chris," she finally said, still giggling. "Thank you for that. Really, I feel so much better."

Now I dropped my head. "Okay, point taken. I guess maybe that sounded a little dark."

She brought her thumb and pointer finger together in front of her face so they were almost touching, and said, "Just a little."

I could feel my face getting hot, turning all shades of red. "It was supposed to be a comforting idea," I tried to explain.

Her nose scrunched up in this way, her features contorted in an expression that hovered between amusement and horror. "How?" she shouted.

"Like what if it's only natural that things don't last? So then maybe it doesn't have to be such a terrible thing. Right?"

She laughed silently again, clamping her lips together as she shook her head.

"No?"

"No."

After another bout of laughing, she looked at me, her eyes lit with this inner glow, and said, definitively, "You're weird." Except, the way she said it, I had never felt more normal.

MAIA

I WATCHED CHRIS WALK BACK ACROSS THE FIELD, AND I pressed my hands against my cheeks, opening and closing my mouth, all the muscles in my face strained from laughing so much.

Dad was in the kitchen washing his hands at the sink, his microwave dinner box sitting open on the counter. Glancing over his shoulder at me, he said, "Everything work out?"

"Yeah," I told him.

He turned around and grabbed the dish towel that was hanging off the handle of the stove. "Good."

"Daddy?" I couldn't help thinking back to our last interaction in the kitchen the night before, the look on his face when he walked away. "Thanks again for helping."

"You're welcome." He dried his hands, looking down once again, like he was stopping himself from saying more.

"You know," he added. "You could've just asked me for help to begin with."

Really, could I have, though? Instead I said another version of the truth: "I didn't want to bother you."

"Bother me?" He smiled—actually smiled, for the first time in I don't know how long. "What do you think dads are for?"

I'm not sure anymore. But I didn't say that either.

"Well, thanks again. I'm sure you saved us hours of not knowing what we were doing."

As I started to walk away, he called me back. "Wait, Mai?"

"Yeah?"

"That boy," he began. "Nice kid. Seemed, anyway."

I shrugged, nodded. "Yeah, I guess so." I didn't want to appear too enthusiastic. About Chris. About this conversation. About anything, really.

"Is he . . ." He paused, and looked at me, hard, like he was waiting for the word to magically appear in the air between us. *"Funny?"* he finally finished, uncertain.

It took me a second to make sense of his intonation. I thought maybe he had heard us laughing, but no, he wasn't talking ha-ha-comedy funny. I was going to make him say what he meant—that's what Mallory would have done.

"Hilarious," I replied, crossing my arms.

He rolled his eyes, either at me or himself, I couldn't tell. "You know what I mean."

"No." I looked up at the ceiling, pretending to consider it. "I don't think I do."

He lowered his voice and said, "I meant *gay*, Maia."

"Gay?" I repeated more loudly, and I saw him look over my shoulder toward the door, just in case Chris was still out there or had somehow developed superhuman hearing. "You know that's not a bad word, right?"

"I know that, thank you very much." He turned back toward the counter and unpacked the plastic tray of frozen food and held it between his hands, picking at the edge of the plastic film. "I was just wondering. Something about him, I don't know. I just thought—maybe?"

My parents were weird about plenty, but never stuff like this. They were pretty liberal. They taught us to be too, so I had no idea where this conversation was coming from, or where it was heading.

"Dad, how would I know?" I finally answered.

"Okay, okay," he said, holding his hands up. "I won't bring it up again."

"Wait, why does it even matter?" I demanded. "Since when do you care about stuff like that?"

He lowered his chin and looked at me like I was the one who was completely clueless now. "Since never. I'm just trying to decide how worried I need to be."

"Worried about what?"

"About you running around town with some kid nobody knows."

"Oh," was all I could say.

"Is that a problem?" he added pointedly, echoing the words I'd said to him, except the way it sounded coming from his mouth was totally different. Playful, not spiteful like mine had been.

Dad could surprise me sometimes.

I wanted to say, *Touché, Dad, way to stand up to me,* but that would have killed the moment. Instead I said, "No, it's not a problem."

"Good." He placed his dinner in the microwave and closed the door. "Glad to hear it."

"Well, I honestly have no idea if he is or not."

And just as I was thinking, *I hope not,* Dad said, "I hope so."

I pulled my hoodie down off the hook in the hallway. I was about to leave, but I ducked my head back in. "I'm gonna go for a bike ride. I won't be late," I told him.

He said, "Be careful."

I knew he wasn't only talking about the bike.

This was the first glimmer I'd seen in months—years, really—of Dad trying to be a dad. He was thinking about reclaiming his title. It was a sign of life. A sign that underneath that sad exterior there was still a part of him that was someone other than the guy who screwed up so bad, he would be willing to serve penance for it for the rest of his existence.

I was pedaling faster than I think I'd ever gone before. My legs felt strong and solid, powerful. Maybe it was the twilight falling around me—the urgency of the day ending—that was propelling me, pushing me forward.

As I breathed, my lungs felt light and loose. From laughing with Chris. Or maybe it was a result of all that debris that got washed away between me and Hayden. Or whatever had just been cleared out with my dad.

Maybe Chris was right, and things didn't have to seem so terrible.

I thought about that car ride, the way it felt to have the windows rolled down, the wind blowing against my skin and through my hair—that was as free as I'd felt in a while. A long while. Maybe ever. I let go of the handlebar with one hand and reached up to pull the elastic band out of my hair. My hair fell down and whipped all around me in the wind, just like the other night.

I passed Bowman's and the school and Bargain Mart and the gas station. I wished I could ride all the way out to New Pines. I wished there were more light left in the day. I made my way back along the exact route I'd come by.

Riding past the PRIVATE PROPERTY sign that designated Bowman's, my thoughts drifted once again to Chris. Maybe it was Hayden's words still on my mind, or my dad's. Whatever it was, instead of turning off the road into my driveway, I turned onto the gravel path that led up to the gray, wooden house I'd lived across from my entire life.

Up close, it was more disheveled than I thought—chipped paint and weeds, and the roof over the porch looked like it could cave in at any moment. I stopped my bike in front of the house and was debating about what exactly I was even doing there, when I heard a voice above me.

"Test driving the new wheels?"

When I looked up, Chris was leaning over the railing of the balcony on the side of the house, the one I could see from my bedroom window. Walking over to where Chris was, I backed up so I could see him better. Behind him there was a telescope.

"Are you looking for your bipolar stars up there?" I called up to him.

"Binary stars," he corrected.

"I know," I told him.

He laughed a little—he got it.

"The tires are good," I offered.

I liked the way he was looking at me, with this easy smile. I liked the way he was leaning, with his elbows propped on the edge of the railing. There was something inviting about his face, his stance, his everything.

"I was not looking for *bipolar* stars," he told me, lifting his head to gaze out somewhere above the tree line. "I was looking at Saturn." He raised his arm and pointed.

I turned around and tried to follow his gesture. The stars were multiplying by the minute as the sky grew darker. I had absolutely no clue which bright spot was Saturn.

When I turned back toward him, he was no longer looking at the sky; he was looking at me. "What?" I asked.

"Do you want to come up and look with me?"

It's always strange entering someone's house for the first time. The kitchen was clean and minimal—not a bunch of gadgets and things lying around. It was dated, for sure, but nice. He led me into the living room, where Isobel was sitting in an old armchair sleeping.

It was strange to see her—this woman I'd seen around town forever—in her own home. "Aunt Isobel works these insane hours at the hospital," he whispered as we headed up the stairs. "So she sleeps at weird times."

"Oh," I replied, suddenly feeling shy and awkward. Because in that instant, not only had Isobel become more real to me, Chris had as well.

"Be careful in here," he said as we walked down a narrow hallway and entered another room. "I have the lights off so we can see better—I mean, see the stars better."

My eyes adjusted quickly. I could make out a bed, a mirror, a dresser, two nightstands, a lamp, and a closed closet door. The only light was coming in through the open door that led outside.

"Can you see okay?" he asked, holding out his hand. "Do you need me to turn a light on?"

"No, I think I'm okay." But I reached for his hand anyway. Only our fingertips touched, just for a moment, with this weird electric thrill.

Out on the balcony, the breeze was stronger than it had been on the ground. I looked across the field at my house. Dim light was coming from the kitchen window; it was the light above the sink. My house looked so small from here. Like a toy house. Not something real people could live in.

"So, what are we looking at?" I asked, trying hard to push aside the thoughts of my house and its inhabitants—I wanted to be here, fully here, in this moment with Chris.

"Well, it's really clear tonight, so you have your pick." He raised his arm and pointed out at the sky, starting at the far left of our field of vision. "We have Jupiter." He moved his arm to the right. "Saturn." Right again, "Venus, and Mercury."

"Jupiter," I answered.

He leaned over to look through the eyepiece, adjusting the position of the telescope. As I watched him, I wanted to reach out and touch his hand again. He reminded me of Mallory, the way she would get quiet as she concentrated on twisting the lens and getting her shot just right, like the whole rest of the world had disappeared and it was just her and the camera and the thing they were looking at.

"Okay," he said, stepping aside, "take a look."

As I leaned over and peered through the eyepiece, just as he had, I was fully unprepared for it. "Oh my god," I whispered. I opened my mouth again, but my speech was impaired by what my eyes were seeing. When the words finally came, they were halted and stiff. "I. Can't. Believe. What. I'm. Seeing. Right. Now."

"You've never looked through a telescope before," he said. Not a question but an observation.

"No," I whispered, looking at him.

"It's pretty amazing, right?" His face lit up. His reaction to *my* reaction was almost better than the actual experience.

I looked up at the sky and then back through the telescope.

"Look again. Do you see those two dots on either side? One is kind of to the right, and the other is lower, to the left?" I saw exactly what he described. "Those are two of Jupiter's moons."

I looked up at him again. "I—I just—this really is amazing."

"Okay, if you think that's cool, let me show you something else." He adjusted the telescope again. "Jupiter gets all the attention because it's the biggest, but this has always been my favorite."

He moved aside so I could look again.

"No," I breathed. "This can't be real."

"You see it?"

"It's Saturn." I laughed. "I can see its rings. Like actually see them, right there."

"I know," he said.

"All right," I admitted. "Now I can see where your whole theory comes from. Not the depressing one, but what you said the other night. About how things just work out. Now you almost have me believing it."

We were standing so close and there wasn't much room to move around, with the telescope taking up most of the space, and I swore, for a moment, when our eyes met, I felt us moving even closer.

I should look away, I thought. But I couldn't. He was watching my mouth. I felt my lips wanting to part slightly. He leaned in. I so badly wanted him to kiss me. But right before that point of no return, that one instant before it was going to happen, something caught my eye. I looked over his shoulder, breaking the spell.

Chris cleared his throat and looked down quickly, raking his hand through his hair as he backed away from me. He glanced behind him to where I was looking. It was almost like the door had moved slightly, pushed open a mere fraction of an inch by the breeze. The light caught the glass and reflected like a tiny spark.

Once again, I could not believe what I was seeing.

This was *the* door.

It was nearly impossible to drag my gaze away from the stained glass window that I'd barely even had a chance to search for, yet here it was, delivering itself to me.

When he turned back around and met my eyes again, I was the one to look away.

The moment passed—this perfect, magical moment—and it was my fault. I had dropped it, let it slip through my hands, and it shattered, lying there in pieces on the floor.

"So," he said, putting an end to this excruciating silence. "You should know"—he paused, and my heart thumped hard as I waited for him to finish—"you might be a bit of an astronomy geek."

I laughed nervously. So he was going to ignore what had just happened, or didn't happen, between us. I was equally disappointed and relieved.

I followed suit: "You might be right about that."

Things seemed to settle back into place around us. The door moved again, ever so slightly, accompanied by a tiny creak I'm not sure Chris even heard.

I looked out across the field in the direction of my house again.

"So, I should probably get back," I said. "Um, thanks again. That was—"

"Yeah, it was," he said, finishing the sentence I couldn't.

CHRIS

TODAY I WAS RUNNING TO FORGET.

Sure, maybe it was fun to have a crush. But her hair, and the standing close, and god, we almost kissed. This was real. Not a crush. I knew if things went much further, I'd have to tell her I'm trans—not even for her sake, really, but for mine. It hurts too much to be in relationships where you can only show one part of yourself—I have seventeen years' worth of proof stockpiled on that. But it would also hurt too much if she decided she didn't like me if she knew the rest of me.

I picked up my pace, focused on my breathing. In breath. Out breath. In breath. Out breath. Left. Right. Left. Right. My footfalls, light on the pavement, tapping out the beat like a bass line.

I was running to forget about the scent of oranges on her hair and the way our fingers touching sent a jolt through my whole body. I needed to forget because where I was in my life, *who* I was, I did not have the luxury to be entertaining those thoughts. All that stuff—girls and sex and relationships—could wait. It *had* to wait. Between Mom and Dad not being able to reach an agreement about me going back to school this year, and Mom still not being able to forgive Dad and me for steamrolling her into signing the stupid paperwork so I could start on hormones, and not to mention the fact that I could barely manage a long-distance friendship with Coleton at the moment, *romance*—or whatever these feelings were—was the last thing I needed to be thinking about.

Things were too hard right now, too complicated. Judging from my phone call with Dad this morning, I didn't see things becoming less complicated anytime soon.

Dad: "Are you having a good time there?"

Me: "Yeah. I've been driving around a lot. Yesterday I helped Isobel's neighbor change her bike tires." (I was careful not to call her by name, or to even call her a friend.)

Dad: "You knew how to do that?"

Me: "Yeah. Besides, her father helped."

Dad: "Oh." (Awkward silence.) "How's that station wagon holding up?"

Me: "Good, I guess."

Dad: "Good. Do you have enough money left?"

Me: "Yeah. Thanks."

Dad: "Well, do you want to say hello to your mother? She's right here."

Me: "Um."

Background: (Mom whispers "No," repeats "I said no," then silence.)

Dad: "Chris? You know what, you just missed her."

Me: "Oh."

Dad: "Listen, why don't we give you a call later?"

Me: "All right."

Dad: "Wait, Chris? Are you there?"

Me:

I was running to forget not only this crush on Maia, but a whole array of other things: like me being in Carson, me being the thing that was driving my parents apart—me being stuck in between who I was and who I wanted to be.

I didn't want temporary anything; I didn't want something in between. I didn't want casual. I didn't want any more lies or hiding.

The toe of my sneaker caught on a loose chunk of pavement. I tripped and stumbled forward but caught myself. I tried to keep moving, but it was too late, I'd lost my balance.

I was going down.

In slow motion.

Falling.

I put my hands out just in time and came down hard on my wrists.

I saw the blood on the pavement before I felt the searing pain igniting different parts of my body at once. The palm of my left hand, my right elbow. Both of my knees.

"Shit," I hissed.

"Fuck!" I yelled.

I limped home. I wasn't hurt too bad, I knew that. It was all superficial. I'd be fine in a couple of days, but damn it stung.

MAIA

I WAITED UNTIL THE NEXT MORNING. MOM AND DAD had already left. I watched out my bedroom window, fully dressed, sneakers tied, Mallory's camera strapped securely across my body. I saw Chris come out of the house and take off running down the long driveway. Fifteen minutes later, Isobel stepped out, dressed in her scrubs, balancing a purse and car keys and travel mug as she made her way to her car. As soon as she pulled out of the driveway, I was racing down the stairs.

I let the screen door slam behind me and jumped from the second step of the porch, walking as fast as I could without actually breaking into a jog. The long wet grass in the field between our houses grazed my calves, and the morning dew soaked through the canvas of my sneakers.

I made it to the ladder that led up to the wooden balcony. I tested one of the rungs to be sure it was sturdy enough.

This is so stupid.

But I pulled myself up, rung by rung.

I felt Mallory standing at the top of the balcony daring me, egging me on, challenging me to be more adventurous, braver, more like her. I made it to the top and scrambled to the platform on my hands and knees. If anyone was watching, they'd think I was, well, a lot of things:

1. graceless
2. clumsy
3. sloppy
4. psychotic
5. a solid reason to call the police

But I was done caring about what anyone thought. Because there was the door. It's not as if I was there to spy or lurk or sneak around. I wasn't doing anything wrong.

I'd committed the uncropped photograph to memory. I looked down at my feet planted firmly on the wooden planks. Mallory had been up here. I raised the camera and peered through the viewfinder. It wasn't right. I backed up a step. Still not right. I backed myself up until I could take no more steps backward.

Carefully I leaned back against the railing—it was digging into my spine. I checked again. I still needed to be farther back, at a higher angle.

I placed my hands on the railing. I looked down. I shouldn't have looked down—but I knew the second I did, that Mallory must've been sitting up on the railing of the balcony when she took that picture.

My hands were shaking. I took a breath and stepped up onto the lower railing. But when I pushed myself up, I found that my wrists were stronger than I'd thought they were, more capable, and I leaned over the edge, maneuvering myself in that graceless, clumsy, sloppy way.

Don't look down.

I managed to twist around so that I was sitting on the top railing, facing the house. My heart was pounding, but I had done it. I hooked my right foot underneath the bottom railing to give myself a little more leverage. Suddenly, up high above the ground without a safety net, I felt more stable and balanced than I usually did with both feet firmly planted on solid ground. The wind blew against me and the air whistled past my ears. Careful not to move my lower body, I brought the camera to my face once more.

Yes.

This.

This was really it.

I could imagine Mallory hoisting herself up there without a second thought, as easily as she used to hop onto the countertops in the kitchen. Just a simple jump, not worrying about the very real possibility of falling over the edge.

The sun was catching the colors of the glass and reflecting them back out onto the wooden planks like beautiful little stains. But it was outside the frame. I wondered if Mallory had seen them too. I let the camera rest in my lap and looked out across the untilled field at my house. The barn. My bedroom window, and Mallory's room next to mine. I wondered if that was originally why she'd come up here, to get this view of our house. I hadn't found a picture of it, but that's not to say she didn't take one.

I turned back toward the door.

I steadied my hands and pressed down on the shutter release. It snapped. But there was another sound underneath the click and clap of the shutter, below me. A door closing. Carefully, I unhooked my feet from the lower bar and jumped down from the railing. I leaned over the edge, trying to see, but I couldn't tell what or who was responsible.

There was movement from inside the house, a shadow behind the glass window. I darted to the side of the door and plastered my body against the wall. I clutched the straps that hung on either side of my neck, the camera like some kind of magical armor I was trying to use to make me invisible.

I heard noises from behind the door. Shuffling, like things were being moved around, drawers being opened and slammed. Chris was usually gone longer. Or maybe I had lost track of time. I closed my eyes, breathing deep, tried to calm myself.

I peeked into the window. If he'd left the room, then I might have a chance to escape. That's the only thing I was thinking when I decided to look.

Through a thin perimeter of clear cut glass I saw Chris standing in front of the mirror. His back was to the door, but I could clearly see his face in the reflection. He leaned in and examined his arm in the mirror. His elbow and the back of his forearm were scraped and bloody. He bent down and pulled one leg of his running pants up above his knee, which was scraped up as well. He did the same to the other leg. He brought his hand in front of his face, and as he touched his palm gingerly, his face twisted in pain.

I inhaled a sharp breath just at the of sight it, like for a moment his pain was mine.

I kept watching. At first I was curious about what had happened, how he got hurt, concerned about whether or not he was actually all right.

He nudged his sneakers off and pushed them aside with his foot, one right next to the other. Pulled each sock off and placed them on top of his sneakers. It seemed so methodical. Practiced. Like he had a routine and he would not deviate. He pushed down his running pants and folded them neatly on the edge of the bed. He was wearing those boy boxer briefs. I couldn't see anything, but I knew I should look away at this point.

He stood there, very still for a moment, with his back to me. Like he was thinking. Then, at last, in one quick movement, he pulled his T-shirt up over his head and let it fall to the floor, so haphazard in comparison to the other articles of clothing.

He was wearing something underneath, like some kind of a vest, an undershirt. At first I thought it was a brace or something. He turned away from the mirror then, away from me. As he took it off, I could see, even from the other side of the door, the red marks it left on his skin, like it was tight, very tight.

I remember thinking how strong and slender his back looked as he maneuvered out if it. *I shouldn't be watching this.* I was about to duck again when he turned, his arms folded across his chest. That was when I saw that his hands were pressed deep into a flesh I knew so well. And as he reached down into the open dresser drawer to retrieve a clean shirt, I could see in profile, the gentle curve of his chest as he bunched up the shirt and wrapped it across the front of his body, holding it in place as he exited the room.

I sank down under the window, against the door. I waited. I didn't move a muscle, didn't make a sound. I'm not sure I was even breathing. Close by, through the open window around the corner of the house where I couldn't see, I heard the sound of water being turned on, full force. Then it switched to that unmistakable spray of a showerhead.

I don't know how I made it back down the ladder, and I don't remember crossing the field to get home. But I was in my room, Roxie sitting there patiently at my feet, as I looked out my window. I wasn't sure what I had just done, or what had even just happened, or how I could ever justify any part of me being there.

I tried to break it down logically: Chris had breasts. Chris was a girl. But he also wasn't a girl. He was . . . Chris.

Does it matter? Should it? Does it change anything? I didn't have answers for any of the questions that were running on a loop in my head.

The one person I would have really liked to talk with about this—really, the only person in the entire world who could help me with those answers—was Mallory.

The alarm on my phone had been going off for over an hour and I never even heard it. It took me several minutes to realize *why* my alarm had been going off in the first place.

I had stayed up way too late the past two nights. But as soon as my brain put all the pieces together, I jumped out of bed, rushing to get ready, looking everywhere for my Bargain Mart shirt, only to find it in a ball at the bottom of my hamper, all wrinkled and gross.

I was going to be late to work. Again.

I grabbed my bag and put Mallory's camera inside it. Then I raced my bike down the road and into town. The whole time, I was still thinking about what I had witnessed. It had only been two days since I'd last seen Chris, but it felt as if I'd lived through ten lifetimes. It had taken me that long to come up with answers, except they weren't very helpful.

Does it matter?

I don't know.

Should it?

I don't know.

Does it change anything?

I don't know.

I locked my bike up and tried to slip through the automatic doors without being spotted. I maneuvered stealthily, ducking down empty aisles to make my way to the back room, where I silently clocked in twenty-two minutes late for my shift. I was almost home free, but as I was coming out of the double doors, my manager was coming in. We both stopped short.

"Morning," he said, not mentioning the fact that this was the fourth time in two weeks that I'd been late. He clicked his tongue and sighed, then brought his hand to his chin, regarding my wrinkled T-shirt with disdain, before semi-sternly instructing me: "I need you to go help out over in clearance today."

I just shrugged.

For hour after mind-numbing hour, I was at it with another punished coworker. Our conversation faded quickly, overtaken by the clicking sounds of the pricing guns and the gentle soft rock humming over the speakers, interrupted every five minutes by a prerecorded movie-trailer voice announcement of the "Daily Deals." The recording had just finished cycling through for about the seventy-fifth time when I heard my name.

"Maia?"

When I looked up, there was Chris. The person I had not stopped thinking about for the past forty-eight hours.

"Hey," he said, smiling as he looked down at me.

"Hi." I stood up quickly, suddenly very aware of my dingy Bargain Mart shirt, my dirty jeans and old sneakers, my glasses and my hair. More than any of those things individually, I was concerned about the fact that I honestly couldn't remember if I'd even bothered to look in a mirror before I ran out of my house this morning.

He squinted and turned his head. "You're wearing glasses."

"I usually wear contacts, but"—I inadvertently pulled the trigger on the pricing gun, and a ninety-nine-cent sticker popped out—"I was running late this morning."

"I like 'em," he said, nodding.

"Oh, I don't know." I took them off and examined them

as if I'd never even seen them before. I felt the need to avoid looking directly at him, for fear my face might give me away and show all the things I was not supposed to know. "I mean, thanks."

"I used to *want* glasses when I was a kid," he offered when I said nothing to keep the conversation going. "I'm jealous. It kinda sucks to be cursed with perfect vision."

I didn't want this to be awkward, but I suddenly had no idea what to say to him, so I forced out a tiny laugh. It sounded fake and sat there between the two of us.

"Well, I was just here and saw you. So hi."

"Hi," I said yet again, and as I glanced at the items he was holding—a box of extra large bandages and a tube of Bargain Mart brand triple antibiotic cream—I blurted out the only thing I could think of: "Not another oven mitt emergency, I hope?"

He laughed.

There. Maybe it didn't have to be weird. Maybe it was possible to fall back into that rhythm we had been cultivating. Maybe things didn't have to change after all.

"No, I'm just clumsy," he said, raising his arm to reveal a line of small Band-Aids leading up to his elbow, too small to cover up the extent of the scrapes.

I winced.

"It's nothing." He shrugged. Of course, he didn't know that I also knew about the equally severe scrapes on his knees too. "But you would think, living with a nurse, she'd have something more in the way of first aid other than the teeniest, tiniest Band-Aids ever created."

"Yeah, really," was the best I could come up with. *Stupid.*

The silence between us hung there, waiting to be filled, but then he glanced down the aisle—at my fellow clearance aisle casualty, who was blatantly staring at us, and said, "Well, I'll see you around, I guess."

As he started to turn away I could almost feel Mallory nudging me again, whispering in my ear, *Chickenshit, say something!*

"Hey, wait." He turned back toward me, and it took me a second to realize I was the one who had spoken. "I get off in like twenty minutes," I continued. "I mean, if you feel like hanging out or something. And you don't mind waiting around for a little."

"I can wait around."

"Okay," I said, and accidentally pressed the pricing gun trigger again.

"Okay," he repeated, "I'll be outside."

As soon as he started walking toward the front of the store, I looked over and my coworker just nodded and said, "It's all good. Go."

So, I abandoned my post in the clearance aisle. I zigzagged a path to the back room, grabbed my bag, and locked myself in the family restroom, where I could be alone and get myself together.

"What are you doing?" I whispered to my reflection, gripping tightly to the sides of the enamel sink.

The girl staring back at me offered no response.

I twisted my hair back into a bun and splashed my face with water. I gargled and spit, patting my face dry with scratchy brown paper towels I pulled from the dispenser. I took the camera out and set it carefully on the sink. Rummaging through my bag, I found one individually wrapped mint floating at the bottom—I must've picked it up from one of the two restaurants in town at some point. I tried to remember how long it might've been there, whether it was still good or not. But my mouth tasted gross, so I didn't care. I tore open the wrapper and set it on my tongue anyway. I dumped everything onto the dirty floor of the bathroom, and out poured crumpled receipts and a broken pencil, a marker, nickels and pennies, a safety pin, and finally what I was searching for: my strawberry lip balm.

I picked it up with two fingers and centered myself in front of the mirror. I removed the cap and pressed the waxy tip against my upper lip, gliding it along the right side, then the left. I kneaded my lips together and stood back.

"Yes," I whispered this time.

CHRIS

THERE WERE PARTS OF THE SCRAPES THAT WERE still pretty raw from being ground up by the pavement. I applied the ointment and used two new, big bandages to cover it again. It already felt better, shielded from the sting of the air.

Then I pulled up one leg of my jeans and removed the haphazard arrangement of little bandages, and did the same thing. Again, for my other knee. And then one last bandage for the palm of my hand. I crumpled up all the paper backings and wrappers and stuck them in the plastic bag.

There was a garbage can by the entrance, so I walked back over and threw the bag away, then went back to the car. I sat inside at first, but I thought maybe that looked too weird, like I was expecting her to get *in*, which I wasn't. So then I got out and stood next to the car, but that looked stupid, so I tried to lean against the hood instead. But I thought that looked like I was trying to be a James Dean impersonator or something—as James Dean as one can look next to a station wagon, that is.

So I decided to walk back toward the building. I leaned against the cart rack, in the shade, and waited. As I stood there, I tried to smile at the customers coming and going—I thought people were supposed to be friendly in small towns—but hardly anyone smiled back. Most of them gave me these cool, sideways stares. So I pulled out my phone, to have something to stop myself from getting too nervous.

She asked me to hang out, I tried to remind myself. *As friends*, I silently added. *Just friends.*

Cole's last text to me was two days ago. He had said: Guess what?

It came in after I had that spill in the road, and I didn't feel like guessing, so I ignored him. I was ignoring him too much lately. It had taken me a couple of days to rally, but I was back. I was feeling better now.

What? I typed, then deleted.

Hey Cole. Delete again.

Hey, how's it going?

Stupid. Generic. Lame. Delete.

Hey, sorry man.

That one, I sent. I watched the screen for at least a full minute, but there was no indication he was going to respond in the near future.

I was still looking at my phone when a shadow fell in front of me. As I looked up at Maia standing there, I wasn't sure if it was the light or the shade or what, but I was having trouble remembering the "just friends" part of my agreement with myself.

"Okay," she said as we stood at the edge of the parking lot looking out at the sparsely arranged cars. "So I can give you the official tour of our sprawling metropolis, featuring our very own Historic Downtown Carson, but that wouldn't take very long."

I waited before speaking, just in case she wasn't finished.

"Or we could do something else," she added. "It all depends on how much time you have."

"I've got time," I told her.

"And I've got"—she reached around and opened her bag so I could see inside—"the camera today, so I was wondering if you felt like heading back over to New Pines."

I pulled my keys out of my pocket and jingled them. "Let's go."

On the drive, she was extra quiet. I kept feeling her staring at me. Every time I would turn to look, she'd glance away or act like she was watching something outside the window.

"Everything okay?" I finally asked her when I could take it no longer. *Were we going to have to get the whole near-kiss thing out in the open? Would that make it better or more awkward?*

"Yeah, everything's fine," she said, but her voice was all high and she was talking faster than she normally did. "Why?"

"It just seemed like—were you just staring at me?" I asked.

"Staring at you? No." She was shaking her head. "No. No, not at all."

"One more 'no,' and I'll believe you," I tried to joke. "Do I have something on my face or—"

"No," she said, and even though she smiled, a flush was creeping across her cheeks.

"Okay, okay, I believe you."

She laughed, and said, "Sorry, I wasn't staring on purpose."

"No, it's okay. I just wanted to make sure you didn't feel weird or uncomfortable about the other day."

"The other day?" she echoed. "What do you mean?"

"In my room."

Now her face went pale, abruptly draining of color. "In your room? What—what do you mean?" she repeated.

"When you came over the other night."

She exhaled, and it seemed like that tightness in her body relaxed.

"It's just that you left pretty quickly and I didn't know if you felt weird about"—I paused, willing the silence to convey the word I was too shy, too embarrassed to say out loud—"anything," I finished, instead.

"Oh." A flash of recognition passed over her face, the corner of her mouth curving into the smallest hint of a smile before she bit her lip to make it stop. "No, I didn't feel weird."

"Okay." Shit. Now I really didn't know what to say. "Good."

"Did you?"

"Did I what?"

"Feel weird?"

"Oh," I said, accidentally mirroring her response. "No."

"Good," she said, looking straight ahead.

. . .

We parked not far from where we had only a few days earlier. It was busier today. More cars on the road, more people on the streets. It was almost bustling, for a small town. The sidewalks were shaded under a canopy of lush foliage that arced over the street, with the leaves from the trees on opposite sides meeting in the middle.

Maia got out of the car in less of a hurry than she had on our first visit. She took her camera out of her bag and put the strap around her neck, just like it was that very first time I saw her on the road. Someday I would work up the courage to ask if she would show me the picture she took of me that day.

For now, we stood on the sidewalk next to the station wagon, looking around.

"Where to?" I asked her.

She looked right and left, then stepped out into the street. We crossed to the other side, where the fence of the cemetery lined the sidewalk. "I really wanted to get a picture of those gates," she said as I followed along next to her.

When we got there, she placed her hands on the bars, like she had the other day. Then she glanced over at me and cleared her throat as she stepped back, pointing the camera at the gates. She kept taking steps backward, past the sidewalk, onto the grass, and then finally, balanced with only her toes on the curb, she looked through the camera for what seemed like a long time. I stood back to give her space, but even several feet away, I could tell she was holding her breath.

Just when I thought she was about to take the picture, she lowered the camera and looked down at her feet. She repositioned them in the slightest way, more like she was moving her feet inside her sneakers rather than making her sneakers move.

At last her finger pressed down on the button and I heard the clap of the shutter. Even after it released, she didn't move for a moment. She was so focused; it was kind of mesmerizing to watch her. When she lowered the camera and looked at me, I realized I was the one who was staring at her now.

"What if we went in? Just for a few minutes?" she asked. "No zombies, I promise."

"Yeah, sure," I answered. "But I got your back, just in case."

She looked at me as she pushed through the gates, and smiled in this way that made me wish we really had kissed the other night—if only so that I could kiss her again right now.

It felt like we were walking into another world, another little city inside the town. There was a wide road made of old cobblestones that stretched out in front of us, and smaller pathways that curved around to the left and right, connecting to an even wider network of paths. The abundance of gigantic trees distracted from the smaller monuments that dotted the ground. Old roots had long cracked and lifted the stone walkways. The smell of flowers in the air made it seem like we were entering a park, not a cemetery.

We walked down the main road, both of us taking in the otherworldly scenery. Names and dates on the headstones were engraved in a script that was hard to read, some of the markings worn away altogether.

"A lot of these headstones date back to the 1800s," I said.

"Yeah," she replied, but she wasn't paying attention to the graves we were passing. She had her eyes focused out into the distance.

"People died so young back then." I was unable to stop myself from automatically performing the birth year to death year calculations in my head. "Nineteen. Twelve. Four. Eight months." I pointed at each grave as we passed. "Two days."

"Crazy," she said half-heartedly, still distracted.

"So, are you looking for anything in particular?"

Finally she turned her head in my direction. "Statues," she said immediately, but then followed up with, "I think."

"Statues?" I repeated, and I found myself scanning the landscape for them too. "How about those, over there?"

"No, not Jesus and Mary type statues. Something more . . . unique."

We veered off the main path, toward one of the pockets of taller headstones and monuments. I stayed on the walkway while she went to inspect a crowd of what appeared to be nearly life-size saints and angels, carefully stepping between the rows of headstones.

"No." She sighed, shaking her head, as if one of them had asked her a question.

"What?" I called over to her.

"Let's head back more toward the middle."

As I followed her, she looked at me and asked, "Do you think this is weird?"

"No, it's . . ." I tried to choose my next word carefully. "Interesting."

We walked toward the middle, and she looked at the

statues along the way, but none of them was right, apparently, because she had yet to take a picture.

I tried to go with it, but we had been walking for quite a while, and I had to ask:

"So is this a statue you've seen before?"

"I have," she said. "I just don't know where. But I know I'll recognize it when I see it."

"Okay," I said, but I was having a hard time searching for statues because I couldn't keep my eyes off her.

"Are you getting bored?" she asked as we ambled along the path.

"Not at all," I said, looking around. "It's sort of peaceful here. I like it."

"Me too." She brushed her hand along the bark of a tree we were passing, and then said, "Hey, can I ask you something? It's sorta personal," she cautioned.

"That's okay," I told her, even though I wasn't positive it would be okay.

"Being here, I guess it just makes me think about things." She was prefacing her question too much. Her footsteps were slowing down. "Have you ever lost someone? I mean someone close to you, someone you cared about?"

For some reason that was not at all what I'd been anticipating. I was worried maybe I wasn't passing as well as I thought I was—maybe she heard something in my voice or laugh, or maybe she saw something in the way I walked, or maybe my chest wasn't quite smooth enough or my jeans not baggy enough, or she had noticed my fingers were too long and slender and delicate. I had picked apart every last thing I wanted to change about myself as I'd waited for the question. But now that it was out, I didn't know what to say. Her face was open and curious and soft as she watched me, waiting for my answer.

"You lost someone?" I asked. "Who?"

I watched her swallow, like she was having a hard time getting the words to come out of her mouth. But then she finally said, "My sister. Mallory—her name was Mallory."

"What happened?"

"It was last year. She just . . . *died*." She said it like a question, like "died" was a foreign word that she hadn't quite figured out the meaning of. "She had this heart problem no one knew about, and she just died." She waved her hand through the air like she was trying to catch something invisible. "Did you know that already?"

"No, I didn't."

"I just thought maybe you heard, the way people talk around here."

"I don't really talk to anyone other than you."

She laughed, and even though I wasn't necessarily joking, I laughed too.

"I'm sorry about your sister, Maia." And I was sorry. "Really, that sounds awful."

She looked down at her feet, and said, quietly, "Thanks."

"Are you okay?" I asked her, and I could barely stand how much I wanted to take her hand right now, how much I wished I could put my arms around her.

"No," she answered. "But I think maybe I'm starting to be."

She stopped walking when we came to a fork in the

pathway, and turned a full 360 degrees, shielding her eyes from the setting sunlight that was filtering in underneath the tree canopy.

"What time is it?" she asked me.

I pulled out my phone to check and saw that Cole had texted me back:

Thanks. It's all right.

"It's 8:09," I told her.

She squinted into the distance, shaking her head. "I don't think I'm gonna find it." Her shoulders sloped forward and her hands loosened their grip on the camera that was still hanging around her neck.

"We can always come back again when we have more daylight," I offered, trying to lift her spirits. She nodded and glanced over her shoulder in the direction of the coming sunset, and did a quick double take.

"Wait a minute," she whispered, more to herself than to me.

And then, without another word, she began walking due west, taking a straight diagonal line directly to where the sun was sinking into the horizon.

MAIA

THERE, IN THE SUNSET, WAS A STATUE THAT STOOD IN silhouette, the sun breaking all around it like a halo of golden rays. How could I *not* notice it? Maybe that's what drew Mallory to it in the first place.

My feet made their way, no longer concerned with keeping to the pathways or stepping over the graves. The closer I came to it, the more sure I was of everything. I was sure that this *was* the statue in Mallory's picture. I was sure I was supposed to be here. I was sure that anything I had said or done or thought leading up to this moment was justified. I was sure I was doing the right thing. I was sure, most of all, of myself.

I circled the statue. It stood tall, on a platform. I looked at it from all angles. It wasn't like any of the other statues around. It wasn't a famous saint or an angel with wings. Not any deity I was familiar with. It was just a woman. An ageless woman in a draped garment with flowing, shoulder-length hair. She was larger than life-size, and she didn't carry anything with her that would give any clue as to what or whom she was supposed to represent.

We stood in front of her and looked up at her face. She gazed down, almost as if she was looking directly at us.

"Emily," Chris said.

"What?"

He pointed to the base of the platform. There was a small, rectangular, bronze plaque attached to the stone.

EMILY

DAUGHTER, SISTER, FRIEND

That was all it said. No last name, no dates.

"Wow," was all I could manage to say.

Maybe the statue really was just a person, an ordinary human being who once lived and who was once loved enough for her family and friends to erect a statue in her memory.

I readied the camera and stood where I imagined Mallory must've also stood. Chris walked away from me and the statue, out of what would be the frame if I was really taking a picture, and leaned against a nearby oak whose trunk was so enormous that if he lay down in front of it lengthwise, I think the trunk would still be wider.

I was supposed to take a picture. But as I brought the camera to my face and looked through, the magic was gone. I lowered the camera, and looked with my own two eyes, and I felt the magic simmer around the edges of my vision once again.

I raised the camera again, peered through the viewfinder,

and pressed the button, as was my plan. But I couldn't fight this sneaking suspicion that somewhere along the way I had been missing the point.

I walked over to where Chris was standing, and glanced back at the Emily statue.

"Get what you needed?" he asked.

When I looked at him, I realized I hadn't thought about those questions that had been buzzing around my mind these past two days. "Yeah, I think so."

Once we made it out of the maze of the cemetery and were standing on the other side of the gates, planted back in reality, Chris was the first to speak. He had his hand placed over his stomach. "Are you hungry at all?"

"Starving," I answered.

"Good, me too," he said, relieved. "What do you feel like?"

"Anything without a face. I'm vegetarian," I elaborated.

"I love vegetarian restaurants."

"Well, I doubt we'll find any around here."

No sooner had I spoken the words than he was on his phone, tapping away.

"The Green House," he said, tilting the screen toward me. "Five-minute walk."

"Really?" I asked in disbelief.

He shrugged. "Wanna try it?"

We made it there in four. The outside of the building was painted a leafy green, and there was an outdoor seating area cordoned off with a row of live bamboo plants. We were greeted at the door by a girl with floral tattoos up and down her arms. Her smile was warm as she led us to a table that looked out onto the street.

She pulled a lighter out of her apron pocket and reached for the candle that was sitting in the center of our table.

I read my menu in the flickering light, and tried not to stare at Chris again, at the way the candlelight made him look so vibrant and alive and gorgeous.

"What looks good to you?" he asked.

"I don't know," I admitted, fighting the voice in my head that wanted to answer: *You.* "I've never been to an actual vegetarian restaurant before." These were foods I'd never tried, and had barely even heard of, except for on TV. Like Chili Roasted Garlic Black Bean Hummus with Pita Chips. Crispy Baked Tofu Lettuce Wraps with Peanut Sauce. Super-Loaded Veggie Ramen. Eggplant Lasagna Rollups.

Chris's eyes widened as he leaned across the table toward me just slightly. "Are you serious?"

"Well, yeah. I mean, the vegetarian cuisine in Carson is mainly cheese fries."

I laughed, but he didn't.

"Oh my god, where do we even begin?" he said, studying his menu with a new intensity. "We just need a good strategy."

"A strategy?"

"Yes." He continued flipping through the pages of the menu. "Okay, I think the thing to do is order a bunch of dishes and split them so you can try as many things as possible."

"Um, okay," I agreed.

We took turns ordering something from each section of the menu. The waitress arched her pierced eyebrow when we first started rattling off the list of dishes, but then smiled like she was in on some secret joke.

In a short time, our entire table was filled with plates. We barely spoke while we ate, save for all the sound effects, the "Mms" and "Yums" murmured through full mouths.

I'd tasted some of everything and I'd arrived at a verdict. "Okay, it's official. I want to marry these tofu lettuce wraps," I announced. "But only if the peanut sauce can come too."

"And leave the eggplant things in the cold? Really?"

"The heart wants what it wants," I said, shrugging as I took another bite.

"Okay, then I'm marrying the Vegan Taco Flatbread," he added. "Wait, or the Quinoa Stuffed Banana Peppers."

"Mm, yeah."

The waitress appeared again as we sat there swimming in the table of half-eaten food. "Boxes?" she asked.

On the way back to the car, we took our time, our footsteps unhurried and loose. I watched him looking up at the sky as we walked side by side. I had this sense that, for the first time ever, I was finally a part of the world and not just *in* it. I wanted to hold on to this feeling, whatever it was.

Because for a moment, a sliver of a moment, I wasn't thinking about anything. I had forgotten about Mallory, and the gas station wall, and the spring break party, and Bowman's, and my bike tires, and the cemetery gates, and the whole reason we were here to begin with. I wanted to stop in the middle of the sidewalk and grab on to Chris's arm and make him hold still too. I wanted to put everything on pause while I memorized what it felt like to just be me.

I swung my arm as I walked, so that it bumped against his. He shifted his gaze from the stars to me. I smiled at him as I hooked one of my fingers around one of his.

He looked down at our hands, our fingers weaving together. "Is this all right?" he asked.

My heart was pounding so hard, I could barely respond, but to murmur, "Mm-hmm."

I didn't care that Chris was trans. He was Chris. And there was nothing in the world I would rather be doing in this moment than walking down the street holding his hand.

As we drove home in the dark, the windows all rolled down again, I kept finding myself smiling for no reason. The radio was turned down low, and it was the perfect kind of evening—cool and breezy. I was tired, but in a good way.

Something had happened today. Maybe many things had happened.

I couldn't say what exactly it was, but I suddenly felt as if I'd known Chris for a lot longer than just a couple of weeks. I looked at him now, and it seemed like so much had changed from only a few hours earlier when he'd approached me at Bargain Mart and I'd felt so weirded out, or in the car ride to New Pines, when I couldn't stop myself from staring at him, trying to find traces of what I'd seen through that window. But now, as I looked at him, I wasn't seeing any of that.

"Hey, Chris?" I said. I could be honest with him. I could explain the entire situation. I was going to. It was better to get it all out in the open. But then as he turned toward me and our eyes met, I couldn't do it.

"What?" he asked.

"Nothing," I answered. "It's just that today was the best day I've had in a long time."

He nodded and said, "Me too."

CHRIS

I PULLED INTO THE DRIVEWAY, THE GLOW OF THE DAY on me. I parked and shut the car off and sat there for a minute. It was so stupid, but I missed her already. I held my hand up and touched my palm lightly—I could still feel the imprint of her hand in mine.

Isobel's headlights were shining on me as her car rolled up behind the station wagon. I was holding a paper bag full of my half of the Green House leftovers as I waited for her to get out of her car.

"Did you have dinner yet?" I asked her as she walked up to me.

"No," she said, eyeing the bag. "Where did you get that?"

"Maia and I drove out to New Pines today. We checked out this vegetarian place."

Isobel gave me a look as we walked inside.

"Sit. I'll get the forks," she said as she gestured to the

kitchen table and started pulling out the boxes and opening them. "Okay," she began, picking up a citrus-glazed brussels sprout between her thumb and forefinger, examining it with curiosity before popping it into her mouth. "You gonna tell me what's going on over there?" she asked, tipping her head in the direction of the door.

"Nothing," I lied, realizing that our usual back-and-forth banter was not going to cut it tonight. "We're just friends."

"You sure?" she asked, and I thought I heard something in her tone that was disapproving.

"Why are you asking like *that*?" Wasn't she the one who encouraged me to live my life and not make apologies for trying to be happy? Wasn't she the one who always set that example for me in the first place?

She drew her eyebrows together and narrowed her eyes.

I continued, "I mean, would it be so bad if we were more than friends? I'm not saying we are. God, this would actually be supremely shitty timing, and I'm honestly *not* trying to start anything up, but what would be so wrong with that? Just because I'm—"

"No!" she shouted, cutting me off once she realized what I was leading up to. "Chris, don't be ridiculous. There is nothing wrong with getting into a relationship because you're trans. How could you even ask such a thing?"

I marveled at the way the word could just roll off Isobel's tongue without hesitation or uncertainty; I still wasn't that comfortable with naming it.

"I just want to check in to see where *you* are. If things were moving in that direction with you and Maia, or you and anyone, I'd think that's fucking incredible."

"Okay, fine," I relented.

"I only want to make sure you're okay and you're taking care of yourself and being safe."

"Safe?" I snorted. "It's not like I'm gonna get her pregnant."

"Bad joke, kid." She scrunched up her face and shook her head, giving me the thumbs-down with both hands. She was right. I was being defensive, and that wasn't funny. "I'm talking about you guys being safe, as in safe with your heart and your trust, and yes, okay, your bodies too."

"What, you don't think she's trustworthy?"

"No, that's not what I'm saying at all. But . . ."

"What?"

"Does she know that you're trans?"

I sighed, shaking my head. "You know, it'd just be nice for once to not have to provide some kind of disclaimer before saying hello to someone."

"Hey, I'm not telling you what to do one way or another. I honestly don't know what the answer is, Chris. But . . ." She took a bite of the flatbread and said, in between chewing, "From where I'm standing"—she paused to swallow—"it looks like you're saying more than just hello to her."

She had a point. But every time I thought about having the conversation, it made me want to run.

"When the time is right—*if* the time is right—you'll figure it out." She reached across the table and squeezed my arm. "I wasn't trying to upset you. You know that, right?"

"I know. It's just—"

"Scary?" she finished. "It's always scary to be honest, to show someone who you are. Why do you think I'm still living way out here, all alone?"

"Because you want to be," I answered.

"True." She smiled at the bite of stuffed pepper in her hand. "And you know what? I'm pretty damn okay with my life. But sometimes I ask myself whether I'm alone because that's what I want, or because it's the price of keeping myself safe."

"You are happy, though, aren't you?" I'd never seen Isobel show any self-doubt or even the slightest hint of her life not being exactly what she wanted.

"Happy enough." She nodded.

"Aunt Isobel—" I began, but she didn't let me say any more.

"Oh Jesus, let's not get all maudlin." She waved her hand between us, like she could shoo away all the residue of her words. "The whole point is that I don't ever want to see you holding back just because it's safer that way. I want to see you living your life all in. You know what I mean?"

"Yeah," I answered. "I do."

In my room I changed out of my clothes and got ready for bed. Before I put on my baggy T-shirt and the pair of shorts I always wore as pajamas, I stood in front of the mirror.

I wasn't brave enough to do this every day. But sometimes I could.

I met my own eyes in the reflection. I covered my breasts with my hands.

Being honest was what I wanted not too long ago—I wanted to go back to regular school, I wanted to be out, I wanted to start living again. It was me wanting to be honest with myself and my parents and the world that led to me being here in Carson in the first place. I really wanted to be all in, like Isobel said.

But honesty is a lot prettier in theory.

I closed my eyes and pulled my oversize T-shirt on and didn't open them again until I was facing away from the mirror. I wondered if it was possible to meet the right person, but at the wrong time. I never thought I would have feelings for someone, not when I'd only just started transitioning, not during this summer when everything was only temporary, not before I had my life together.

I climbed into bed and brought the covers up tight around my chest, and finally took out my phone. I texted Coleton: How do you know if a girl likes you?

He wrote back immediately: no idea . . .

Me: Yeah, me neither :)

Coleton: Link: How Do You Know If a Girl Likes You?

Coleton: that's all I got for ya, sorry

I laughed out loud.

Me: Thank you, very helpful!

Coleton: I try

Then, after a minute, he wrote again: So, does she?

Me: I dunno

Coleton: Who is she?

Me: My aunt's neighbor

Me: Maia

Coleton: awesome

Me: Maybe

Me: So what was your 'guess what' about the other day?

He sent a picture of a scoreboard at the Battleground, the arcade we always went to—it was the Transformers pinball machine. Under the top scores it said:

1st CTN

2nd MGF

3rd CTN

4th CTN

5th CTN

This was a major feat. The Battleground was our haunt; it was where Coleton and I became friends, at a birthday party we both were invited to in fifth grade because the whole class received invitations. Of all the games at the Battleground, including mini bowling and laser tag, Transformers pinball had been, for some reason unbeknownst to me, Coleton's Achilles' heel. Only I knew that CTN stood for Cole*tron*, not Coleton.

I felt really shitty for not responding before, because I could clearly imagine him there at the arcade beating the mysterious MGF's insanely high top score that had been on the board for the past six years, and having no one to celebrate with.

Me: Holy shit! You freakin did it!

Coleton: manager gave me free nachos :)

Me: When I get back to bflo I need to see irl

Coleton: cool

Coleton: Alright, gonna crash out. Good news about the girl who *might* like you

Coleton: keep me posted

Me: Thanks! Nite

The thought of being *completely* honest and all in with Maia was still terrifying, but the news of Coleton's pinball victory gave my confidence a little boost. Maybe there was some small part of me that was beginning to let in a sliver of hope. Hope that maybe she could accept me, even if I didn't quite know how to accept myself yet.

As I lay my head on the pillow, a sensation of vertigo passed through my body, like I could feel the axis of my life silently tilting.

Maia was changing everything.

MAIA

I LAY DOWN IN BED AND SMILED AT THE CEILING. Roxie jumped up next to me and panted in my face, wanting me to share this rare light feeling with her.

She curled up next to me, and I ran my hands over her coat, feeling the lumps and bumps and muscle waste of her old age. But somehow everything felt just right. Like things would turn out okay, after all.

The only thing that could've made tonight even better was if I had not looked away when we said good-bye. If I had been bold and brave and kissed him like I really wanted to.

CHRIS

IT WAS FOUR O'CLOCK IN THE AFTERNOON, AND I WAS lying on my bed with my laptop sitting open next to me, trying to not look up any more stupid websites about how to tell if a girl likes you, or trolling for more advice on the LGBTQ social media sites I basically only ever lurked on. There was tons of advice out there. Advice in general. Advice about dating. About coming out. About coming out as trans to a person you want to be dating. When and where and how and if.

The consensus was: There was no consensus.

So I did what I always did when I needed to zone out and forget about my tiny human problems. I pulled out my journal and I turned on the International Space Station Livestream channel. I wrote down the date, and scribbled the note:

Day 21 in Carson, NC

There was so little I was sure of at this particular moment,

I had nothing else to write. Instead I watched the video feed of Earth rotating beneath the satellite. It all looked so calm and clean and orderly from 250 miles above the surface—the oceans seemed so smooth, reflecting the sunlight like a ball bearing. Around the globe, the constants of the planet did their thing: The clouds passed over the land, the Sun rose and fell, the gentle blue halo of atmosphere shimmered ephemerally around it all—Earth transforming into this perfect giant marble where nothing bad could ever happen.

For the first time, I was beginning to wonder about the validity of my big theory, if things really are orchestrated and perfect, like I always thought, or if it's all just random chaos and happenstance and dumbass luck that we happen to be living and breathing on this spinning rock, held in place by invisible forces at this particular time, in this particular place.

The ISS orbits Earth every ninety-two minutes, so every forty-six minutes you're guaranteed to see either a sunrise or a sunset. I had seen two sunsets and one sunrise when I looked up at the ceiling fan. The incessant tapping of the metal chain pull string against the glass light fixture—*tick, tick, tick, tick, tick*—was driving me insane.

I stood on top of the bed but then had to stoop under the fan. I held the chain and found that there was one of those clasps that the tiny metal balls click into. I was struggling to detach it; the joints were stiff and tight from probably never being moved since the fan was installed forty years earlier.

A small hollow knock sounded from the hallway, accompanied by, "That looks dangerous."

I looked over to find Maia standing in the doorway.

"Your aunt told me I should come up," she explained, hitching her thumb in the direction of the staircase down the hall. "I hope that's okay."

"Yeah, I was just trying to fix this stupid—never mind." I jumped down off the bed. The *tick, tick, tick*-ing immediately started up again.

"It's different in here in the light," she said, still standing in the doorway.

She was looking around, at the bare walls and the tops of the dressers, the laptop that was still opened to the ISS footage, my journal sitting on the nightstand.

"Come in," I offered. I was still standing at the foot of my bed. "It's kind of messy, sorry. And hot."

"It's hot everywhere." She walked in, toward the center of the room, and then pivoted on her heel so we were facing each other. The moment our eyes met, she said, "You should see my room—I mean, because it's a lot messier than this. I mean, this isn't even messy at all, so—"

As she stood there in front of me, I noticed that she was clutching the strap of her bag so that it pulled down across her body. I couldn't help but linger a moment on her chest, where the strap was pulled between her breasts, tightening her shirt. I pulled my gaze away suddenly, hoping she hadn't noticed.

"So, what's up?" I asked.

"Nothing really. I got out of work early and I guess I didn't feel like going home. Thought I'd see if you wanted to hang out. Or something," she added.

"Hang out here?" I asked.

She shrugged and pulled the bag up over her head, but didn't set it down.

"Do you wanna sit?" I closed my laptop and moved it off the bed, since that was the only place for sitting. I propped my pillows up against the headboard and leaned into them, and she brought her bag with her as she sat cross-legged at the foot of the bed. She set her bag in between us, and took a breath like she was about to say something, but then exhaled.

Looking around again, she kept nodding—I'm not sure she even knew she was doing it.

"Hey, do you want my number?" I asked her. "Just to have."

In my brain's overdeveloped fantasy cortex, I'd already played out a brief vignette in which I asked Maia that question, and in response she held her hand out to me and let me write my number on that soft, fleshy part of her palm. I'd gotten to the part where I was cradling her hand in mine, about to press the pen against her skin—

Then she pulled her phone out of her bag, and said, "Yeah. Here, save it in my contacts." She handed me her phone, open to a new contact.

I hated my brain sometimes.

I typed in my name and my number and handed it back to her. My phone pinged on the nightstand where it was sitting next to my journal. I tipped the screen toward my face. A message from a number I didn't recognize.

Now you have mine. Hi!

I tapped out a

Hi back atcha

She replied with a thumbs-up emoji.

I added a :)

And then we looked up at each other and smiled.

"What do you want to do?" I asked her—with my voice—wishing I could text her everything I was really thinking instead. It would be so much easier. I'd tell her that I liked her, and I even liked her being in my room, sitting across from me like this. I would tell her that even though I liked her (and I didn't need a website to tell me so), I was scared too—*too scared*. I wanted to tell her how in reality, nothing could happen between us, even though, yes, I did indeed want to kiss her the other night.

Because those are not the kinds of things you say out loud to someone.

MAIA

I'D GOTTEN MYSELF PUMPED UP THE WHOLE WAY TO his house. I was ready to be honest and sit him down and tell him everything—that I'm not the artsy photographer I'm pretty sure he's falling for, that I know that he's transgender and he doesn't have to try to hide it from me, that I *really* like him—but now that I was sitting here and he was over there, all the courage I had worked up inside me was just coursing through my veins, making me jumpy and twitchy.

His question still lingered in the air. It was simple enough, but my thoughts were racing.

"I don't know," I finally answered—because what I had planned on saying sounded weird as I rehearsed it in my mind: *Chris, we need to talk.*

No, that was after-school-special speak.

That would not work.

"What were you doing before I got here?" I said instead,

stalling the inevitable, buying myself a little more time. "Prior to trying to decapitate yourself with the ceiling fan, I mean," I said, looking up at the ceiling.

His smile eased my nerves.

"What, that doesn't sound like a fun Friday night to you?" He picked up the notebook that was sitting next to him, and said, "I was just scribbling—doing nothing, really."

I had an idea—a clear, nonmuddled idea that might just work. I pulled Mallory's sketchbook from my bag, the one I'd found in her things, where I had started making my list of her photographs and their corresponding locations.

"Doing nothing is my favorite," I told him. I opened the sketchbook to where I had dog-eared a corner, and flipped to a clean page. "We could sit here and do nothing together?"

"Okay." He nodded in agreement and opened his notebook in his lap.

I promised myself I would not let one more day pass with all these secrets between us—I'd have to explain the whole story and I'd have to get it just right or he'd never understand why it started, or how me being outside his window that day was not even about him, that I was never trying to intrude upon him. Maybe if I could write it down in a letter, without the chances for miscommunication that would come with trying to say it all out loud, I could somehow make the whole thing make sense, at least enough sense for him to not hate me.

I began: *Dear Chris,*

I drew a line through it and started over with a simple *Chris,* but then I couldn't decide where the actual beginning of this story was. As I pressed pen to paper, the only words that came were the ones that had been spray-painted on the wall at the gas station.

I traced the words, inking the letters over and over again.

I looked up at Chris. He was watching me, but he quickly looked down at his notebook once more, the scratching of his pen loud in the quietness that had fallen over us.

A realization hit me.

I wondered if part of the reason I was feeling so good about him and me and our time together was because he's the only person I've ever known who didn't automatically know already, not only about Mallory's life and her death, but about *me*. Everyone in Carson knows who I am, or rather, who I've been. Sometimes living here felt like I had signed some sort of contract, agreeing to have a certain personality for the rest of my life, and that made it hard to change.

But with Chris, I had no such arrangement. I was allowed to tell him the things I wanted him to know, on my terms, in my time.

There's something to that.

No, I decided, I wouldn't tell him that I knew his secret. Who was I to take that from him?

I would, however, still tell him about the camera and the pictures and what I was really doing. I felt my head nodding, agreeing to the plan I was formulating. When I looked up again, his eyes darted back down to his notebook. He was keeping the pages tilted toward him, like it was a test and he didn't want me to see his answers. Maybe every secret needs to be told on its own terms.

CHRIS

I TRIED TO FOCUS ON MY JOURNAL, INSTEAD OF watching Maia. I flipped to a clean page and started a small sketch—it was scribbly and hesitant—not good at all. That wasn't the point, though.

I wasn't being nearly as stealthy about it as I should've been; she'd caught me staring at her at least a dozen times over the course of the last thirty minutes. When I looked up at her the next time, she had set her pen down and was leaning back on her hands, looking toward the open door outside. I placed my pen in the page and closed my journal.

When she looked back over at me, I asked her, "What were you drawing?"

"I wasn't drawing," she answered.

She studied her sketchbook for a moment, and when she finally turned it around so I could see, I felt my heart in my throat, pulsing. I had seen that quote many times before—it was my mother's favorite. She even had it on several items in our house: a bookmark she always used, the cover of a day planner she kept at her desk, and in my parents' bedroom it was printed on one of those wall plaques that you find in home stores, made of reclaimed wood with the words painted on or airbrushed, or something like that.

Maia licked her lips and read the words on the page out loud, her voice smooth and even: "We don't see things as they are"—she paused, and her eyes met mine for just a moment before she continued—"we see them as we are."

Then she bit her bottom lip as she waited for my reaction.

"Okay, that's bizarre," I finally managed to verbalize.

"Why?" She looked at the page again, then back at me. "Why did you write that?"

"I just saw it, and it's been stuck in my head, is all." She was squinting hard at me, her eyes crinkling at the edges. "What, have you seen this before?" she asked.

I nodded. "It's my mother's favorite quote. She has it everywhere."

Maia leaned forward, inched herself closer to me, like I'd just told her something huge. She was beaming out this incredible smile at me. This was the most excited I'd seen her since we were in the car and she was telling me about her dreams of traveling the world as a photographer.

"What do you think it means?" She was looking so deeply into my eyes, I could barely think straight.

"I—I guess it means . . . ," I began, only to realize that maybe I didn't actually know what it meant. "I'm not really sure."

"Yeah, me neither." She turned the sketchbook back around so that it was facing her again. "That's what I've been trying to figure out."

"Have you checked the interwebs?" I asked.

"Yes," she said, but she was shaking her head. "Hey, maybe you could ask your mom what she thinks?"

I laughed.

"Or not," she added.

"No, maybe I could," I said. "After she starts talking to me again."

"Sorry. I shouldn't have—"

"No, please. It's totally fine, really."

She smiled in this pinched, apologetic way. After waiting a beat, she seemed to have decided to change the subject. "So, what were you writing?" she asked, looking at my journal, which was still sitting closed in my lap.

"Actually, I wasn't," I admitted. "I was drawing."

Her eyes widened, and she sounded surprised when she said, "You draw?"

"No. Not well, anyway!"

She laughed, then inched herself forward just a little more, leaning like she was trying to see over the top of the notebook. Something inside me said I shouldn't show her. If I didn't show her, that old logic told me, then I wouldn't have to feel all the things she made me feel—terrified and hopeful, all at the same time, for wanting something I had been telling myself I couldn't have.

But another part of me, the newer part that somehow had manifested itself in this middle-of-nowhere town over the past month, that part knew it was too late. In spite of my best efforts, I had fallen for Maia. Hard. It was not just a crush, not a simple chemical reaction my brain was manufacturing. This was the real thing.

"Can I see?" she finally asked.

I opened my journal and removed the pen from the binding. I examined the scribbly drawing for another moment. Before I could change my mind again, I turned it for her to see. She reached out and ran her fingers over the indented hatch marks my pen had made, but the way it sent tingles through me, she may as well have been running her fingers over my skin. I watched her face carefully as she leaned into the space between us.

We were so close, I could hear the breath she took before she asked, "Is that me?"

The picture *was* of her. But it was of me, too. It was me seeing her. I wasn't sure how to say that, though, so I just nodded. It was everything. It was too much. I knew what would happen if our eyes met again.

I couldn't. I was a coward. I had to look away.

MAIA

WE DIDN'T KISS.

CHRIS

WE SHOULD HAVE KISSED.

MAIA

IT WAS THREE O'CLOCK IN THE MORNING AND I WAS still wide awake. I had reviewed every single interaction I'd ever had with Chris, many times over. But there were only a handful of things I knew for sure:

1. I liked him.
2. He was sweet and smart and funny.
3. I liked him a lot. And . . .
4. He liked me back.

Then there were all these other things that were more slippery, trickier to know for certain. Like the fact that he had secrets, and not just him being trans, but something else. The vague handful of scraps of information he had shared—the reason he wanted to help me that night at Bowman's, how he had willingly exiled himself to Carson for the summer, the stuff with his parents—these pieces were adding up, and I got this sinking feeling that something had happened to Chris before he came here, something bad, and he didn't want to talk about it.

I had secrets too. But in spite of the fact that there were all these half-truths and half-lies standing in the way, he had somehow uncovered the *me* that had been obscured by Mallory, by the death of Mallory, and even by Carson itself.

I got out of bed and went to my window. His light was still on. I turned mine on too and grabbed my phone.

Me: Are you still awake?

Chris: Yes.

Chris: You can't sleep either?

Me: No

Me: Hey, can you sneak out for a little while? I want to show you something.

Chris: Like right now?

Me: Yeah

Chris: Umm . . . Sure.

Me: I'll meet you by your car in 10, ok?

Chris: Okay

I swapped my pajama bottoms for jeans, twisted my hair up out of my face, put a bra on under my T-shirt, grabbed my keys and my strawberry lip balm from my bag, and put them in the pocket of my hoodie. I kissed Roxie on the head and told her I'd be back soon. In the kitchen I found the pad of paper we kept in the junk drawer and left a note—I doubted anyone would notice, but just in case.

• • •

An owl called out to me while I waited for Chris by the car. It was that four-beat phrase of the barred owl. People say it sounds like "Who cooks for you? Who cooks for *yo-ou*?" I remember when Mallory and I were little, Dad always said an owl meant bad luck, but Mom would argue that it was a good omen.

I guess I'd have to wait and see which was true.

"Hey!" Chris whispered as he skipped down the porch steps.

"Hi," I whispered back.

When he reached the car, he asked, keeping his voice low, "Where are we going?"

"Not far," I told him as I slid into the passenger seat.

He waited until we got out onto the road, past Isobel's house and mine, before he turned on the headlights.

There was no one around. The only bar in town had been closed for hours. And I could almost convince myself that we were the only two people left on the face of the earth.

"Can you give me a hint?" he asked.

The night made me feel invincible, like the world was ours for the taking. I wanted to tell him to just keep driving until we hit water, but that wasn't my plan.

"Are we doing something illegal?" he whispered again, even though it was just us.

I cupped my hand around my mouth and whispered back, "No."

His shoulders bounced in a silent laugh. I couldn't help but look at his arms, the sinew defined slightly as he adjusted his grip on the steering wheel, lean muscle under what I imagined to be smooth, soft skin. For a second I forgot I was supposed to be the navigator.

"Are we at least close?" he said, drawing me back into focus.

"Almost there," I said. "Okay, slow down. Turn in here."

"It looks closed," he replied, but he turned in anyway.

"Drive around to the back of the building."

"Oh god," he groaned. "Why do I just keep doing everything you say?"

"Because," I said. "We're having an adventure."

He pulled around to the back of the gas station, the headlights shining on the brick wall, a spotlight on the words we'd shared earlier. I waited for him to see it.

"It's the quote," he finally said.

I got out of the car and walked around to the front of it, then leaned against the hood.

He shut the engine off, but left the headlights on, and then got out and walked up to the wall and ran his hands along the words.

As he turned around and walked back toward the car—toward me—the light shone on him, illuminating all the features I was growing to love. Not just the crooked smile and the dimple, but his walk and the way he would put his hands in his pockets, how he tilted his head ever so slightly when he looked at me—his everything.

He joined me, also leaning against the hood, with one foot perched on the bumper. We had to stand close to each other so that our shadows didn't get in the way of the lights.

"What do you think?" I asked.

He smiled as he looked at the wall. "I'm really glad you dragged me out in the middle of the night to see this."

"Really? Worth it?"

He nodded, and met my eyes. "Totally worth it."

I adjusted the position of my feet on the blacktop, and the side of my foot tapped the side of his. Neither of us moved away. Maybe it was only an accident, but he shifted the placement of his hand on the hood next to mine so that the pinkie finger of my right hand and the pinkie of his left were touching.

We stayed like that, neither of us talking, simply looking at the wall, and allowing these small points of contact between our bodies.

The air had cooled, and the insects had even quieted down. The only sounds were of our breathing. Now would have been the time to tell him all of those things, to let him hear the secrets I was so ready to get out. But I was distracted by the feeling of his arm, warm against mine, and my shoulder leaned into him.

Any one of these tiny touches could've been an accident, but I felt each one deep inside me, starting in the very center of my abdomen, moving up under the ribs, sending minor shock waves to my heart.

I moved my hand on top of his, each of my fingers gliding over his, exploring the grooves of his knuckles, my fingertips along his smooth nails. His fingers parted, allowing mine to fall between them. I couldn't tell if it was my hand shaking or his.

"Is this all right?" I heard my voice whisper into the night air. I looked up at his face then. He had his eyes closed, but he nodded, almost as if he knew I was looking at him.

He turned his hand over slowly and let our palms slide together, our fingers intertwining like they each had little individual minds of their own. It was like all of the nerve endings in my entire body were concentrated in the places where our skin was touching. We held our hands out in front of us, both of us now watching as they mingled and became one, the backdrop of the brick wall receding into the distance.

I could feel the breath in my lungs moving faster, in and out, and I dared myself to look at him once more.

His eyes were open now, and they were on me.

I felt that magnetic pull again, tugging on my whole body, and he was drawing closer to me too. He'd stopped leaning against the car and was now standing up straight, turning to face me. My eyes followed his movements first, and then my feet followed, until I was standing up as well. His gaze moved back and forth between my eyes, glancing down at my lips.

With his face close to mine, he spoke so quietly that his words were made mostly of air: "Can I?"

I parted my lips. My mouth wanted to answer, *Yes, kiss me. Now, please. Because I've been waiting thirteen billion years for this,* but I couldn't make any words come out, so I nodded into the rapidly shrinking distance between us.

Our palms pressed together hard like there were magnets there, too. His other hand floated against my cheek and down the side of my throat, and his fingertips rested in the hair at the back of my neck. I moved my free hand to his forearm, and pulled him closer.

We were breathing against each other, breathing each other in, and the instant our lips touched, I felt this enormous release, like a sigh escaping, not from my mouth, but from my whole body.

His mouth was warm, his lips soft.

CHRIS

SHE TASTED SWEET ON MY TONGUE.

My heart was pumping, fast and strong and steady, like I was running a race. I didn't care what the repercussions might be for this moment; I was taking it.

We were taking it.

This moment was ours.

If there had been any doubt left in my mind about whether or not she really did like me, it vanished, like the space between us vanished as our lips slipped together. She brought our hands—the ones that were joined—down to the side of her waist, and left my mine there, while hers traveled up my arm, over my shoulder, around to the back of my neck. I let my fingers press through her shirt against the soft part where her waist and hip met.

I felt her breath catch.

We pulled each other closer at the same time.

Her other hand was touching my face, her fingers soft and searching as they passed over my cheekbone and jaw and chin and down the front of my neck and back again, like she was cataloguing their shapes in her memory.

We were breathing the same; my inhale was her exhale, her inhale my exhale. I felt our kisses through my whole body as they grew faster and deeper by the second. Her hands moved down to my hips, and she took a few small steps toward me, steering me backward with her hands. We passed through the bright white light of the headlights, and I opened my eyes to see our shadows moving against the brick wall. She was leading us around to the side of the car, still kissing me.

I pulled my mouth from hers for a moment, but she answered my question before I had a chance to ask: "I just want to be closer to you."

I heard the click of the handle unlatching, and she swung the back door open. I got in first, and I held her hands while she slid in behind me.

I pulled her close, our chests pressed together, and when she tilted her head back, her breathing was just as ragged as mine. I could feel her throat swallowing against my lips as I kissed her neck. She brought her leg up and wrapped it around mine. My hand went to her thigh—I wished I could touch her face and her arms and hands and legs all at the same time.

She was slowly sliding down onto her back, pulling me against her so there was no space in between us. I was on top of her and I tried to hold myself up, but my arms were shaking. My shirt had pulled up a little, and our bare stomachs were touching. My leg was between her thighs, and as she raised her hips and pressed herself against me, I thought my heart was going to explode.

"Wait, is this okay?" I asked her, pulling out of our kiss to look at her.

She was nodding, saying, "Yes, yes. It is, I swear."

Her hands were on my back, over my shirt. I knew she had to have been feeling my binder underneath, and I knew I needed to stop before it went any further, but god, I didn't want to.

I leaned down and kissed her collarbone, then her neck again—her elegant neck—I'd been wanting to do that for so long. I felt her thighs squeeze against my sides. I had my mouth close to her ear. I was going to tell her, *Maia, we should stop*, but before I could, she moved her hands from the small of my back, where her fingertips were touching skin, to my waist, and just as I was going to catch her hand, not let it go any further, she took mine in hers instead and placed it, so gently, on her stomach, under her shirt, and guided my hand up and over her bra.

I closed my eyes and rested my forehead against her shoulder for just a moment while I tried to gather my willpower.

"Is this really okay?" I asked again. Part of me hoped she'd say no, because I was scared.

"Yes," she answered.

I felt her breathing hitch as my hand molded to the shape of her breast. She pulled her shirt up, slowly, over her head. We watched as she tossed it aside and it fell out of the open door onto the ground outside.

We looked at each other and laughed at the same time.

She bit down on her lip, and whispered, "Sorry."

"Don't be," I said. "But are you sure you're—"

"I am. I'm really okay," she said, cutting me off. "I'm just a little embarrassed."

"Why?" I whispered back.

"I've never done anything like this," she said. "Like. Ever."

I nodded. I understood. "You don't need to feel embarrassed about anything." I understood completely. "You are so amazing, and so kind, and smart, and so, so, so incredibly beautiful in every way possible."

She held my face in her hands and kissed me, and I felt so comfortable under her touch that I almost forgot about the thing I could never quite forget about. She let her hands trail down my neck, over my shoulders, and everything felt so right. Until she placed her hands on my chest. I pulled back, recoiled—it was a reflex. She flinched. And almost right away, she moved her hands down to the sides of my waist. She was watching me too closely. I needed to look away, so I leaned down and kissed her shoulder.

"Chris?" She brought her hand under my chin, tipping my face forward, making me look at her. "Is this okay for you?"

I hesitated. She was asking me the question I really needed to be asked right now, only I didn't know how to answer her. There were no simple yes or no answers to that question. I shifted my weight off her and sat up.

So did she.

"It's okay," she said, taking both of my hands in hers, "if it's *not* okay."

"I want this. I want all of this. I really do." I paused. I wasn't sure what was about to come out of my mouth. Part of me just wanted to hop out of the car and run away and just keep running forever, and never face her again. Not if telling the truth meant that everything was about to be ruined. I swallowed hard past the fear that was collecting around all the words that seemed eternally stuck in my throat.

"But I have to tell you something, Maia," I forced myself to continue. "And I don't know what will happen after I tell you. It might change everything for you. It might change everything between us, and that is terrifying to me because I've never felt like this about anyone. I've never even dreamed that it was possible to feel the way I feel right now."

"Okay," she said. "Whatever it is, you can tell me."

I nodded, took a deep breath, and spoke the words I'd practiced saying out loud in the mirror earlier that night after she'd left:

"I'm transgender." I let the words dangle there, feeling the rest of my life hinging on what would happen next. "I just—I needed you to know."

I held my breath as I watched her face for some sign of recognition, some sign that told me she understood what I was telling her, but she just kept looking at me in the same way she had been. All open and soft and patient.

"Maia, please tell me what you're thinking?"

I braced myself, but she reached for my hand and held it in hers with so much tenderness. Then brought my fingers to her lips and closed her eyes as she kissed them. "I'm thinking," she began, looking at me once again, "it doesn't change anything."

"Are you—are you sure?" I asked.

"I'm sure," she said.

She let go of my hands and moved close to me, wrapping her arms around my neck, my shoulders, and I could feel her breath moving in and out of her body. She tightened her grip until I placed my arms around her too.

My hands felt cool against the warm, bare skin of her back.

I felt her relax against me, and just like that, all of the tension I'd been holding on to for my entire life started draining out of my body. We stayed in each other's arms—the door wide open, her shirt on the ground, headlights still shining against the wall—until daylight began creeping in through the night clouds.

MAIA

CHRIS GOT ME HOME BEFORE DAWN. IT WAS 5:55
when he parked at his aunt's house, and he held my hand as he
walked with me through the grass, all the way up to my porch.

He kissed me on the cheek, and looked down at his feet
as he smiled. In that moment I didn't care if we got caught.

I crept up the stairs to the second floor as quietly as
possible, every tiny creak my steps made sounding like doors
slamming. As I passed Mallory's room, I looked in like always,
but Roxie wasn't there. I tiptoed down the hall and into my
bedroom, silently closing the door behind me.

When I turned around, there was Roxie lying at the foot
of *my* bed. I gave her a quick pet and then collapsed. I didn't
bother taking off my clothes or my shoes. I lay on top of the
bedspread and watched the daylight beginning to fill my
bedroom.

If I closed my eyes, I could still feel his hands on my skin.

I rolled over and buried my face in my pillow, but was unable to stop myself from grinning. My hair spread out around me, and as I breathed in, I realized it smelled like him, smoky and sweet at the same time, like sea salt and clean laundry. I inhaled deeply and held the scent there in my lungs until my chest got stiff and my body forced me to let it out.

I wrapped my arms around my pillow and held on tight.

I didn't wake up again until noon. When I came downstairs, Mom was sitting in the living room, which was strange. She didn't normally hang out around the house, what with the risk of having to interact with Dad, and everything.

She had her feet tucked under her on the couch, her hand lazily smoothing Roxie's head, as she read a magazine. She had pulled her hair up into a ponytail and didn't have any makeup on at all, and was clad simply in shorts and a tank top. I found myself smiling at her before she saw me standing there. She looked so normal, at ease. I hadn't seen her like that in a while.

"Morning," I said, sitting down on the opposite end of the couch.

"*Afternoon,*" she countered, but then smiled.

"You look nice," I told her.

She jerked her head back and pulled her eyebrows together, her hand immediately flying to her hair. "I'm a mess!"

"No you're not. You look very chill."

"Chill, huh?" She shook her head, then looked at me more closely, squinting as she took in my clothes and my hair. Could she tell I'd been in the back of a car kissing a boy with my shirt off in the middle of the night?

"You look"—she paused, searching for the word—"*happy*," she finished, uncertain.

"Really?" I asked, and I knew my voice was too high, too excited.

"Yes," she answered, but her smile faded quickly and was replaced by a tight, forced curve of the mouth as she looked back down at Roxie. I could practically smell the disappointment coming off her. I'd violated the cardinal rule. Happy wasn't allowed in our house. In that moment, I would have rather she caught me half-naked in a backseat with a boy's hands on me.

"Are you hungry?" I asked her. "I'm starving."

She tilted her head to the side, checking in with her stomach. "A little, I suppose."

I had my containers from the Green House still sitting in the refrigerator. I took out plates and bowls from the cupboards and arranged the leftovers into two servings. I heated up the ones that needed to be heated, and made them look pretty, like on those TV food shows.

If Dad was home, there was no sign of him, so this would be just a me and Mom thing.

I poured her a glass of the herbal sun tea that she had sitting out on the counter in the giant mason jar dispenser—she'd sworn off Dad's Luzianne, supposedly for caffeine reasons.

"Okay, Mom," I called into the hallway. "Lunch."

She ambled into the kitchen a few seconds later, holding her hip the way she did whenever she'd been sitting too long. Roxie followed behind, sniffing at the air.

"Thank you, honey," she said, and then cleared her throat, almost as if "honey" had slipped out by accident. "I saw that there were some take-out containers in there." She glanced at the fridge. "I didn't know whose they were, though."

She really would do anything to avoid acknowledging Dad's existence.

She took a bite of the vegan taco flatbread, and nodded in approval. "So," she began.

I waited, but I don't think she had a follow-up.

"Hey, do you remember that time when we all went to the beach?" I asked. "It was like six or seven years ago. We stopped in New Pines and went to that old-fashioned ice cream place?"

Her face went slack and blanched.

She opened her mouth, but no sound came out.

Her fork teetered between her fingers, like she was about to drop it. But then she snapped out of it, blinked her eyes fast a few times, and said, "Sure." Her voice was tight, controlled, the color rapidly returning to her face. "Why?"

"No—nothing, no reason." I was inadvertently breaking all the rules. I wished I could roll back time and never have said anything at all. "I just—I went there the other day. With Chris. That's where the food came from."

She speared a citrus-glazed brussels sprout and popped it into her mouth—I could hear her teeth scraping against the fork.

"Well, not the ice cream place," I continued anyway. "But this little vegetarian restaurant we found. There. In New Pines, I mean."

The way she was staring at me, her eyes suddenly all hard and wide, made me so nervous that I was chopping up my sentences into fragments.

"Oh." She nodded, but when she said, "That's nice," I knew I'd lost her.

I was taking a bite of my tofu lettuce wrap when she stole a glance at me. It had to have only been a second, a fraction of a second.

But it was long enough for me to recognize it.

I knew what her gaze meant because that was the way she always looked at Dad. Like I'd done something to betray her, and now she wasn't sure if she could trust me anymore. And I had.

I'd used a forbidden word: "we."

"We," in reference to a time when Mallory had existed.

She took a sip of her sun tea, and then pressed her napkin to the corners of her mouth. Sitting up straighter, she cleared her throat.

"Maia, I wanted to ask you," she began.

She was going to bring up the fact that I'd snuck out last night, that I'd come home at dawn. She'd demand to know what I was doing, who I was with, and I'd cave and tell her every last detail—that's how guilty she made me feel.

"Were you out in the barn for some reason?" she finished. Her eyes were narrowed and squinting, and she was doing this micro head shake, almost like she really wanted me to say no. "I noticed the light had been left on."

"Um." I swallowed again. "Yeah, I—I was, actually."

"Why?" she asked.

"I just—I don't know—I guess I wanted to look around."

I wanted to remind her that the barn was always supposed to be a shared space for me *and* Mallory. That I used to be out there all the time with her. That, technically, I should be allowed in the barn whenever I wanted.

"Well," she said, clenching her jaw as she nodded. "You just make sure you leave it as you found it."

"Oh—okay," I stuttered.

She stood up and tried her best to smile, but it was like her face was cracking, like it was too painful and she could only press her lips together in a straight line. "Thank you for lunch," she said, like it was a business meeting or something. "I think I might go lie down for a little," she muttered as she walked away.

As I sat there looking down at the reheated remnants of the happiest meal of my life, the guilt began tugging at my seams—Mom's words echoing through me like a single thread being pulled.

I'd just finished reboxing up the leftovers once again and placing them back into the fridge when my phone vibrated in my pocket.

It was Chris:

I can't stop thinking about you

I smiled at the words, and imagined him saying them out loud.

Then he wrote: Please tell me I get to see you today?

We were lying on the concrete, the sun falling gently onto our skin through the filtered shade of the trees at Bowman's.

My lips tingled from all the kissing. It had started the second we'd entered the wooded path—kissing while walking, kissing against a tree, kissing while standing on the house's foundation, and sitting, and then lying, with me on top, then him on top. When we were too exhausted and out of breath to keep kissing, we spread out like when you're a kid making snow angels, except it wasn't cold, white snow; it was the warm sun-bleached white of the concrete.

Only our hands were touching.

"This is where we talked for the first time," I said, my head tipping to the side to look at his face. "I already liked you then."

"Really?" he said. "'Cause it seemed like you were completely annoyed."

"Don't you know that was just my cover?"

He looked up at the trees, the blue of the sky punching through the spaces in between the leaves.

"Did you get in trouble for last night?" he asked. "Did they know you were gone?"

I wish. Getting in trouble for sneaking out would have felt a lot better than getting in trouble for remembering, or whatever it was that my mom thought I had done wrong.

I didn't say that, though; I shook my head. "You?" I asked instead.

"No," he said. "It would have been worth it if I had, though."

His fingertips were dancing along the lines of my palm.

It made me remember Mallory, this one night in her bedroom when we were lying side by side on her bed. She held my hand up and traced each line, telling me, "This is your life line. And here, that's your heart line. Your head line. And your fate line."

"What about this one?" I asked Mallory, pointing to the longest, deepest line on my hand.

"That's your sun line," she said. "It's all about fame and fortune."

"Fame?" I scoffed at the idea—Mallory was the one who was going to have all that. "Me?"

"Well, it's also about scandal," she told me, making her voice all deep and throaty. And then she threw her head back, laughing.

"What?" Chris asked, his voice snapping me back to the present.

I opened my eyes. I hadn't realized they were closed.

"What?" I repeated.

"You just laughed," he told me, smiling.

"I was thinking about last night," I told him, not a lie exactly.

He nodded, saying, *"Mmm."*

"That was pretty scandalous, wasn't it?"

His cheeks flushed, and he buried his face in my shoulder. "It was," he agreed, letting his hand rest on my stomach. He lay back, and we switched positions: my head against his shoulder, his arm around me. I was careful of where my hands were. He hadn't told me so, but I knew from the way he'd pulled back when we were in the car, he didn't want me touching his torso. I placed my hand low on his stomach, near his hip.

"Is this all right?" I asked.

"Yes." Then with his hand over mine, he moved it gently, up his stomach, so that my fingers were just grazing his lower ribs.

"Okay," I said. I wanted him to know I understood he was showing me what was okay.

It was quiet for a while, just the sounds of leaves rustling and birds, the occasional muffled rumble of a car passing on the road.

"Can I ask you something?" I said, propping myself up on my elbow so that I could see his face.

He looked up at me and nodded.

"I know you didn't want to talk about it when I asked you before, but why are you really here?" I said.

The expression on his face changed in the most subtle way—from smooth and relaxed one moment to tight and rigid the next. I could feel him trying to control his breathing—making it slow and steady. I could see him swallow as he calculated what he would say to me. He inhaled deeply, like he was trying to hold the air in his lungs, and just when I thought he was going to begin speaking, he exhaled again.

Finally he cleared his throat, meeting my eyes for only a moment before looking up at the sky again. "Last year, this thing happened at school and it kind of completely fucked up everything in my life."

I waited.

"I got beat up," he finally said. "I guess it was pretty bad. I mean, it was three against one."

"Oh my god," I breathed.

"I couldn't go back to school for a while," he continued.

"And then, I don't know, things just started happening fast. I ended up coming out to my parents, and they just didn't really get it, so by the time I *could* go back to school, they wouldn't let me. They still don't really get it, I guess."

"Chris, I'm sorry. Are you—"

"I'm fine now," he interrupted, locking eyes with me again. "I promise. I barely even think about that anymore." But he was being too confident, too nonchalant about it; I knew he wasn't telling me the whole story. I could fill in the blanks. I got the picture.

"I just had to get away from everything for a little while," he concluded. "That's all."

He shrugged like it was nothing, and even though I wanted to ask so many more questions, I just nodded, and tried to conceal the way my hands were trembling, my body unable to contain how angry I was for him.

CHRIS

I WAS IN DEEP. IT HAD ONLY BEEN A WEEK SINCE THE first night we'd kissed, and I was all in. We spent every day this week alternating between my bedroom and hers, depending on whether or not Isobel was home during the day. Maia even called in sick to work Tuesday and Wednesday so we could be together. She switched with someone, Thursday for Friday.

I hadn't run in days, but now that I was on hormones, my body could hold on to its muscle, whereas before, I would've already felt my calves and quads and hamstrings breaking down. It was the little moments like this that kept surprising me—I was no longer constantly fighting a losing battle against my own body. Which meant I could take three days off to spend it in bed with my girlfriend—*girlfriend*—and not worry about immediately turning all soft and curvy.

I was in my running clothes, stretching, while I watched

from my porch as Maia's mother and father left for work, one and then the other. As soon as I could no longer see them on the road, I jumped up and jogged across the field just as Maia was closing her front door behind her. When she saw me coming, she waited on the top step, smiling.

"Morning," she said, leaning down to kiss me, her hair falling over her shoulders and grazing my face.

"You heading to Bargain Mart?" I asked her.

"Unfortunately," she groaned. "I'd rather be spending the day with you, though."

"I thought I'd run while you bike?" I told her. "Keep you company on the way there."

She nodded, and again, her smile lit up her eyes like there was a tiny white-hot star living somewhere deep inside her.

If there really were, I honestly wouldn't have been surprised. Because every time I was near, I felt my body pulling closer to her, millimeter by millimeter, like she was magnetic north and I was just a rule of nature.

Out on the road I ran, and she pedaled.

"You can go faster, you know," I told her. Maybe I wanted to show off a little. I was strong, I could handle it—I wanted her to know that.

"*Okay,*" she sang, standing up on her pedals and pumping her legs harder.

I ran faster. I could keep up. Even though there was a stitch needling through my side.

She slowed down again, and said, "I don't want to get there sooner."

We made it passed Bowman's, and the school I'd only driven

by. As I looked at the building—all brick and institutional-looking, I could almost imagine myself there, walking through the doors, holding Maia's hand. I didn't say anything, but I hadn't run this far since I was still on the track team. She was like fuel for me.

When we reached Bargain Mart, she slowed to a stop and got off her bike. I was struggling to catch my breath, when she hooked her finger around the collar of my shirt, asking, "See you later?"

I wanted to tell her to please call in sick again. I didn't know how I'd wait until later to see her. But I just said, "Absolutely."

When we kissed good-bye, she pulled me closer to her, even though I was sweaty and panting. It felt amazing, being out in the open like this, telling the world—or at least Carson—that we belonged to each other.

No perfect grades or first-place medals had ever made me feel like I mattered as much as when she looked at me the way she was looking at me. I stood there and watched her wheel her bike through the parking lot, and then lock it up in the bike rack next to the building. She waved to me as she disappeared through the sliding glass doors.

I started jogging again—I'd take it easy the rest of the way.

A truck passed me after a while, but I didn't pay much attention until a couple of minutes later when it circled back in the opposite direction.

My thoughts were a million miles away, reliving every intoxicating moment of this past week with Maia, when I heard the engine of that same truck, pulling alongside me. I turned to look, and when I saw who it was, I tried to increase my pace, just a little, even though I knew if this went bad, there would be no outrunning him.

"Hey, Chris," Neil said as his truck crawled along next to me.

I didn't answer him. I looked straight ahead.

"Hey, man," he called out the open window. "Hey, sorry about that whole thing the other day."

I just kept running.

"I was an asshole, okay?" he shouted. "I know that."

Left, right, left right. I tried to concentrate. I would not break rhythm for him.

"Dude, I was wasted," he said. "Come on, will you stop a minute?"

I slowed down. I told myself I was only slowing down so that I could tell him exactly what I thought of him.

"What?" I finally yelled back.

"Look, I got no problem with you, all right?" he yelled out the passenger side window.

"Can't say the same," I yelled back.

"I just wanted to warn you, okay?"

"Warn me?" I repeated.

"Maia," he said, shaking his head—the sound of her name on his lips stirred something up inside me, this fire in my chest.

"She is one fucked-up girl, okay?" he said, eyes all wide, raising his eyebrows. He pointed a finger at me. "You watch your back with her, all right?"

I stood there, dumbfounded, silent, in disbelief. By the

time my brain told my mouth to say *"What?"* he was already driving away.

"Hey!" I yelled. "Get back here!"

But he was long gone.

I ran the rest of the way home, took a shower, dressed, and ate sandwiches with Isobel in the kitchen before she had to go to work. I even went for a long drive, but none of those things helped to get Neil's words out of my head.

I knew I shouldn't let him get to me. This was the same guy I'd watched push Maia around at that party, the same guy who'd slashed her tires. Someone who does those kinds of things was not worth my mental energy. Yet he was in my head, under my skin.

I knew she wouldn't be home until later in the afternoon—she said around four—but every little noise I heard outside made me jump up to the closest window or door.

As soon as the time changed from 3:29 to 3:30, I debated driving over to pick her up, but we hadn't planned on that and I didn't want to overstep. We'd never actually made a real plan.

Then four o'clock hit.

I stood on the porch.

No sign of her.

Around four, I repeated in my head. That could mean anywhere from three thirty to four thirty.

I went back inside and messed around on my phone—I could be patient a while longer.

I watched as 4:10 passed. Then 4:15, 4:20, 4:25, and 4:30 came and went.

I was driving myself crazy. I set my phone facedown on the coffee table, and sat on the couch. I closed my eyes and vowed to not look at my phone again until I'd completed five cycles of that slow deep breathing Isobel had taught me when I was rehabbing from my broken ribs.

Inhale. Exhale. One.
Inhale. Exhale. Two.
Inhale. Exhale. Three.
Inhale—

We'd been walking awhile off the path, and I can't remember now if anyone was talking or not. Just as I became aware that I could no longer hear the sounds of the coaches' whistles and yelling back at the school, we came to a clearing. Everyone stopped and stood there, looking at me.

"What?" I said when no one made a move. "So, who has the fireworks?"

They snickered and smirked at one another with these sideways glances.

"Why are you pretending to be a boy?" Ben asked, ignoring my question.

My heart started racing. *Run*, that voice said again, louder this time.

"I'm not," I answered.

"You're not pretending, or you're not a boy? Which is it?" Ben countered, barely able to get through the words without laughing. He placed his hands on his hips and rocked back on his heels, waiting for an answer I couldn't supply. "Can't be both."

"You know what? Fuck you," I mumbled, knocking my shoulder into Ben's as I started to walk away from them.

Run.

Fuck you, I told that voice in my head too. I wasn't going to give them the satisfaction of running away. He grabbed my arm, though, and yanked me back so hard that I thought my shoulder dislocated. I went to push him away, but I was too slow, or he was too fast, and now he had both my arms. I thrashed around, convinced I could shake him off, but that only made him hold on tighter.

"Let go of me!" I yelled, hating myself for the way my voice was shaking.

"You don't wanna fight me, *Christina*," he said, his voice set at a tone that was both a warning and a dare. He twisted my wrist and shoved my hand against his jeans, rubbing against his penis so roughly that it felt like the zipper cut the skin of my palm open on its metal teeth. "You feel that?" he shouted over Tobey and Jake clapping and laughing and hooting—but what I remember the most was the way his breath felt on my face.

I got my arm free, but before I could do anything, Tobey jumped in and grabbed it. He got me in one of those wrestling moves from behind, looping his arms under mine and pressing down on the back of my neck so I couldn't move. I'd seen this one before, some kind of nelson—half nelson, full nelson, I couldn't remember. I knew there was a specific way to get out of it, but right then, I couldn't remember that either.

Ben stepped in toward me and grabbed me between my legs, his fingers probing through the layers of sweatpants and boy shorts and girl underwear from my back-to-school shopping trip, harder and harder, until I had no choice but to wince, biting back the scream. "Feel the difference?" he yelled. "You got nothing there!"

I kicked him in the shin as hard as I could. I was aiming higher, but it was enough to make him take his hands off me, and when he bent over, I kneed him right in the face. Then I stomped on Tobey's foot and he let go of my arms.

And, finally, I ran.

I didn't even know if I was heading in the right direction, but I kept going. I could hear them trampling through the dry leaves, breaking branches off the trees as they ran behind me. "You're dead!" one of them shouted, I couldn't tell who. All I cared about was putting distance between us.

I was fast, the fastest—didn't I have a whole wall of track-and-field ribbons at home to prove it? I knew I could beat them out of the woods. But my foot caught on a rock that was unearthed, and I tripped. I got up quick, but the second my left foot hit the ground, excruciating pain soared up my leg, through my spine, all the way to my brain. I kept moving, even though I was pretty sure I'd at least sprained my ankle. It slowed me down too much. I yelled "Help" as I tried to keep going, but my voice got swallowed up in the trees and leaves and stillness. They caught up. When I turned to face them, Ben's nose was gushing blood.

He walked up to me slowly, like an animal. I held my arms up, ready to fight, wishing I had taken tae kwon do with Coleton over the summer instead of going to astronomy camp. But I hadn't, and so I had very little idea of what the hell to do other than protect my face. Ben moved in closer and in one swift movement he punched me in the stomach so hard, it sucked all the air out of my lungs. I keeled over, but Tobey and Jake each grabbed one of my arms and pulled me upright. Ben punched me again. And again. Then he punched me in the face, once, twice, ten times, I don't even know.

And when they realized they didn't need to restrain me anymore, Tobey and Jake joined in. They didn't hold back at all. They kicked my ass like I really was a guy. When I finally went down, I hit the ground hard. And they started kicking me in the stomach, the back, legs, everywhere. When they stopped, I opened my eyes and looked up at them. Except they weren't looking at me like I was a guy. They were looking at me like I was a girl and they weren't about to let me forget it.

Ben got on top of me, one knee on either side of my hips, and he ripped the zipper of my track jacket open, then jerked my T-shirt up, peeling it over my head. It got tangled with the jacket sleeves that were still clinging to my arms. I could feel the air and the ground against my bare skin. *No.* I counted the layers he would still have to get through: spandex tank top and two sports bras to go, each so tight that even I had trouble getting them on and off every day.

"What the fuck?" Ben spat the words. "All this just to hide your tits?" I felt his hands moving up my stomach, then reaching down, to the elastic band of my sweatpants.

"Get off her!" It was Coleton's voice. They all looked up at the same time. I tipped my head back to try to see if it was really him. Everything looked blurry and fuzzy, but he was definitely there, standing a good twenty feet away from us, holding his phone up in the air. "I just called the police, you fucking scumbags!" he screamed, his voice cracking.

I let my eyes close.

When I opened them again, the boys were gone and Coleton was kneeling over me, pulling my shirt back down. "Can you sit up?"

I moaned—I hurt too much to talk. I could feel my body curling in on itself, and I wondered if I was actually going to die. Every inch of me felt like it was on fire, yet somehow I was so cold. Coleton took his track jacket off and folded it under my head, and then he stretched the end of his shirtsleeve down over his hand and wiped my mouth. When he pulled his hand back, there was blood all over it. The look on his face scared me, so I let my eyes drift shut again. I could hear sirens wailing in the distance; that was the last thing I remembered.

I heard the dog barking. My eyes flew open. I jumped up and ran to look from the kitchen window. Roxie was outside. Maia's bike was there next to the porch where she always left it.

MAIA

I HADN'T BEEN OUT TO THE BARN ALL WEEK, AND I would only have a little time before Mom and Dad would be home from work.

The file folders were still out, haphazardly stacked, just the way I left them. I took a few at a time and placed them back in the desk drawers where they belonged, only I couldn't get them to fit right.

Her camera was sitting out on top of the desk. I wondered if my mom knew that wasn't where it was supposed to be. It felt heavier than usual as I picked it up. I opened the bottom left desk drawer and set the camera inside, where it was the first time I came out here.

I closed the drawer, then turned the key that was still sitting there in the lock.

"Mallory?" I said out loud.

I held my breath, waiting.

Waiting for a sign from her, for a flicker of the lights or a cold breeze. Aren't those the kinds of things that they say happen when there's something supernatural afoot? I wanted her to tell me that I wasn't doing anything wrong, that she liked me here, among her things, remembering and trying to make sense of it all. I wanted her to tell me that I was doing exactly what she wanted.

Unlike all those times I felt her pushing me forward, nudging me along, whispering in my ear, making me do things I never would've dreamed of doing, I couldn't feel her now.

I laid my head down on my folded arms and breathed in that tart yet buttery scent of linseed oil that was soaked deep into the wood table. As I closed my eyes, the images started like a slide show, rolling over a darkened screen in my mind: each picture, but mixed in with my own memories.

Gas station, riding my bike, the open road, clouds with silver lining, tires screeching, the sound of the shutter clamping shut, then opening back up, skinning my knees, falling out of the tree, Neil, the windows rolled down, the breeze blowing through my hair, the green grass at the cemetery, Emily, the taste of exotic foods, laughing, rain, Saturn, hands touching, the damp night air, graffiti, Chris, kissing, tires flat against the pavement, camera strap around my neck, the scent of weed, the scent of incense, the scent of Chris in my hair, lying on the warm concrete, the lines of my palm, hands light on my bare skin, my breath catching, strawberry ice cream dripping, wrought iron gates, strawberry lip balm, Chris—

One after another, faster and faster, until I was spinning, my head dizzy.

It was like a dream, but I could still feel my body planted in the chair, solid and heavy, grounded and drained. My arms were sticky against the wood. My forehead sweaty against my arm. Part of me was still here.

I heard my name being called, over and over, but I couldn't answer, couldn't move.

"Maia?"

All at once, the images stopped.

"Maia," the voice said again.

Not Mallory.

The table was hard and cold beneath me. I opened my eyes, raised my head off my folded arms.

"I was knocking," he told me, standing in the open doorway. "Were you asleep?"

I sat up, beginning too slowly to understand what was happening.

Chris.

"You okay?" he asked, taking a step over the threshold of the doorway.

He can't be in here.

I'm barely allowed in here.

My heart revved up to hummingbird-wing pace in a matter of seconds.

I was on my feet. I tried to regulate my heartbeat, my pulse. But I couldn't. I could feel it pounding forward with my footsteps as I walked toward him.

"Oh my god," he whispered, looking around. "This is completely badass."

He wandered along the rows of old built-in shelves that

lined the side wall, running his fingers over the glass jars that crowded each level. Each one full of a variety of random objects Mallory was always collecting: acorns, pinecones, dried flowers, stones, old burned-out lightbulbs, rusty bent nails, broken glass, seashells.

He picked up one of the jars—smooth gray stones—and examined them, turning the jar toward the light. "Wow," he said. "Are these actually sea urchin fossils?"

"Chris," I said as I approached him, but I was having trouble figuring out what to say next. "Don't," was all I could come up with as I reached for the jar he was holding.

The air between us moved like water, like currents, like he was making waves, rocking everything—shifting all the things that I'd worked so hard to keep still.

"Sorry," he said softly, gently letting go of the jar.

I set it back on the shelf, directly within the circle of dust that had formed around it. I crossed my arms, then quickly uncrossed them.

His eyes focused somewhere above my left shoulder, and his feet followed, stepping past me. I turned around too. He was looking at the wall of pictures.

All the lies were palpable, hanging in the air between us.

I took careful steps toward him, until we were standing in front of each other, and then I wove my fingers between his. I wanted to grab his hand and lead him out the door and go far away from here. I wanted to cast some kind of spell and make him forget he'd seen any of this.

I closed my eyes. Pressure was building in my chest, an ache pounding through my entire body. I'd waited too long to tell him the truth, and now this whole thing was toppling over.

He let go of my hand.

No, wait.

I nearly said the words out loud.

Can't this hold still just a little longer? I silently prayed to whomever or whatever might be listening. But even the ghost of Mallory couldn't stop what had been put in motion. It was happening. Ending. Right now.

My body tensed. I braced myself for the rocks and rubble and dust and debris that would be coming any second. But all I felt were his hands, cool on my face. I dared myself to open my eyes. And when I did, Chris was still there, right in front of me. Everything as it was.

"Maia," he breathed. He shook his head slightly, and I didn't understand what that meant, until he continued. "You are so talented."

As I watched Chris take in all the magnificent photographs that lined the walls of the barn, exactly as Mallory had arranged them, I did understand. I understood that if I couldn't bring myself to tell him they were not mine, right here, right now, then I was most likely dooming us.

But if I did, what then?

If I told him I wasn't this creative, talented person he was falling for, who would I tell him I was instead? The only true thing I was sure of about myself anymore was the way I felt about him. That didn't seem like enough.

"Can I ask you something?" he said, stepping away from me, toward the wall with the graffiti picture in the center.

I cleared my throat, but it still cracked when I answered, "Yes."

"Can I see that picture you took of me?"

"What—what picture?" I asked.

"From that first day on the road? When I almost ran you over?" he reminded me, as if I could ever forget that moment. "I just—I thought I saw you take a picture of me. Didn't you?"

He was still scanning the wall, not finding the nonexistent photograph.

"Will you show me?" he asked again.

"I can't," I said, nearly whispering.

"Why?" he asked, smiling in this way that melted something inside me.

I opened my mouth, but before I could say anything, Roxie barked outside. I heard tires coming up the drive. Suddenly my feet came unglued from the spot they'd been stuck to, and I rushed to close the door so it was open only a crack.

It was my dad pulling in, which wasn't a problem in and of itself, except it meant that my mom wouldn't be far behind. And I couldn't let her see us in here, not after the warning she'd already issued.

Chris came up behind me and placed his hand on the small of my back.

"Why are we hiding?" he whispered, his breath warm against the side of my neck.

Dad slammed the door of his truck shut and walked to the house, Roxie following behind him.

"We're not," I told Chris, opening the barn door once again. "Let's get outta here," I said, taking his hand.

I shut the lights off and secured the door behind us.

As I led us out of the shade of the barn and into the sunlight, this whole situation felt manageable again. I pulled him along, across the field, in the direction of the gray house.

"Is your aunt home?" I asked him.

He shook his head.

Halfway between his house and mine, I pulled him close to me and kissed him. Hard. He hesitated, surprised at first, but then he kissed me back, his hands on my waist—a part of my body I'd always felt self-conscious about, but which was quickly becoming one of the places where I wanted to be touched the most. As we pulled apart, I looked at him, *really* looked at him.

He knows who he is, I thought as our eyes searched each other. He is authentic and confident and sure of himself and what he wants. For some reason, one of the things he wanted was me—I could see that. Part of me thought, if I paid close enough attention, maybe he could teach me to know myself in that way too.

Chris was doing something to me—from the outside in or the inside out, I really wasn't sure. I kissed him again, lighter this time, slower.

When I opened my eyes, I saw my mom's car pulling into our driveway.

I had been thinking that this thing with Chris was one more item that should fall under the category of things my parents shouldn't know for their own good—because I was living, I was moving on in a way they couldn't—but in that moment I didn't care if they found out about us.

CHRIS

THE RAIN SOUNDED LIKE WHITE NOISE. BUT UNDER-neath the hum I could hear the echo of individual drops seeping through the weak spots in the roof above us. Underneath that, I could hear the sound of my own pulse drumming in my ears, and Maia breathing softly as we lay side by side.

It was almost enough to drown out all the things Neil had said to me.

Just when I'd worked up the nerve to ask her one more time about all the stuff with Neil, the unspoken history, she said, "If you were home right now—in New York, I mean—what would you be doing?"

I rested my head against the smooth bare skin under her collarbone, between her shoulder and her chest—it was the perfect shape. "Probably playing video games. Or reading," I told her, but then rethought my answer. "Or something else that is actually exciting."

"Nothing wrong with that."

I loved that she really didn't believe there was anything wrong with that. I loved that I didn't have to pretend to be anything I wasn't with her. Not anymore.

"What would you be doing if you weren't with me right now?" I asked her, letting my fingers brush against the subtle curve of her waist.

"I honestly don't know," she said, her hand trailing up my arm, fingers as soft as a feather.

"I could imagine you in the barn working on your photography right now," I told her. The thought of it made me smile, but I could feel her body tensing all around me. "You didn't like me being out there today, did you?" It had been bothering me, and I wanted her to know I got it—I would respect her privacy if that's what she needed.

"It wasn't that." She paused, her hand stilled against my skin. "It was just—"

"It's okay. You don't have to explain." I lifted my head to look at her face. "I meant what I said, though—you really are talented."

She shrugged.

"And brave," I added.

"I'm *what*?" she shouted, laughing through the words. "I'm not brave at all."

"Are you kidding? Yes you are." I propped myself up next to her. This was not a point I could make lying down, not when it was one of the things that I admired most about her, one of the things that made her stick in my mind from the very beginning. "When I think of you going out and taking all those pictures—up in that tree at the party and when I saw you out in the road—you're fearless. I mean, I almost ran you over and you weren't even scared, Maia!"

She was laughing like I'd told her a joke.

"I'm scared of tons!" she exclaimed.

"Yeah, like what?" I teased, and even though this time I *was* joking, she suddenly got quiet again.

"You," she answered.

Her smiled faded, and I felt mine melting away too.

"M-me?" I stuttered.

"Not *you*, you." She sat up before continuing. "But . . . *this*."

She grabbed my hand—*this*.

I was scared of this too, but I said, "Don't be."

"I'm trying."

She kissed me, leaning into me until she was pressing me down onto my back. I moved my hands to her waist at first, because that's where she was always putting them. As I pulled her closer, I could feel the muscles in her back as she moved against me. My fingers traveled up under the band of her bra, where the clasps are, and my hand rested between her shoulder blades.

She held still for a moment, and lifted herself up, looking down at me.

"What's wrong?" I asked her.

"Nothing, but—" She gazed at the lamp on the table next to the bed. "Can I turn this off?"

I nodded.

She reached across me and pulled on the string that hung

from the lamp. The room went dark. Too dark to see at first, but as she sank back on top of me, my eyes adjusted to the moonlight shining through the stained glass door, the lines of pale lavender seeping in through the spaces in the blinds.

I felt her bending her arm to reach behind her back, her hand brushing against mine, her fingers feeling for the clasp.

She let out a short laugh, and said quietly, "Can you . . . ?"

We looked at each other as my fingers worked the little metal hooks. They released one by one, and as the two halves of the band fell to her sides, the straps sliding off her shoulders, she closed her eyes.

Even though she wasn't watching, I kept my eyes on her face as I pulled the straps down her arms. "You know we don't have to do anything else," I whispered.

"I know," she said. "I want to, though, if you do."

She let her weight come down onto me again. I wished I could feel her skin against mine, her breasts against my chest. I pulled my undershirt off over my head. I still had my binder on, and my underwear, but my midsection was bare—the cool air was a relief against my skin as it rushed between us.

She rolled off me then, covering herself with her hands until my hands took their place. I'd never touched her like this, not without a barrier of clothes between our skin. It felt like everything switched to slow motion, and I wanted to savor every moment—but then my stupid thoughts turned once again to Neil, remembering the way he had gotten so rough with Maia the night of that party, and then my thoughts inevitably turned to that day in the woods, to the memory of what it felt like to be touched out of violence, out of hate.

I made my touch as light and gentle and smooth as possible.

She was breathing, deep and slow.

It brought me back from those dark spaces in the corners of my mind.

"Chris?" she said softly, running her hands along my back.

"Yeah?"

"Will you take this off?"

"No," I answered immediately. "I—I'm sorry, I just can't."

"Okay," she said right away. "It's okay."

Her thigh slipped between my legs—I felt a tiny fire igniting inside me, in a way I never had before, not even when I was all alone in my bedroom. I didn't need to tell myself to pretend to be anything. I was just me, feeling her hand reaching down, against the thin fabric of my underwear.

The truth was, *this* scared me, but scared me in the most amazing way—that thrilling way you get scared when you know you're actually safe, like when you're on a roller coaster.

"Tell me to stop if it's not okay," she said. "Okay, Chris?"

"Okay," I told her, and I hoped she knew I meant okay, I'd tell her to stop, *and* okay, it *was* okay.

I let her touch me until I could take no more.

We were both breathing heavily now.

She took my hand in hers, moved it down her stomach—she had to have known I was too shy to do it myself, even though I wanted to—and she guided my hand until my fingertips tucked under the thin elastic band of her panties, inching into uncharted territory. As my fingers slid down and against her, she tilted her hips toward me.

I listened to her breath and her tiny moans. I listened to the way her body moved against mine. I didn't know what I was doing, not really, but it didn't matter. After, as we lay there side by side, I wanted to say something, to tell her how much this meant to me—that it meant love—but not even that word could do justice to the way I felt.

"Come here," she said, pulling me toward her, so that I had my head resting once again in that soft spot near her shoulder. "I just want to feel you close to me."

That's what she'd said the night we first kissed. I wondered if she remembered that.

I would've asked her, but I didn't want to crush the quiet as our breathing slowed to normal again. She was the one to speak first.

"I know you don't want to talk about it, and you don't have to, but . . ." She paused midsentence.

"Talk about what?" I asked.

"About what you told me the other day—what happened to you back home." Her voice sounded strained, and when I looked at her, I could see that her eyes were filling with tears. "Sorry. I just hate the thought of something like that happening to you."

"I'm fine, though," I told her again, but she shook her head and blinked hard, like she was willing the tears to go back from where they'd come, and they did.

"I just want you to know, it wasn't your fault," she said, her voice solid and firm. "I know you know this, but you didn't deserve that, okay? Nobody deserves that. Ever."

I did know that, of course, but no one had actually ever said it to me before, not in that way. "Okay," I whispered.

I set my head back down in its spot, and there was this calmness that settled in all around us. I lay there, listening to the air filling her lungs and then emptying, over and over, until I knew she had fallen asleep. As slowly and quietly as possible, I slipped out of her arms. Making sure she'd stayed asleep, I sat on the edge of the bed and quickly wrestled out of my binder. I covered myself with my arms, then bunched up the sheets around the front of me, and lowered myself to the bed on my stomach.

My back was facing her when I felt her hand, smooth and cool, against my skin.

"Chris?"

"Yeah?"

"Are you sure?"

"Yes." I swallowed hard—I was trusting her with everything. "Just don't—"

"I won't," she said. "I promise."

I nodded, and then both of her hands pressed against my back. Then her lips kissed, openmouthed, over my shoulders and between my shoulder blades, where I had let my hand rest on her earlier, then down the length of my spine, to the small of my back. It felt incredible, even more incredible than her hand kneading between my thighs, because this was something I could've never even imagined myself allowing to happen.

After she'd run her hands over my entire back, she pressed her body up against me. I felt her stomach and her breasts and her hips, and her face against my skin.

"Chris?" she whispered, her breath against the back of my neck, right behind my ear.

"Yeah?" I whispered back.

She inhaled deeply like she was breathing me in, and then she said the words that I never thought anyone would say to me: "I love you."

I didn't hesitate, because the words had been on the tip of my tongue for weeks already. "I love you too."

The whole night, I never let go of the sheet I had clutched to me, but even so, I'd never felt more alive, more free, more understood, in my entire life.

PART THREE

august

MAIA

WE WERE STANDING OUTSIDE THE DECREPIT OLD movie theater, waiting for Hayden and Gabby. Chris was holding my hand a little too tightly. Or maybe it was me. There was something in the air between us, like an itch just out of reach.

Hayden and Gabby had gotten relentless in their efforts to meet him. I chose the movies. It's a controlled environment: two hours of not being able to talk. Because talking meant the risk of someone saying something about Mallory or me or the stupid lie I had let take on a life of its own this summer.

"Are you all right?" Chris asked me. "You seem a little tense."

"No, I'm fine," I said, forcing a smile. But he was getting to know my different smiles, and he squinted hard at me like I was glass he could see right through.

"You're nervous about me meeting your friends, aren't

you?" he asked, but before I could respond, he added, "It's okay, so am I."

"I'm sorry," I told him, and I was. "I should be trying to make you less nervous, not the other way around."

"You want them to like me—I get it."

"No, I already know they'll like you." Which was the whole problem, but I couldn't say that, so instead I leaned in and kissed him on the lips quickly. I was determined to make this evening go smoothly, and as we looked into each other's eyes, I was convinced for a moment that it would.

"Hey, I was waiting to tell you this until I knew for sure," he began, and took a deep breath before continuing. "But I'm trying to get my parents to let me stay."

"Stay?" I felt this massive thump in my chest. "Stay *here*?"

"Yeah, stay here in Carson and live with my aunt and go to school with you this year."

All the blood in my body ran cold.

"Think about it; it's the perfect solution," he continued. "My parents are too scared to let me start school back home. This way, there's not all the baggage from everything that happened. But more importantly"—he held on to both of my hands now—"we get to be together."

I once saw this video of a snowboarder who got trapped inside an avalanche. The snow began cracking all around him like glass, and then the mountainside just collapsed, swallowing him up in its hundred-mile-an-hour current. It's not always the massive explosions or earthquakes that cause avalanches; they can be triggered by something small, like the movements of animals, or new rain or snow.

I could feel the ground cracking all around me.

It was one thing for Chris to be here and not know anyone else or talk to anyone else and simply exist with me in this dreamworld we had created—I was worried enough about being able to successfully shepherd two hours of silence in a darkened theater with my friends—but if he was really going to stay, he'd find out within one day every last thing I was keeping from him.

"I mean, you want me to, right?" he asked after I still hadn't responded.

"Yeah, of—of course," I stuttered. "Yes, you just—I—I'm surprised. I didn't know you were even thinking about that."

His smile returned as he brought my hand up to his mouth and kissed it.

"You think your parents will really let you?" Even I could hear my voice shaking as I spoke the words. But before he could answer me, a pair of footsteps approached on the sidewalk, accompanied by Gabby's booming voice:

"Hello, lovebirds!"

I turned to look, and so did Chris. He was already waving at my friends, and I felt myself getting swept away in the undertow, being carried farther and farther from them.

Gabby stood in front of Chris and said, "At last, we get to meet the person responsible for stealing our girl away from us all summer."

Chris looked to me—I was supposed to make the official introductions, but I couldn't. I was being buried.

"Gabby, right?" Chris said, pointing at her, and then pivoting toward Hayden. "And Hayden?"

"Nice to finally meet you, Chris." Hayden glanced over at me, and I managed to give her a smile. "So," she said. "What do we wanna do?"

"Movies?" I uttered, pointing above us to the giant marquee theater sign half lit up in neon.

"Oh yeah," Gabby chimed in. "Hayden and I decided that sounded really boring, so—"

"You can't just decide that," I argued. "We made a plan."

Hayden raised her voice above ours. "Then let's vote. Those in favor of the movies . . ." We each looked at one another, and I was the only one raising my hand, until I locked eyes with Chris, and then he put his hand up too. "All in favor of doing something, you know, *fun*, where we actually get to hang out?"

Hayden's and Gabby's hands shot up, and as I crossed my arms to signal our stalemate, Chris slowly raised his, extending just one finger at first, shrugging, as he spread all five in a full hand raise. "Sorry," he said, his face cringing.

But before I could respond, they all started laughing.

I took a deep breath—I would have to deal with one disaster at a time. In comparison to the time bomb Chris had just dropped into my lap, I guessed I could handle one unscripted evening. I exhaled, looked at Chris, and said in my best make-believe-yet-actually-very-real defeated voice, "Traitor."

To which he wrapped his arm around my shoulder and leaned in to kiss my forehead, prompting Hayden and Gabby to respond in a chorus of "Awww!"

"Let's get something to eat," Hayden said, and they walked away from the theater. We were headed toward DairyLand, but to get there we had to pass some abandoned storefronts, and then Miss Teresa's Antiques, which was basically a giant indoor yard sale. I was traversing the same stale geography I'd been surrounded by for my entire life, except this time it was buzzing with the unknown, here with Chris by my side, and my friends just ahead.

"Oh wow, look at this!" Chris stopped walking, and was peering into the overcrowded storefront window. It was an old telescope mounted on a wooden tripod, the original box sitting on the floor next to it.

Hayden and Gabby backtracked to join us, and Gabby said, "Let's go in."

A buzzer chimed as we walked through the door into a world of forgotten items. The sharp scent of mothballs and mildew and old books immediately brought back a hundred different memories of all the times I used to come here with Mallory in search of the perfect photo prop or vintage combat boots or antique costume jewelry. My head began to ache, that old familiar dizziness settling in the pit of my stomach.

Chris went straight to the telescope, and while he was inspecting it from all angles, he murmured to himself, "Wow" and "sweet." Hayden whispered in my ear, "Adorable." Gabby gave a not-so-subtle thumbs-up. I batted at them with my hand and silently mouthed at them to *Stop*. They dispersed to go rummage through the clothing.

I wandered to the jewelry display by myself. I was looking through the glass case at the antique engagement rings and expensive one-of-a-kind brooches and pins when the shopkeeper approached—Miss Teresa herself. "Would you like to see anything?" she asked.

"No, I'm just—" I started, but then a necklace caught my eye. A locket engraved with a crescent moon encircling a star with a missing stone in its center. "Actually, can I see that?"

She pulled it out and laid it on top of a swatch of velvety fabric. As I ran my fingers along the tarnished gold chain and the grooves of the locket, I could feel my mouth curving into a smile.

"That would look so pretty on you," Chris said as he came up behind me, placing his hand on my back.

I turned over the tiny paper price tag that was tied around the chain by a loop of string—sixty dollars. "I can't spend that much on a necklace."

"But if you really like it . . . ?" he asked, letting the question dangle there.

"It's vintage. Worth every penny," Teresa added, pressing down on the tiny lever, popping open the locket to reveal a mark engraved on the inside.

"I like it 'cause it reminds me of you," I said to Chris. "I don't need it, though. I already have you. Thanks anyway," I told Teresa.

"Maia! Chris?" Gabby called across the store. She and Hayden were dressed up in clothing from different time periods. Hayden waved us over, donning long white gloves up to the elbows. Gabby was in a fur shawl and had a sequin clutch.

"We're being beckoned," he said, thoroughly enjoying himself.

I groaned as I trudged toward them.

"You can relax," he said close to my ear, and his voice was so soothing, I almost believed him. "It's going well. I really like them."

Hayden and Gabby were standing there with this old jacket they found, the kind with elbow patches. "Here, Chris," Gabby said, holding the jacket open. "Try this."

"Guys, come on," I said.

"What?" Hayden asked as Chris threaded his arms through the sleeves. "He looks great!" Then she placed a fedora on his head, setting it on a tilt.

"Really?" Chris looked at me as he straightened the jacket out.

"You do," I told him. "You look great." He did, and for a second I wasn't worried about the giant mess I had created; I was more worried about keeping my hands off him in the store. His smile was contagious. I watched it spread from Hayden to Gabby, and then finally to me.

He took the hat off and placed it on my head, telling me, "And you look amazing."

I wasn't sure how I could be so immensely happy while also being so profoundly sad—I was drowning. "I'll be right back," I said, pushing the hat into Chris's hands.

"Where's she going?" I heard Hayden ask as I rushed to the bathroom.

I had to run, had to get away. I locked the door behind me and turned the faucet on full force. I tried to slow my breathing, but I couldn't. I was gasping for air—I couldn't seem to get enough in or out. I was dizzy. I sat down on the floor because I was afraid I'd fall. My hands were shaking.

Someone knocked.

"Just a minute," I yelled.

It was Hayden's voice on the other side of the door. "Are you okay?"

I scrambled to my feet and shut the water off. I looked in the mirror for only a moment before I swung the door open—I had a twinge of that old sickening sense of not recognizing myself again.

"You okay?" she repeated as I came out.

"Yeah," I told her as we walked back to where Chris and Gabby were waiting. "Just not feeling great."

Everyone had removed their accoutrements. And Chris was holding one of those really old box cameras, saying, all excited, "Maia, check this out. And look, there are these old lenses over here." Just when I thought I was back on solid ground, it began rumbling and vibrating under my feet again.

"*Chris.*" I hadn't realized how sharp my voice was until the word was out of my mouth and everyone was staring at me. "Um, Chris," I said again, softer, taking the camera from his hands and setting it down on a stray dining chair. "Look, we have to go, okay?" I whispered to him. "Y'all, we have to go, all right?"

"Wait, what? Why?" everyone was saying all at the same time. But I couldn't answer any of those questions; I couldn't deal. I started walking toward the door instead.

CHRIS

I KEPT CALLING HER NAME, BUT MAIA WOULDN'T TURN around. "Hey," I said, finally catching up with her out on the sidewalk in front of the theater. "What's going on?"

"Nothing," she said, but everything about her was shouting the opposite: her crossed arms, her wide eyes, the way she was standing so rigid, looking everywhere except *at* me. "I just—I didn't want to do this tonight, and—and I don't like getting steamrolled by everyone, and I don't feel good, okay?"

I tried to keep calm, but I'd never seen her rattled like this and it was scaring me. "Should we at least tell your friends—"

"No!" she interrupted. "I'm sorry. Please just take me home. Please?"

"Okay, we can do that." I started walking along next to her, toward where we'd parked, but when I tried to reach for her hand, she pulled away. I glanced behind us; her friends were on the sidewalk in front of the store, watching us leave.

I didn't try talking to her again on the way home. She just stared out the window, facing away from me the whole time, biting her fingernails.

I parked the car in her driveway and turned off the headlights, waiting for her to say something first. She leaned her head back against the seat, finally looking at me as she reached for my hand, and said, "I'm sorry." But her voice sounded ragged and strained, like she had been screaming all night.

"What's wrong? What can I do?" I asked.

She shook her head. "Nothing."

"Is it me?" I debated the questions I really wanted to ask for a moment, and decided to only say half of it. "Maia, you're not . . . embarrassed of me, are you?" The other half, the half that was harder to say, was, *You're not trying to hide me, right? You're not afraid of your friends finding out I'm trans, are you?*

"No, it's not you." She unbuckled her seat belt and slid across the bench seat, and leaned close to me with her face against my neck. "I'm just having a bad day," she whispered.

I nodded. I got it.

I had bad days—days when the past is biting at your heels, about to catch up with you—and I figured she must have them too, but I'd never heard her talk like that before. I put my arm around her and said, "It'll be okay."

She held on to me even tighter, and said, "Chris, I really love you."

"I really love you too," I replied.

• • •

I couldn't sleep at all. Maia's sadness had crawled inside me, and I couldn't shake the feeling that something was very wrong—that not only was she not okay, but somehow *we* weren't okay either.

I texted her in the morning to see how she was feeling, to ask if she wanted a ride to work, but I never heard back, and an hour later I saw her leaving her house on her bike, wearing her Bargain Mart shirt.

I went for my run. I showered and got dressed, as usual. I thought I'd go for a drive, clear my mind. But when I drove past the antiques store, I stopped.

The bell dinged as I entered, just like it had last night. The woman who had been working then was there again. "Morning," she called over to me from across the store, where she was organizing a row of knickknacks on top of an old desk.

"Good morning," I answered.

She gave me a knowing look and walked over to the jewelry counter. I followed behind, and before I could even ask her any questions, she pulled out the necklace Maia had been looking at. "This is what you came for, isn't it?"

"How'd you know?" I asked.

She shrugged and said, "Just a hunch. Tell you what, I'll give it to you for fifty. How does that sound?"

I would've gladly paid sixty—that was how much the vintage telescope was going for—and I would've paid a lot more than that if it meant making Maia smile today.

I nodded, and she took a tiny, square, plastic ziplock bag out from under the counter, carefully dangled the necklace over the opening, and let it collapse neatly inside. She sealed the enclosure and handed it to me. I couldn't wait to give it to Maia—I kept imagining her reaction, so I decided to surprise her at work.

I walked up and down the aisles, before I texted again.

Did you make it into work okay?

She wrote back immediately: Yes, I did. Thank you, sorry forgot to text back earlier.

I wandered through the clearance aisles, and the clothing departments. It was a big store, but not so big that I shouldn't be able to find her. When I walked by the fitting room for maybe the twentieth time, the older woman working there asked if I needed help finding anything.

"Actually, yes," I answered. "I'm looking for Maia. Is she around?"

The woman pursed her lips and turned her head, saying, "No, that poor girl. She's out sick today."

I left the store and walked around to the side of the building. Her bike wasn't in the rack. I pulled out my phone and looked at her text again—yes, she had clearly said she was at work.

She'd lied to me.

Back in the station wagon, my mind was flooding over with the events of the last day—nothing was making sense. I wanted to go talk to Hayden and Gabby, but I didn't know how to reach either of them. As I drove past the gas station, I slowed down.

Neil's truck was parked at one of the pumps.

I pulled up behind him just as he was coming out of the building. He stopped when he saw me standing there waiting for him, and approached me cautiously, looking around.

"Chris?" he said. "What's up?"

I skipped the pleasantries and got right to the point. "What were you talking about the other day?" I asked, but he just cocked his head to the side like he was confused. "The thing you said about Maia, what did you mean?"

He walked over to the side of his truck, removed the gas pump from the tank, and returned it to its cradle. Holding his hands on his hips, he leaned against the side of the truck bed and looked at me closer. "What do you want to know?"

I wanted to know whatever it was he thought I should know about her, whatever it was that made him tell me I needed to watch my back. "I guess for starters," I said, "why did you go off on her like that at the party?"

He sighed and shifted his gaze away from me. "Look, we've all been messed up about what happened to Mallory. And I know that Maia is her sister and all, but she was *my* best friend. To have to see Maia going around doing all this crazy, cruel shit like she's the only one who loved her—it's not right."

"What crazy, cruel shit?" I asked.

"You know she burned all of Mallory's work?" he said, and he was starting to talk in this labored, halted way—not out of anger, but sadness, almost like he could start crying at any moment if he let himself.

"No," I said. "I don't know what you're talking about."

"She burned all her pictures!" he shouted. "And if that wasn't bad enough, then she's gonna walk around with her camera—it's just not right," he repeated.

"Wait, I'm confused. Were they pictures of her sister?" I was really trying to work with what he was giving me, but the pieces weren't fitting together. "And why shouldn't she be able to walk around with her own camera? What am I missing?"

He stood up straight then, arms dropping to his sides as he turned to face me. He shook his head slowly and held one hand up as if he was trying to ward off the words I had spoken. "Hold on. Are you saying Maia told you that camera is *hers*?"

I stared back at him, and I watched his mouth drop open as I nodded in response.

"Jesus," he mumbled, rubbing his hands across his face. "We should sit."

MAIA

I WAS LYING IN THE SUN AT BOWMAN'S. I STOPPED before work this morning, but I couldn't force myself to face the rest of the day. I was falling in and out of sleep when Chris texted me yet again: Where are you?

I started tapping out a lie—at work—when his next message came.

I know you're not at work. Come meet me. I'll be waiting in the barn.

I clambered to my feet, heart instantly pounding out of rhythm.

As I raced my bike home, every part of my body, inside and out, was vibrating. I hopped off my bike while it was still moving, and it crashed into the side of the barn. I barged through the door to see him standing in front of the wall, looking at the photos.

"Please," I said, trying once more to slow the unending

advance of the catastrophe I had created, but could not stop. "Just let me—" *explain*.

"Maia, show me the picture you took of me that day," he demanded, finally turning to look at me.

"Chris, I—"

"Where is it?" he interrupted. "Show me that picture, Maia."

"I can't."

"Why?"

He looked at me in a way he never had before. It wasn't that his expression was blank, but more like his face was stripped of all emotion. Beyond that was something more sullen, bittersweet: He was hurting. No, I was hurting him. It was only a matter of time.

"You already know why," I said, and I could feel my eyes burning, filling with tears, because this was it. It was over. It had finally caught up with me. "Don't you?"

"I know, but I—I don't . . . *understand*," he said, his speech choppy and broken.

"I wish I could explain it to you; it's just so hard—"

"Well, try!" he said, raising his voice.

"It made me feel closer to her," I said, trying. Really trying. "Like she wasn't really gone."

"More," he said, shaking his head. "I need more."

"I liked that you thought I was special, okay?" I knew I had no right to be yelling at *him* right now, but if I didn't yell, I was convinced I would melt onto the floor in a puddle of my own self-loathing and never be able to put myself back together. "I liked that you thought I had these amazing talents and dreams and—"

"So you lied?" he yelled back. "You lied to me this whole time, Maia!"

"But I—"

"But nothing!" he interrupted. "How am I ever supposed to trust you again?" He came closer, watching me, waiting for an actual answer to his question. The thing was, I didn't have one.

"I don't know," I finally said, taking a step closer to him.

"Great," he scoffed, looking around at all of Mallory's photos.

I reached out to try to touch him, but he twisted away from me.

I've heard that the sheer amount of snow that lands on a person trapped in an avalanche can create confusion— you don't always know which way is up. Sometimes the victims are found suffocated and dead, having dug the wrong way.

It must've been the disorientation that made me say, "Fine. You can hate me and never trust me again if you want, but don't pretend you don't have secrets too."

"What are you talking about?" he snapped. "I've been totally honest with you—more honest with you than I've ever been with anyone in my entire life."

"I knew, Chris. I knew almost from the very beginning."

"Knew what?"

"*Knew*. About you. I spied on you. Just like a perfect little photographer would. Just like Mallory would have done. I knew. I saw you."

He shook his head. "I don't—I don't believe you." He

was trying to hide it, but I could see this sheen cast over his eyes, water filling the corners.

"I'm just saying, how do you think *I* felt when day after day, as I'm falling for you—*hard*, I might add—I knew you weren't telling me the truth?"

"This cannot be real," he whispered, looking at me in a way that sent chills up my spine, like we were strangers, like there was nothing between us. That was when I remembered that I'd forgotten to tell him the most important part: how I trusted him anyway.

"So all those days when we were running around together searching for the perfect shots, all those conversations, everything we shared—that was, what, a lie?" His voice was small now, quiet, and I knew that was worse than the yelling.

"No. No, that wasn't a—"

"And that night when I told you. Everything you said. How you were so understanding. And you said that—you said that nothing changed—were you just laughing at me on the inside?"

"*No*, I wasn't!"

"That night meant everything to me," he said, his voice trembling, "and it was all a lie."

"How I feel is not a lie, Chris," I said, my voice thickening with my own tears about to spill over. "I'm sorry, okay? Wait, just let me try to explain. I shouldn't have said it like that."

Too late, Mallory whispered in my ear.

CHRIS

LOGICALLY, I KNEW THAT THE FEELING IN MY BODY was only adrenaline—heart racing, palms sweating, the electric buzz coursing through every vein and every cell—but another part of my brain honestly wondered if I might spontaneously combust.

I needed to get away from her, or I was afraid that fire inside might actually kill me.

"Leave me alone," I yelled as I busted out the door and into the open air.

But she wouldn't. She was following me, saying, "I'm sorry," trying to get in front of me, blocking my path.

"Get out of my way!" My voice sounded hard, mean. She opened her mouth again but never even got a word out before I cut her off. "Just. Get. Away."

"No, we need to talk. I'm not explaining anything right. I just—it all came out wrong. I'm sorry," she said again.

She didn't get it—I was done talking, done trying to understand. Her words, the supposed truths she had just told me, were all jumbled in my head, repeating themselves over her simple apologies. Underneath that, I still had all of Neil's words running on a loop too. My head felt too full. I just had to make it back to Isobel's, then I could think again.

"I'm sorry?" I tossed the words over my shoulder at her. "That's so weak, even for you."

"I know. I know it is. But you have to believe me, I do love—"

"Don't." She didn't get that word anymore. It wasn't hers to have. Not with me.

"I love you," she finished, rushing to keep up with me.

"Stop saying that!"

"That's the one truth I had this entire time—I love you."

I didn't know much truth, but I knew one of my own had arrived in this very minute. I reached Isobel's porch; at last, I had something solid to hold on to. "You love me? That's great. But guess what, I don't love you!"

"Yes you do," she said quietly, standing on the ground looking up at me, which for some reason only made me want to yell. I opened my mouth again, but I had no words left to say. They were all lodged in my throat, hard and stinging and threatening to suffocate me. So I did the only thing left to do. I turned around to go inside. She kept calling my name and trying to grab on to me, but as she tried to follow me in, I pushed her away.

I slammed the door closed and locked it, with her on the other side, saying words I could barely hear over all the noise in my mind. My head pounded, my eyes stung, my ears ached, the bones in my legs felt like they'd shattered, but I ran up the stairs anyway, and finally I sank onto the floor, those stupid burning pinpricks stabbing behind my eyes.

No, I was not going to cry. No fucking way. But I brushed my face and found it already wet; without meaning to, I had shown her tears. I hated her for that, too.

I stood up, and without thinking or planning or weighing out the pros and cons, I started packing a bag. I opened the closet and grabbed handfuls of my clothes, tearing them off the hangers and shoving them into a duffel bag. I had my laptop, my journal, my phone. I looked at my telescope. It would have to stay for now; it would take too long to disassemble. And I needed to move.

I ran down the hall and into the bathroom and scooped all of my things into the bag, not bothering to make sure the cap was closed on my hair gel or that the lid on my toothpaste was snapped shut.

Then I barreled down the stairs. *I should write a note for Isobel, at least.* But there was no time. I had to leave, and it had to be right then. She'd understand.

I burst through the screen door, and there was Maia, waiting for me on the porch, crying, trying to stop me. I brushed past her like I was a ghost. Or maybe she was the ghost. I threw my bags into the back of the station wagon and slammed the doors, Maia behind me the whole time, telling me to stop.

I started the car, put it in reverse, pressed on the gas too hard, and flew backward. I shifted into drive and turned the wheel hard, the tires kicking up gravel. When I looked up, Maia was standing in front of me in the middle of the driveway. I laid on the horn, and she jumped. I tapped the accelerator, and the car inched forward. She stood there and looked at me through the windshield, just like she had the first time I ever saw her.

And because I needed this moment to end, because I needed all of the moments with her to end, right now, forever, I slammed the horn again. It echoed through my skull and down my spine, sending a chill through my whole body. I'm sure somewhere out in the cosmos the sound waves of this moment will be rippling away for eternity.

She stepped out of the way.

I put ten hours, seven hundred miles, and four states between me and Maia, but I was sure my heart never stopped racing the whole time.

Both of my parents' cars were in the driveway. The outside light was on, which meant they were expecting me. I parked the station wagon on the street. I swung my backpack over one shoulder and decided to leave the rest of my stuff in the car. As I walked up to the house, I shoved my keys in my pocket, only to find that I still had that damn necklace sitting there in the tiny plastic bag.

The light from the TV was flashing through the darkened living room when I walked in, but otherwise, the room was empty. I locked the front door behind me, and was prepared to run directly for the stairs, when I heard my dad.

"Chris?" I turned to look. He was entering the living room from the kitchen. "Isobel called us."

"Oh." It was all I had.

"Are you—" he began to ask, but I cut him off immediately because I was not okay or all right or any other fill-in-the-blank word he might have used.

"I'm exhausted." I heard my own voice, all frayed and raspy, and I knew it was the truth. He started walking toward me; I needed a shield, an out, so I said quickly, "I'm just gonna go to bed, if that's okay?"

"Okay," he said, standing still halfway through the living room. As I started up the stairs, he added, "Chris, we're happy you're home."

When I got to my bedroom, the light was on. I walked in to find my mom bent over my bed, tucking in the sheets. I stood there and watched her being so careful, smoothing out the wrinkles, pulling the comforter tight.

She gasped when she turned around and saw me standing there. "You scared me," she said, bringing her hand to her chest. "I was just putting clean sheets on your bed."

I nodded, mumbled "Thanks" as I walked past her, and dropped my bag next to my desk.

"Well, I'll leave you alone." But she was still standing there looking at me. "Unless . . ." She hesitated, then took a step closer. "Unless you want to talk?"

"I don't."

"Okay," she whispered, reaching out to touch my shoulder as she left my room.

I closed the door behind her, fished the necklace out of my pocket, opened my desk drawer, and tossed it in—I needed that thing, and all that it meant, out of sight.

MAIA

THE THING ABOUT AN AVALANCHE IS THAT THERE'S no outrunning it once it starts; there is only surrender. So I sat down on the steps and waited.

I waited until it got dark. Until his aunt came home. She parked the car, pulled two plastic Bargain Mart bags out of her backseat, and as she approached me, she turned her head and frowned.

She sat down next to me, and I was so thankful she didn't say anything.

We stayed like that for what seemed like forever. Both of us waiting.

"He's not coming back," I finally said, "is he?"

"I don't know."

"Did you talk to him?"

"No," she said, holding up her phone. "Voice mail."

Then she put her hand on my shoulder, and said, in such a gentle way, "Are you gonna be okay?"

I shook my head. And then I stood up and said, "If you talk to him, tell him . . ."

"Yeah?"

"Never mind."

Mom was standing in the kitchen pouring herself a drink. Tonight it was brown and in a short glass with ice cubes. I slipped my sneakers off in the hallway and mumbled "Good night" as I passed her.

"You're in for the night?" she asked, surprised.

I backed up a step so that I was in the doorway of the kitchen, facing her. "I'm in for the night."

She looked at me—she had to have noticed my puffy red eyes—and I thought when she opened her mouth, she would ask what was wrong, but she only said, "Okay," and then flipped the switch to the light above the sink.

Roxie fought me when I scooped her up off the living room couch into my arms and carried her up the stairs with me. She never liked being picked up, even when she was young, but especially now, with her aches and pains and arthritis, she couldn't stand being held. She wriggled and tossed her head and clawed at my arms, but I didn't put her down until we were in my bedroom with the door closed.

"Sorry," I told her as I set her on the bed. I lay down too, and curled up into a ball around her. She was prepared to give me the cold shoulder until I pressed my face into my pillow and started crying. Roxie's warm tongue licked the arm that was covering my face, so I reached out and hugged her tight to my body. She gave in and let me hold her there, never moving the whole night.

I woke up at six thirty in the morning and reached for my phone.

Nothing. At least, nothing from Chris. I had messages from both Hayden and Gabby, though. "Shit," I hissed.

The latest were simple and to the point:

Gabby: ???

Hayden: Not cool, M :(

I swiped the messages away—I'd deal with that mess later.

I called him for the hundredth time. His voice mail was full now from all the messages I'd left. I lay back down, and though I tried to stave it off, uncertain if my body could handle any more tears, I started sobbing all over again.

CHRIS

THE RATTLING OF MY PHONE VIBRATING ON MY nightstand jolted me awake. I reached for it, and for a second I forgot everything that had happened, and almost answered. Then the memories came crashing over me as my bedroom came more sharply into focus.

I turned my phone off altogether and lay back down. But I was already wide awake. The sun wasn't up yet, but there was that early-morning glow coming through the windows. I thought about going for a run—clear my head before I had to deal with my parents and their inevitable list of questions.

My brain told my body to get up, dust itself off, carry on, keep going, *now*. But the only movement my body would agree to was rolling over and falling back to sleep.

When I woke the next time, the light was coming in, bright and strong.

I heard Mom's voice, muffled from behind her bedroom door down the hall.

"I know—" she said sharply, then, "Don't you dare tell me what's good for Chris!"

I was sure it was my parents arguing. I untangled myself from the sheets and jumped out of bed, swung my door open, and marched down the hall. I was prepared to barge in and tell them to just stop it once and for all, but there was quiet, a pause, followed by, "No, you're wrong. Yes, I knew this would hap—" followed by another silence.

It wasn't my dad she was yelling at. She was on the phone.

"All I know is, I sent my kid to you for two months and he comes back to me heartbroken and—"

I didn't even hear the rest of her sentence because she'd said "he."

"Yeah, fine, Isobel. Bye."

I heard her footsteps approaching the door, so I turned around to try to make it back to my room before she saw me, but it was too late.

"Chris, wait," she called after me.

I turned around slowly. "Yeah?"

"How are you feeling today?" she asked, as if it was just some kind of stomach bug that had me down.

"Fine," I lied, shrugging for effect. She was wearing jeans and a T-shirt, her hair pulled back in a ponytail, which made her look younger than she had in a long time. "You're not working today?" I asked.

"No, I took the day off. Well, I'm showing a house at

six—third time, so fingers crossed—but I thought maybe we could spend some time together today?"

I opened my mouth. I was going to tell her I didn't feel like it. Tell her that referring to me as "he" once didn't make up for this whole summer of her treating me like a pariah. Remind her that she never did apologize about our fight. But she kept talking.

"I thought we'd head over to the waterfront, go to that place you like with the really good fish and chips?" She stood there in front of me, smiling.

I crossed my arms. I could see what she was doing. She wanted to act like it was old times between us. Every once in a while, when I'd be going through a particularly rough patch, she'd let me stay home from school and we'd spend the day together, at the waterfront, or she'd take me to the latest superhero movie even though she hated them. Or this one time when we went to Niagara Falls and pretended we were tourists—bought the T-shirts and the sunglasses and hats and a souvenir snow globe for Dad, and even took the *Maid of the Mist* boat tour—despite the fact that we'd both been to Niagara Falls a million times before, all to get me out of my head for a day.

Well, I couldn't pretend. Not this time. Not anymore.

"Mom," I said, looking her in the eye for what felt like the first time ever. "You do know that you and I, we're not okay. Right?"

She looked down and let her shoulder lean against the wall. "I know, Chris. And I know it's my fault too. I'm just trying to—"

"What, make me feel better?" I interrupted. "You're a little late."

I turned away from her and walked back down the hall to my bedroom. Closed the door. Put on my headphones and fell into bed.

MAIA

Maia's Greatest Hits of the Year (So Far)

1. Alienated friends. *Check.*
2. Got drunk and made a fool of myself at a party. *Check.*
3. Got not-drunk and made an even bigger fool of myself at yet another party. *Check.*
4. Got my tires slashed out of revenge. *Check.*
5. Fell in love. *Check.*
6. Felt like an actual person for a little while. *Check.*
7. Lied my ass off about everything in my life and subsequently destroyed the best thing to ever happen to me. *Check.* And *check.*
8. Perfected the art of staying in bed for fourteen hours at a time. *Check.*
9. Failed at life. *Check.*

I was staring at my ceiling, trying to think of one last item to add to the list to round it out to an even ten, when I heard Roxie barking downstairs.

My parents were at work, because it was no doubt afternoon already, so I had no choice but to get out of bed. Roxie barked again, and I yelled to her, "I'm coming." As I started down the stairs I realized how weak my body felt, how achy my muscles and joints were from lying around in bed for the last three days. I shuffled into the kitchen. There was a puddle of pee in the middle of the floor, but no sign of Roxie.

I'd made her wait too long.

She was scratching at the door. I tried to reach down and pet her—a peace offering for leaving her alone down here all morning, but she was not interested; she just wanted out.

I opened the door, and she hobbled down the steps faster than I'd seen her move in a while. I went back into the kitchen to clean up the pee with a bunch of paper towels and the spray cleaner we keep under the kitchen sink. I washed my hands and watched out the window as Roxie disappeared around the side of the house, on the scent of something.

I walked out onto the porch and stood there, letting the afternoon breeze move through my hair and my slept-in clothes. My eyes set, as they inevitably do, on the gray house across the field. The house that used to just be the view from my window, but was now the place where I felt like my entire life began and only a short while later ended. The place I could never go back to. I walked down the steps, the wood warm against my bare feet, something pulling me out onto the grass and into the sunlight.

It was hard to tell how long I'd been standing here. I looked around for Roxie, but I didn't see her. I whistled and clapped my hands and called her name, but she didn't come. My legs jumped into action. I rounded the corner where I'd last seen her. No Roxie. I circled the entire perimeter of the house. Nothing.

"Roxie!" I called again. Just as I was preparing to panic, worried that she got confused and wandered off into the woods or out toward the street, I saw something flicker out of the corner of my eye by the barn.

She was there, lying in the sun, right in front of the barn door. She lifted her head to look at me as I walked over to her, probably wary of me trying to pick her up again. I sat down in the grass beside her, and she fell asleep as I pet her, snoring softly.

Just then I watched as a car turned off the road and into our driveway. It was Hayden in her mom's little sedan, and as she pulled up closer to the house, I could see that Gabby was there in the passenger seat.

With all my sleeping and crying these past three days, I hadn't found the time to apologize to them or explain my reasons for bailing on our outing the other night. Roxie grumbled as I stood to go meet them—she lifted her head to see who was there but then laid it back down immediately when she saw it was only Hayden and Gabby.

"If you're coming to yell at me—I know I deserve it, but— can you please not? Not right now anyway," I pleaded as they got out of the car.

They didn't say anything as they advanced toward me, and

I couldn't make sense of their solemn expressions.

"Please?" I added.

When they reached me, they both opened their arms and smothered me inside a giant group hug. We rocked back and forth as I lost and regained my balance. When they finally released their hold on me, Hayden said, "We heard Chris left."

"Yeah," Gabby said. "We're sorry."

There was something inside me that pulsed at the sound of his name, like another heartbeat. "How'd you hear that?" I asked, but I knew—if the population of Carson fluctuates by even one person, it becomes common knowledge.

"Never mind that," Hayden said. "We're here on a mission."

I let out a laugh, a dusty choked sound, from not having so much as cracked a smile in days. "A mission?"

Gabby looped her arm with mine and began steering me toward the house. "More like an intervention."

"We're getting you into the shower and out of those clothes, which it looks like you haven't changed in weeks, and then we have a surprise for you," Hayden explained as they led me up the stairs to my bedroom.

"Thanks, but I really just want to crawl back into bed."

"We know." Gabby was opening and closing my dresser drawers as she spoke, looking for something in particular. "That's why we've gotta get you out of here." She held up my bathing suit from last summer and stuffed it into my hands. "Hurry up and shower—make sure you brush your hair, please—and then put this on. Meet us in the car in ten minutes. Got it?"

Clearly, there would be only one acceptable answer.

"All right," I finally relented, and was then ushered into the bathroom.

Hayden was speeding, going seventy in a fifty-five. I had been spending so much time in the car with Chris, who always obeyed the posted speed limits, that I forgot how fast people drive around here. The rapid movement sent tingles to my fingers and toes, like they had been asleep. I knew exactly where we were going, and they knew I knew, but we all acted like it was a surprise.

Every summer we had three major excursions. Each of us chose one, and every year they were the same.

Hayden chose the beach.

Gabby chose the amusement park.

And I chose river tubing—I always thought it was the perfect way to end each summer: just two miles of nothing to do but be taken slowly downriver by a gentle current, no choices to make, no mistakes, no worries.

I suspected they had already gone to the amusement park without me while I'd been occupied with Chris, but that was okay—I was never a fan of roller coasters and spinning in circles.

Gabby twisted around in the passenger seat and reached across the car to slather streaks of thick, pasty sunblock across my cheeks and down my nose, and then she pulled out my big floppy straw sun hat, which she must've found somewhere in my room, and planted it on my head.

I cleared my throat—an explanation was in order. "Y'all?

I know I've been acting crazy. I know I haven't been a great friend lately—" I began.

Hayden interrupted me. "We don't have to do this, all right?"

Gabby added, "We understand."

"No, I want to say this. I think I've been more messed up than I wanted to admit since Mallory"—I paused to give her name a moment to breathe—"and then the whole thing with Chris, it was—*he* was what I needed. I didn't mean to disappear on you. And I didn't mean to fuck everything up with him either. I just—I don't know. . . ."

"We know," Gabby reiterated. "It's forgotten, okay?"

I nodded, because if I opened my mouth again, I was afraid I would start crying, and I was afraid that if I started crying, I wouldn't be able to stop. So I just nodded and looked out the window, letting the wind blow against my face.

Forty more minutes of loud music and no talking, and we were there.

The River Adventures sign pointed us down a long dirt road that fed into dense forest surrounding the river. We pulled up to the cabin, and a boy who could not have been much older than us rented us three tubes and took us to the drop-in point in an old beat-up truck with the faded company logo on the doors, mumbling that he'd pick us up at the exit point in a few hours.

He sent us downriver, and Hayden began distributing refreshments. She came prepared with an inflatable floating cooler full of snacks and tea and bottled water—she could always be counted on for things like that.

She poured us each a plastic cup of tea from a gallon container I'm sure she had made fresh especially for this outing. After she distributed them, she raised hers in the air and announced, "To a fresh start!"

"To a fresh start," we echoed, tapping our cups together, and as we floated away from each other, I took a sip and immediately spit it out over the side of my inner tube into the river.

"Oh my god," I coughed. "That is not sweet tea!"

"It is too," Gabby said. "It just also happens to have some gin and vodka and tequila and cola."

"Oh Jesus!" I moaned, taking one more tiny sip. "Ugh, that's terrible."

Hayden was drinking hers with a straw, and said, out of the corner of her mouth, "Tastes better the more you drink."

I sipped slowly as I pulled my sunglasses on, then I tipped my hat forward, and lay back, letting my hands dip into the cool water. The sun soaked into my skin, warming me from the outside, the hard tea warming me from the inside as I rocked back and forth on the water. There was hardly anyone else on the river today. It was quiet, peaceful.

"If there is a heaven . . . ," I began, my voice lazy and sun baked. "I mean, if we all get our own private paradise when we die, this would be mine."

This is what I said every year as we floated downstream in the current, holding on to each other's hands. Only this year, I meant it in a new way, because there was a part of me that really wanted—no, needed—to believe it. I wanted to believe that one day I'd be doing this, and there along the shore I'd see Mallory again, waving to me in her two-piece bathing suit, holding her camera up to take a picture, shouting, "Smile!"

"Yeah," I heard Hayden say in response. I opened my eyes and sat up. Ahead of me, she was floating along, using her arms and legs to turn herself in circles, creating tiny waves that lifted my float up and down.

I looked all around, but Gabby wasn't there. Her tube was floating alongside me, empty. Before I could say *Where's Gabby*, I felt hands pushing against my butt and back and thighs.

"No!" I screamed.

I tried to call out Gabby's name, but I was already flipped over and under the water—river water up my nose and in my mouth—before I could get any sound out. Underwater, I was reminded of that avalanche feeling once again, of not knowing which way is up or down. But something inside me, some instinct I was not familiar with, turned me around and forced me to kick up toward the surface, which I broke, gasping and shouting and splashing at Gabby, who was already climbing back into her tube.

"New rule," she said. "Anyone talks about dying, they get flipped!"

"Not funny!" I yelled, still gasping for air and dripping wet, fishing for my hat and sunglasses as I maneuvered myself back into the inner tube.

Hayden paddled herself closer to me, and said, "Kinda funny." She hooked her foot under my tube and then reached out to grab the handle on Gabby's. She arranged us in a line, placing me in the center. We floated like that, not speaking, until we reached the end point.

As I looked up at the sky, seeing the clouds moving slowly the way we were moving slowly down the river, I wondered about our toast, whether or not it would really be possible to get a fresh start, to put it all behind me: Chris, and the pictures and Mallory, and my parents, and Neil, and my two best friends whose hands I was holding, and all of the messed-up shit that had happened between all of us.

Was it that simple? Just let go, and float away?

CHRIS

EARTH IS 4.5 BILLION YEARS OLD. THE SUN IS 4.6 BIL-
lion. The Milky Way galaxy is 13.5 billion years old. Life on
Earth, like single-celled bacteria life, began 3.8 billion years
ago. Humans only evolved 200,000 years ago. Civilization
itself is only 6,000 years old. We're barely a blip on the cosmic
radar. The course of even the longest human life is essentially
nothing in the grand scheme. So one fucking summer is less
than nothing.

Which is all to say: I'll get over her.

I'll forget this whole thing.

Any moment now. I'll get her out of my head.

That was what I was thinking about as I watched Coleton
trash-talking the Transformers pinball machine at the Battleground. Each time he tagged the ball with the flipper and it
ricocheted throughout the course, the bells and alarms went

off, lights flashing, all of it mixing with the noise of the other arcade games.

After a long run that ended in the ball sliding up and over a side barrier—a truly frustrating conclusion—he glanced over at me, leaning against the machine next to him while he waited for the playout of his final score so he could start his second game. "Why don't you play something?" he said.

I looked down at the machine I had my elbow propped against—it was the Twilight Zone pinball. I'd played this one a million times while waiting for Coleton's endless tries against the Transformers table. I was pretty damn good at it too—older machines are harder. I was the number three name on the scoreboard, or at least, I used to be.

I fished in my pocket for a quarter.

My hands were in position, hovering over the buttons on either side of the machine. For a second, I even felt a little thrill of excitement. Maybe being back here wasn't the worst.

As I pulled back on the bulky trigger, I prepared myself to slide into the swing of the game. I knew the goals and objectives by heart. I knew exactly which loops and ramps would maximize my points. I knew just how hard to nudge the machine with my hips to shift the ball and avoid a tilt. I knew that if I only triggered one flipper at a time, the hit would be stronger, the ball would fly more accurately. I knew I'd have at least ten, fifteen uninterrupted minutes of play as the unspoken rule of pinball came into effect and not even Coleton would direct conversation at me, as I needed everything to concentrate on the trajectory of that shiny metallic orb.

But the metal ball sunk right between the two flippers. Once. Twice. Three times.

Every shot just sent it straight into the gutter, and somehow I was too slow or off target to keep the ball in play for even a minute.

Coleton scored next to me, shouting, "Woo!"

I kicked the machine.

"Dude," Coleton said.

It felt good. I kicked it again. Harder.

"Hey!" I heard a voice shout behind me.

I turned around. It was the manager, the one we'd known for years, who let us play free on our birthdays, and who gave us free nachos when we won at something. Only, now he was yelling at me.

"What?" I said.

"You got five thousand dollars lying around?" he shouted.

"*What?*" I repeated, not nicely.

"That's how much that machine cost, so I suggest you find something else to beat up."

"Fine," I snapped. "That's fine, I'm outta here anyway."

I stormed out. Marched across the parking lot to the station wagon.

"Chris!" Coleton had followed me out.

I spun around and yelled, "What?"

"What is your problem?" he said. He looked confused, and that made me feel even angrier. I didn't want to explain anything to him; I didn't have to explain anything, because no one deserved anything else from me.

"Forget it, Cole," I said, turning away from him to open the car door.

"I mean, what happened to you?" he said, actually concerned. "Is it the girl?" And while I was thankful he didn't say her name, he didn't have a clue what he was talking about. He'd never lived outside his little make-believe world. He couldn't understand what I was going through.

It made me burn hotter. I spun around to face him again.

"Yeah, it's the girl." I could taste the hostility in the air around me. "And me. And *you*. And my parents. Everyone— it's all bullshit!"

I was about to apologize, when he came back at me with, "Oh, so I'm bullshit, you're bullshit, everything's bullshit?" He was yelling—he never yelled. In all our years of friendship I had actually never heard him yell. "You know what *I* think is bullshit?"

"Can't wait to hear," I said, because this was officially a fight.

"You bailing on me for the whole summer, cutting me out, treating me like shit, and then you're back and I don't even call you on any of it, and now you're acting like some kind of aggro douchebag!" He stopped to catch his breath. "That's bullshit."

I had nothing for him.

"This isn't you," he added. "What, you really wanna be this person?"

Maybe I did. Maybe I wanted to take this feeling, the buzz of it, and simmer in it for a while, because anger felt so much better than the crushing, debilitating sadness that had been threatening to consume me.

"Yeah," I answered. "And while we're at it, why don't you find your own ride home," I told him. I got into the car and slammed the door behind me.

I looked straight ahead as I turned the key in the ignition, but I could still see him out of the corner of my eye standing next to my window, holding his hands up toward the sky, saying, "Seriously? Real mature!"

I wanted to speed off. I wanted to leave him there in the empty parking spot, watching him wave his arms over his head in the rearview mirror while I went off to find someplace better. But as I moved my hand to shift into gear, I turned the car off instead. And as I sat there staring at the building, it got all hazy and mirage-like. I blinked and blinked again, but my vision only blurred more. *No.* I wanted to stay like this, but that anger was collapsing all around me. I folded my arms over the steering wheel and let my head fall against them.

I didn't look up when I heard Coleton opening the passenger door and getting in. I didn't look up when he asked, "Are you okay?" And I didn't look up when he squeezed my shoulder for just a single pulse, and then said, "It's gonna be all right."

"God, I'm sorry," I mumbled into my flesh. "I fucking hate crying." And it wasn't just a stupid macho thing. Crying made me feel physically ill—my eyes would swell up and my stomach would hurt and I'd already felt nauseous for days and I didn't want to do it anymore.

"Yeah, so do I," he said, like it was no big deal. "But . . . you gotta let it out."

MAIA

ROXIE WAS THE ONLY ONE WAITING UP FOR ME. SHE followed me up the stairs and into my bedroom, and watched closely as I changed and got into bed. I patted my hand against the mattress to get her to jump up, but she paced the floor next to me instead. I let my hand dangle off the side of the bed and gave her a half-hearted scratch behind the ears. Eventually she lay down on the floor next to my bed, and I fell asleep to the sound of her soft snoring.

It was one of those nights where it felt like I had only blinked and it was morning all over again. That relentless sun rising even though I wanted it to stay night forever, because I knew already how fresh starts work, how each day would be one more day since the last time I saw Chris, and I would count the days until the number got so high, I couldn't keep track anymore.

I knew, because that's what happened with Mallory.

Roxie was still lying there on the floor in the same position she fell asleep in. I sat up, even though every bone in my body resisted. I swung my feet around, and as they touched the floor, she didn't stir. As I stood, I realized the carpet was wet. I leaned forward to get a better look, and I could smell pee. She'd had another accident during the night.

"Roxie," I cooed. "It's okay, girl."

I crouched down next to her, my fingers moving through her fur, down to the skin, and then my hand pulled away. I let out this sharp scream—a reflex. Her skin was stiff and taut and cool. I fell backward on my butt, right into the pee. It was cold and it instantly soaked through the back of my shorts. But I scrambled to my hands and knees and rushed over to her, touched her chest and her face, brushed back the scraggly fur around her nose and mouth. I tried to lift her head, but she wouldn't budge.

I didn't know if I was screaming words or just screaming.

"Maia?" It was my dad. I heard his footsteps as he came running up the stairs, yelling, "What in god's name is going on up here?"

That was when I looked up and saw that my mom was already standing in the doorway, motionless. Her makeup was done, but her hair was still wet and tangled from her shower. Both of her hands were clutching her chest, and her eyes were blank, the color slowly draining from her cheeks. Dad burst into the room, his face flushed, breathing heavily. He looked at me, then Roxie, then Mom.

"Do something!" I yelled at them both, even though I knew there was nothing to be done.

Mom stood in the same spot, not even blinking.

Dad walked over and knelt down on the floor next to me, placing his hand on Roxie's rib cage—we all watched as her chest remained completely still.

He shook his head.

I heard a low whine—a sound that could've come from Roxie, only it hadn't. It was my mom, standing behind my dad and me, both hands now covering her mouth, but still that small animal sound escaped. Dad stood up again, and Mom immediately fell against him. His arms folded around her as she buried her face in his neck. It was a silent grief—I only knew she was crying because her whole body was trembling. As she moved her mouth away from my dad's shoulder, I could hear her saying over and over, "I can't. I can't. I can't."

And Dad spoke into her hair as he smoothed it back, repeating, "I know, I know."

I had never seen my mother like this, not even after Mallory died.

I needed to get away. I looked back at Roxie's motionless body once, and then I left her lying there with my parents. I ran into the bathroom and stripped out of the pajama shorts that were now soaked with urine, and threw on the pants that were lying at the top of the laundry hamper. I went downstairs, grabbed my bike.

But I couldn't get far enough away.

I was back in the middle of the road. Waiting. For a sign, or for Mallory, or for Chris, I wasn't sure. But nothing was happening. The sky was all wrong, too clear and cloudless, bright and blue. Nothing like the picture, nothing like that day we met.

I rode past Bowman's and the Gas n' Sip and the school and Bargain Mart and the railroad tracks.

Mallory was gone. Chris was gone. Now Roxie was gone too.

At the stoplight I pulled my phone out of my pocket. I wanted to call Chris again. But I knew that wasn't fair to either of us. I scrolled through my contacts—I knew the number was there from years ago, for getting ahold of Mallory when she'd let her phone die, which she always did.

It went to voice mail; I was expecting no different. I waited for the tone to leave my message:

"Neil, this is Maia. I know I'm probably the last person you want calling you, but I need to tell you something, or ask you something. Please call me back. It's about Mallory."

That evening, as the sun went down, Mom and Dad and I stood around a mound of freshly tilled soil under the big oak tree in front of the house.

Mom and I had waited on the porch with Roxie's body wrapped in a white cotton blanket while Dad dug a three-foot-deep hole in the ground. He scooped the blanket up in his arms, and we followed him to the tree, and he set her inside the red clay earth.

We each said our own silent, private prayers as we took turns covering the blanket with dirt. Just when I thought we would all go back to our separate quarters, never to speak of this again, Mom knelt down on the ground, and sat with her legs crossed, looking out at the setting sun. Without a word, Dad sat down next to her. So I did too.

"It feels like yesterday that you brought her home, doesn't it?" she said, turning to my dad.

He nodded and stifled a laugh.

"You were so mad," Dad said, and whistled. "I brought her home and you came barreling down the front steps yelling at me."

"Why?" I asked—I hadn't heard this story.

"Because we had a one-year-old and a three-year-old, and we'd agreed to wait until Mallory was in school and you were at least walking before getting a dog!" Mom shot Dad a look that was filled with, for once, something gentle.

"And you wanted one of those golden retrievers, not a stray. But then what happened? Tell her," Dad teased. "Thirty minutes later, your mother was sitting on the kitchen floor with the puppy, calling her Roxie, feeding her ground beef she cooked special just for her!" He laughed like I hadn't seen him laugh in years.

Mom busted out laughing too. But as her laughter slowed, she sighed, and said, "She was with us through everything, wasn't she?"

Dad's smile faded then, and so did mine.

We knew what "everything" meant—she was there through the good, short-lived times, there through the bad years that fell on either side of Mom and Dad's split, and then there through the excruciating—Mallory and everything since.

"I just don't know what to do without her," Mom managed to get out before losing her voice to the tears she was trying hard to hold back.

Dad gave me a look—we both knew Mom was talking

about Mallory now. He put his arm around Mom's shoulder, and I got on the other side of her and held her hand. It was a strange configuration, one we hadn't been able to contort ourselves into until now for some reason.

"None of us do, Mom." I wanted her to know that she wasn't the only one hurting—that Dad and I were in pain too, just like she was. But I also wanted her to know that she wasn't alone, like she seemed to think.

She clasped on to my hand and breathed the words, "I know."

We stayed there like that until the sun was going down. When we returned to the house, I made us grilled cheese sandwiches and we sat at the table, the three of us at the same time, and ate our first meal together, without Roxie, without Mallory.

I went to bed before them.

I couldn't sleep, though; I just kept tossing and turning. I got up in the middle of the night and saw that Mom's bedroom door was cracked. I stuck my head in—I wanted to see if she was awake too, but she wasn't. She was lying there, still in her clothes from earlier. But Dad was there too, still in his clothes as well; even his boots were still on. He was spooning Mom, with his arms around her.

I tiptoed across the room, careful not to wake them up, and I crawled into bed next to Mom, something I hadn't done since I was six years old.

Without a word, Mom placed her hand on my arm and pulled me closer.

CHRIS

WHEN I RAN TRACK AT SCHOOL, I REMEMBER COACH
telling us about practicing mindfulness while running, not
to let your thoughts wander. Focus on your breathing, your
footfalls, she told me. There was even this metronome app
for musicians she said I should try—the repetitive *tick-tock*
would help keep the pace.

That was always my one downfall, she had told me many
times: distraction.

Maia was one black-hole-size distraction.

I woke up at 5:00 a.m. like I used to, put on my sneakers,
and went for a run without anybody trying to stop me or ask
me where I was going or when I'd be back. I'd come home
when I was good and ready, shower, and then go through
the daily chore of getting dressed without having an anxiety
attack.

Because I had a new plan now, a real one—to not let

anyone get in my head and distract me from the important stuff, which was going back to school and making it to my eighteenth birthday. After that the next milestone would be making it to graduation, and after that, making it to college, where I could finally begin my life. I'd gotten into a good routine. I made it farther every day, building my endurance.

I'd even started running twice a day: in the morning at sunup and again at sundown.

I was thinking maybe I'd run a marathon in the fall—that would look good for college. I had my eyes and my thoughts and every last shred of energy I possessed focused toward the future. That was all that mattered. And it was working.

When I started running again after I got hurt, I was at an eight-minute mile. Which you hear about all the time as some kind of standard, but it is nothing special. I honestly wondered if I'd ever be able to run on a team again. When I got to Carson, I was at seven minutes, which is still barely competitive, but it was progress. All summer long I'd been stuck at six. I tried to cut myself slack—I hadn't been training with a team in over a year, I had my injuries slowing me down, and I had Maia. Even on my best days there I couldn't break it.

The fastest I'd ever run in my entire life was at a meet right before I got hurt. I ran a 4.51.34 and won by five whole seconds.

That evening, on my second run of the day, I ran a 4.50 mile. I had once thought that Maia was the right person at the wrong time. But now I was thinking that it was my whole life that was at the wrong time. The right time was coming, though. Every day that passed brought me one day closer to it.

By the time I got home, it was getting dark, the streetlights blinking on as I turned onto my street. I went into the kitchen for a glass of water, and Mom was there at the table hunched over her day planner, working on her schedule of showing houses and meeting clients.

"Hi," she said to me as I walked in. "Dad's working late, so I was thinking of ordering some pizza?"

"Okay," I replied.

"All right, good." I could feel her eyes on me as I went to the cupboard, then to the refrigerator. "He'll be home soon," she added, almost as if she needed something else to say.

"Okay," I repeated.

"Chris, sit," she finally said, closing her planner. "Will you?"

I took the seat opposite her.

"So, how are you doing?" she asked.

I shrugged.

She nodded, and said, "I talked with Isobel the other day. She told me about your girlfriend."

"She's not my girlfriend anymore, Mom. And I really don't want to talk about it. Ever." I started to back my chair away from the table, but Mom reached her hand into the space between us, as if she could pull me closer.

"Wait, Chris. Don't—don't leave. You don't have to talk about her, okay?" I sat back down, and Mom continued. "I just wanted to tell you I know what you're going through."

I laughed, shook my head. "I really doubt that."

"Believe it or not, I remember what it was like to be seventeen. I remember being so heartbroken and devastated and feeling like I'd never get over my first love—"

I had to stop her there. "I thought Dad was your first love."

"He was—and he was with someone else."

"But you got him in the end," I pointed out. "That's nothing like this."

She sighed. "Yes, I did get him, but that was years later. Isobel likes to tell a melodramatic version of the story, but they had been broken up for a long time before we ever got together. I still had to get over him. And I did."

I bit down on the inside of my cheek to stop myself from speaking—I didn't want to have this or any other conversation with my mom, but I was desperate for advice, even from her. "How?" I muttered.

"Oh, I went off the rails for a while. I did all kinds of crazy things—I used to be cool, you know," she said, grinning at me.

"Yeah? What crazy things?" I asked, more as a dare than a suspension of my contempt.

"Oh god, I partied, and drank. And smoked pot," she whispered. "I even vandalized the gas station once," she added, immediately amending with, "None of those things are cool, by the way."

"You vandalized?" I prompted.

She nodded. "Yep, graffiti. Me. Can you believe it?"

The quote—it was her. Of course it was.

I wanted so badly to smile, to let her know what it meant—that she had built that link between me and Maia. But at the thought of Maia, I felt a pain in my chest. "Well," I said, standing up. "I'll try to avoid spray paint."

"My point is, you're not alone," she said, standing as well.

"It feels like the worst thing in the world right now, I know—I remember. But it will get better, I promise."

"That's just it, though. It's not the worst thing, Mom," I said, and I was even surprised by my bluntness. "I've felt worse than this before." I didn't need to clarify—the stricken, pained expression on her face, the way her shoulders bowed inward just a little—she knew I was talking about her.

She cleared her throat and picked her planner up off the table. "I'll let you know when the pizza gets here," she said as she walked past me into the living room.

MAIA

THE RUMBLE OF NEIL'S PICKUP COMING DOWN THE driveway echoed in the barn like young thunder. I closed my eyes for a moment before I went to the door. He was on his way to the house, but stopped in his tracks when I called his name.

He walked toward the barn slowly, squinting his eyes, turning his head like he was trying to see the whole situation better, in a way that was more than suspicious; it was almost like he was afraid.

"Hey," I called out to him, waving my hand.

He stopped several feet away from me, and said, "Well, I'm here. What is it?"

"Come in," I told him, pushing both of the barn doors open all the way, letting the light inside.

He crossed the threshold, still looking at me like I might pull something shady, but then, once he was inside, he stood still, looking around. It was nearly the same as when he had last been here. Close enough, anyway. He turned in a circle, and then his eyes set on me. He shook his head and raised his arms toward the ceiling.

"Why?" he said, his voice shaking. "Why did you lie to me?"

"I don't really know," I said, but that wasn't true. I did know. I knew that I had been in so much pain that I'd felt the only way to get rid of it was to push some of it off on someone else. He was there. It was as simple as that.

"Not gonna cut it," he snapped.

"Because I was jealous of what you had with her. And I was angry and hurting and scared," I answered—all of those things were part of the truth. "I hated that she belonged to you more than she belonged to me."

He looked down at his feet. "She didn't belong to anybody."

"You know what I mean," I insisted. "I was so angry that I never got a chance to make things right with her, and I took it out on you because things *were* right between the two of you."

"You know she didn't think like that," he argued.

"Do I? I feel like I don't know anything."

"Yes you do," he countered. "So maybe you weren't tight in the last year. So what? That doesn't take away the other sixteen years that came before!" he shouted, gaining steam. "And don't think I don't have regrets too. Things weren't right between us either." He paused to take a breath. "There's so much I wish I would've said to her. A million things!"

"I—I didn't know that," I tried to tell him, but he kept talking.

"You know, you were right about what you said to me that night."

I knew immediately what night he was talking about.

"I loved her," he admitted. "Yeah, maybe it was obvious. Maybe you and everyone else in the world thought I was pathetic. But you were wrong when you said she'd never love me back."

"I know," I said.

"You don't get to take that away from her. You don't get to take that away from *me*. Because she did love me. No, maybe not in the same way, but she could've. If I ever worked up the nerve to tell her, maybe she could've."

He rubbed his eyes with the back of his hand.

"I'm sorry," I told him, even though I knew "sorry" didn't come close to being enough.

He turned his back to me and walked up to the big wall of photos.

"What was your question?" he asked, clearing his throat. "In your message. You wanted to tell me something and ask me something. I'm guessing this was what you wanted to tell me, so . . ."

"Right. You said before that you knew which ones were important, which were her favorites." I paused, swallowing my pride, my guilt, and all those other troublesome emotions that I usually let hold me back.

He pointed out at least a dozen photographs, which I couldn't have picked out if I'd tried (and I had). Not one of them was among the pictures I had singled out over the past three months.

"You look disappointed, or something," he told me.

"No, it's just those weren't the ones I was thinking were most important."

"You know what she would say to that," he said, but he was stating it as a matter of fact, not a question.

"No. What would she say?" I asked.

"I dunno. She'd probably say something like . . ." He switched his voice to be higher and wispier like Mallory's, and he got this far-off look in his eye. "What *you* think the important ones are is the only thing that matters." He smiled sadly, and said in his regular voice, "Something about the eye of the beholder, or whatever. I don't know. Sounds like her, though, doesn't it?" He let out the smallest of laughs, and then shut his mouth tight.

"Yeah," I agreed, laughing. "It does."

"Well," Neil said. "I'm really glad you're a pathological liar, Maia."

He was standing there, uncomfortably, putting his hands in his pockets, then touching his eternally over-gelled hair, then crossing his arms. He looked younger, somehow, than the last time I was this close to him. Or maybe it was that I suddenly felt a lot older.

He was making his way to the door, when I asked, "Hey, what's your favorite, then? If that's really the important thing, like you said."

He stared at the wall for a moment, held his finger in the air as he walked over to the corner next to Mallory's darkroom, where there was a metal chest of long, narrow drawers. He was opening them, one by one.

"I didn't know there was anything in there," I said, following behind him.

I looked over his shoulder—he was lifting sheets of tissue paper that separated all these black-and-white prints, drawer after drawer, searching for one in particular.

He pulled out a stack of photographs wrapped in a folded sheet of white paper, and set them on top of the drawer. He opened it to reveal dozens of the same picture—two tree trunks side by side, and they had a strand of barbed wire that was embedded into the bark, the trees having grown up around it, so close together that they had even grown around one another.

"This one," he said finally. "She took it last winter when we were up in the mountains."

"Take it," I told him.

"Really?" he asked, narrowing his eyes at me uncertainly.

"I mean, isn't that what she would've wanted?"

He nodded, whispering, "Yeah, I think so." He took his photograph, holding it gingerly, like a baby, as he crossed the barn and headed out the door.

"Hey, Maia?" he said, stepping into the light. "Mallory never hated you. That was *my* lie, okay?"

I think maybe somewhere deep in my heart I knew that, but I was thankful to hear it anyway.

After Neil left, I searched the metal drawers for the graffiti picture and found it almost right away. There were dozens of this one too. I picked up a copy of the photograph and held it gently at the corners.

My entire motive for asking Neil over was to find out what these words meant, but he had already told me without even realizing it. They meant whatever I wanted them to mean. They meant that anything, everything, only means what you say it means. You are who you believe you are, no more, no less.

In a moment of clarity, I knew exactly what I had to do.

I'd already decided I was going to call in sick to work today—I couldn't handle the clearance aisle or fitting room duty. I needed to start living again. I needed to stop thinking about how badly I'd fucked everything up and do something about it. Because getting a fresh start doesn't mean you can just forget about everything that came before.

After waiting in the shadows of her porch, I ambushed Isobel when she got home from work that night.

"Good god, girl!" she shouted when she saw me standing on the top step. "You scared the hell out of me."

"Sorry," I said. "I was waiting for you because I wanted to ask a favor."

She side-eyed me, handing me one of the tote bags she was carrying, so she could open the door. "A favor involving Chris?" I followed her inside as she turned the kitchen light on and set her armfuls of things on the table.

"Sorta."

"Go on," she said as she took her shoes off and lowered herself into one of the dining chairs.

"I have something I want to send him, only I don't have his address." I flashed her my best fake Bargain Mart smile. "Please?" I added, my smile nearly collapsing. "It's important."

She narrowed her eyes at me, then reached over to one of the kitchen drawers and pulled out a notepad and slapped it onto the tabletop. She reached into the drawer, her fingers disrupting its contents, until she found a pen.

The next morning, I was waiting at the post office when it opened. On the back of Mallory's photograph I had written Chris a message:

> I *think* I *finally understand what it means.*
> *Please call me.*
> *Love, Maia*

I hoped the photograph would signify to Chris that in spite of everything, *he* saw me for who I was and I saw him in the same way. I sent a silent prayer out into the universe as I slid the envelope across the counter and into the hands of the postal worker. I paid extra to have it delivered overnight. I watched closely as she weighed the envelope and placed the postage in the upper right corner before tossing it into a bin behind her.

"That's it. You're done," she told me, since I was still standing there.

I left. I went home.

I'd wait to hear from him.

I could do that. I was capable of waiting.

CHRIS

MOM SLID A LARGE RECTANGULAR ENVELOPE ACROSS the kitchen counter in my direction. "This came for you today."

I stared at the handwriting in the center of the envelope that spelled out my name. Then my eyes tracked a line to the upper left-hand corner. To *her* name.

My fingertips grazed the surface of the letters, the slightest indentations from where her pen had pressed down. I closed my eyes, and I was instantly brought back to that day in the car when I first saw her write on her palm.

I picked the envelope up and held it my hands. It felt substantial, more than just paper. The postmark was from Carson, NC. Red capital letters across the front spelled out:

DO NOT BEND

I walked directly to the garbage can and stomped on the foot pedal. The lid swung open like the mouth of a whale, ready to devour. The corners of the envelope collapsed as I stuffed it in, and I felt the bubble wrap inside crushing and snapping under my palm as I pressed it toward the bottom of the garbage.

Mom shouted, "Chris!"

I didn't acknowledge her. I simply went to the cupboard and pulled down a glass—the afternoon sun shining through the window exposing all the spots and streaks left behind by the dishwasher—and filled it with water.

I gulped it down, trying to drown out whatever was boiling up inside me. I swallowed hard several times and washed it away. "I'll be upstairs," I told her on my way out of the room.

I took the stairs two at a time. I closed the door behind me. I exhaled. No sooner had I taken one step inside than my mom pushed the door open, walked in, and slammed it shut again behind her.

"Look." She planted her feet firmly into my carpet. "Love is messy. It's painful and confusing and fucked up—"

"*Mom.*"

"Well, it is." She thrashed her arms around. "Nobody knows how to do it right, okay? It takes a lifetime to figure it out."

"I don't want to talk about this."

"That's just too damn bad!" she shouted. "You wanted space, I gave you space. But enough is enough."

"Not to me, it's not enough."

"You know what, Chris? I've known you your entire life, from the moment you came into this world—"

I had to interrupt her. "A lot's changed since then, Mom."

"And a lot hasn't," she countered. "I see this girl, this Maia, trying so hard, and you're just shutting her down."

I winced at the sound of her name.

"You have no idea what happened, Mom."

"You're right. Maybe I don't. But I know *you*. Whether you believe it or not, I know you."

I shook my head. "I appreciate the fact that you're trying to help or whatever, but you don't understand," I told her.

"I know that you expect people to always know the exact right thing to do and say, the exact right way to feel and love and be."

"No I don't," I snorted.

"Oh, Chris." She smiled, but it was not a smile. *"Please."*

"Who are we talking about, anyway? Me and Maia, or me and you?"

"Both, all right?" She tossed her arms up in the air, and as they fell to her sides something in her softened. She brought her hand to her forehead and held her face at the temples between her thumb and the rest of her fingers. She walked over to my bed and sat down.

"Please," she said again, but this time it wasn't a "give me a break please"; it was simply a request, as she patted the empty space next to her. "I'm not gonna try to pry it out of you, okay? You don't have to tell me what happened with her. I just want you to listen."

"Fine," I relented.

"I love you. You're special. And beautiful—"

"God, Mom, please don't—"

"No, I mean beautiful in your soul, honey." She reached out and placed her hand above my heart. "It has nothing to do with appearance or being a girl or a boy, or anything like that. It just *is*." She held my face between her hands so that I was forced to look at her. They felt so soft and cool, and I couldn't remember the last time she had touched me with this kind of tenderness.

"I wouldn't change a single, minute, microscopic thing about you," she said. "Do you understand that?"

I pulled away from her. "I don't believe that for one second, Mom."

She sighed, and rubbed her temples once more. "You challenge me. You make me think and question and doubt myself, and that's *good*. You force me to do better—you force everyone around you to do better, you always have. And that's what I'm trying to do here."

"Then why do you look at me like you . . ." I'd thought the word so many times, but looking her in the eye, I was having trouble getting it out of my mouth. "Like you hate me?"

"No, no, no." She just kept repeating it as she pulled me in toward her, and I gave in and let my head fall against her shoulder. *"NoNoNoNoNo,"* she whispered, like the chorus to a song.

My forehead was touching her neck, and her skin was so cool, it reminded me of being a kid, back when she'd have defended me and whatever I wanted to the death. I suddenly felt a million words I'd never been able to say to her bubbling up from somewhere deep within me, crawling up through my stomach and into my throat, getting lodged there in one giant lump I needed to release before it strangled me. If I could convince myself I really was just a kid again, then maybe it was okay to cry just one more time.

She let me, rocking me slowly, not saying anything, not trying to make me feel better or find the magic words or tell me any of her old standby white lies about how this will pass and how great I am and how one day everyone will see it too.

She was silent.

I lifted my head, and wiped my eyes, and laughed at myself because I was embarrassed. But she didn't laugh or smile or frown; she looked me in the eye and repeated, firmly, "I could never hate you."

"Then why have you been so hard on me?" I finally asked the question I hadn't been able to bring myself to utter this whole past year.

"When you're a parent, you'll understand. You are everything to me—it's like you're walking around with my heart inside your chest. And I am terrified for you, Chris. I am terrified of what could happen to you because of other people's hatred and ignorance."

"I know, but—" I argued.

"Chris! You were not just beat up. You were targeted, and those boys could've raped or killed you. I know you don't want to believe that, but it's true, and you were so very lucky that you weren't hurt worse than you were."

"Mom, that's not what was going to—" I tried once more, but her words sent this tingle crawling along the back of my neck that prevented me from finishing.

"And then I see you wanting to just put yourself back out there in this big, bold way and it's terrifying," she continued. "I was so angry at you for so long."

"But why? That's what I don't understand. It wasn't my fault. I can't help being who I am!"

"I know it wasn't your fault. You weren't asking for it. You did not deserve what happened."

"Then why are you so angry at me?" I said again.

She shook her head with purpose. "It's not about you being trans. It truly isn't. It's taken me all year to realize this, but it was about me. I think it felt like as you were rejecting being a woman, you were rejecting me—"

"That's not what I was doing, Mom."

"I know that now," she said. "But it was more than just my fragile little ego." She paused and grabbed my hand, her voice low when she said, "I loved my daughter something fierce. You know that."

"Yes," I agreed—that was one thing I knew for sure.

"You have to understand"—she gripped my hands tight—"you were taking her away from me. That's why I was angry. I had to get all mama tiger on someone, and that someone was you." She coughed, trying to hold back her tears. "And I think I was grieving too, mourning you. I was holding on so hard to the person you used to be, I didn't realize you were still here. But that's what you were telling me all along, wasn't it?"

I nodded.

"I never wanted to hurt you, Chris—I wanted to protect you, even from yourself."

"I know," I told her. And this time I did.

"I'm sorry, and I will try my best to be what you need," she said, her voice shaking. "I don't want to lose you."

I suddenly felt all these walls crashing down around me. Walls I didn't even know were there. I swallowed hard and told her the truth: "You won't."

MAIA

I WAITED THREE DAYS. STILL NOTHING FROM CHRIS. I called Hayden and Gabby to come over. It was an emergency, I told them. I needed a favor—a big one—and they agreed before even knowing what it was.

We told our parents we were heading out to the beach for one last hurrah before school started back up.

But that was a lie.

We got into Hayden's car at daybreak and drove.

We only stopped twice for gas and food, then one last time when we were twenty minutes away so I could change my clothes and brush my teeth and fix my hair, and pretend like I hadn't just spent the last ten hours in a car.

CHRIS

THE UNIVERSE IS FULL OF PARADOXES. IT'S THE nature of reality. Black holes are both creative and destructive. Mom—protecting me from myself by hurting me—was also a paradox.

I was trying to concentrate on my breath, on keeping my pace, on beating my last time, but my mind kept drifting to that envelope that was sitting on my desk unopened, slightly crumpled after Mom had fished it from the trash, smoothed it out, and handed it to me. I had taken it without fighting, a silent acceptance of the olive branch we had both built together. That battered envelope with its hand lettering was yet another paradox.

There was this physics lesson I learned about when I was a kid: Schrödinger's cat. In 1935, this physicist, Schrödinger, devised an experiment—a theoretical experiment—all about paradox. You're supposed to imagine a cat sealed in a metal box with a flask of poison. I used to know all about it, the quantum mechanics of it all, but the bottom line is that as long as the box remains sealed, the cat is both dead and alive.

The envelope was like that box. And I wasn't sure I wanted to know the truth of what was really left inside. I wanted to love and hate Maia at the same time, with equal passion. I knew it was fucked up, but it was the only thing that made sense to me.

I must've run five miles: past the elementary school and the playground and the grocery store. I didn't know where I was going until I got there. I slowed to a jog as I approached the trailhead behind the high school. I followed the path, the pull growing stronger and stronger, until I found the exact spot where I'd veered off the trail nearly one year earlier. I looked around just like I had that day. I tried to quiet the world around me so I could listen to that inner voice I had ignored before. It wasn't telling me to run this time..

Carefully I traced the path I'd taken then, noting all the ways it looked different in the full bloom of summer, as opposed to the chill of fall. My fingers grazed the trunks of the trees as I waded deeper into the woods, their bark my own personalized braille, telling me the story of myself.

The closer I came to the clearing, the slower my pace became. Without warning, my memories began to spark one by one, fired up by some kind of electrical charge that was still bound to these woods after all this time. I could see it and hear it and feel it all around me. I followed along behind Ben and Jake and Tobey until I was standing there in the same spot where I'd been standing then.

The scene played out before me like a panoramic movie, and I could do nothing to stop it. I couldn't rewind or fast-forward or do anything to change it. But I was watching it all from a different perspective, I realized. Because now I could see all the parts that I couldn't see then. I could see how hard I was trying to be tough and cool and calm, making myself ignore all the signs. The way the boys kept glancing at one another with these secret exchanges.

I watched as they grabbed me and held my arms—this time I could see the look on *my* face, how scared I was. And I could also see the way I looked to *them* as they chased me, because I was following along too. I saw the rock I tripped on and I watched my ankle turn, watched how I fell, then got back up and limped a few more steps. I followed behind as they caught up, screaming after me. And then I watched them beat me, until I folded to the ground—it had felt fast, I remember that, but this time it happened in slow motion.

While Tobey and Jake were kicking me, I was covering my head with my arms. That's why I missed the part when Ben had already unbuttoned and unzipped his jeans. I missed how the other boys were laughing. I missed what they were planning to do to me. And I missed that Coleton had stood there, frozen, for several seconds before he made the phone call to the police.

I don't think I realized until now how much hate they had inside, how much it wasn't even about me, not anything I did or didn't do. If not me, they would've found someone else to fill my place. The hologram played forward until it was just

Coleton and Chris there on the ground. Coleton was crying, muttering something to himself or to me. I stepped closer now and looked down. My face was so bruised and swollen, I could barely recognize myself.

And I knew for certain something I had suspected but couldn't be sure of until now: This thing, this terrible thing that had happened, happened to me. Not someone else I used to be, but someone I still was, always was, always will be. Not someone who was the weak, wrong part of me, but someone who was, is, strong and real. All of my running away had finally brought me back here to see that, to remember, and to finally lay it to rest.

The vision vanished and it was summer again and I was alone, standing on this grave. I looked around, and my eyes set on the rock, the one that had tripped me. I lifted it out of the dirt and brought it back to the spot where I'd lain. I crouched down and dug at the earth with my fingers and set the rock inside, packed the dirt up around it like I was planting something new. The smooth, round dome just breached the surface.

I walked home slowly. And I got this feeling like I was lighter, like maybe I'd been carrying the past of me around on my back all this time and now I was finally walking into the rest of my life. I couldn't help smiling. In fact, I was laughing softly to myself when I entered my front door.

But I stopped in my tracks when I looked up and saw Maia sitting there on my couch in my living room with my mother.

I opened my mouth, and I didn't know what would come out. Because, while my mind told me I should still be mad, told me that I *was* still furious, another part of me was so damned happy to see her.

MAIA

WHILE I WAITED FOR CHRIS TO GET HOME, HIS MOM
and I talked about Carson and growing up there and how
little has changed since she lived in that gray house. We talked
about which teachers were still at the school and the creepy
DairyLand Fairy logo, and a million other small-town girl
things. We specifically did *not* talk about Chris. If she knew
what I had done to him, she didn't let on.

When he finally walked through the door, I braced myself
for whatever was about to come my way.

He stood in the entryway and looked at me from across
the room, his expression smooth and even, not giving anything away. He didn't look surprised or happy to see me, not
even angry; it was almost like he'd been expecting me.

"Well, I'll leave you two alone," his mother said, standing
up. "Nice meeting you, Maia."

I stood too, and thanked her for the soda she gave me. As

she exited the room, I felt myself being pulled, once again, toward Chris. I took a few steps closer, but he remained in the same spot.

"So what are you doing here?" he said in a disconcertingly casual way, looking down as he wound the cord of his earbuds around his phone.

"I didn't think you'd call," I answered.

He looked up at me then, and there was the tiniest hint of a smile twitching at the corner of his mouth. "So you drove seven hundred miles?"

I shrugged.

He took exactly two steps and stopped short like there was an invisible barrier dividing the room and we were on opposite sides of it.

"I'm not here to try to start over or pick up where we left off, but I couldn't leave things the way they ended—we deserve better than that, after everything," I tried to explain. "I mean, don't we?"

He sighed, and then nodded in the direction of the kitchen, where his mother had disappeared, and said, "Come on." Then he turned around and started toward the stairs. I followed him to the second story of the house, the carpet plush and soft under my feet, the handrail smooth and cool against the palm of my hand.

He led me down a hall and into his bedroom—his real bedroom, not the room at his aunt's house where I had spent so many hours with him.

This room was completely different, his walls full of posters, and endless books on bookshelves and a desk with his notebook and laptop and pens and pencils and a huge lunar calendar pinned up to a corkboard on the wall in front of it.

There, propped up on top of the desk, under the calendar, was the envelope with my handwriting on it. It looked a little worn and wrinkled, but intact. Unopened.

He closed the door behind us and stood there, waiting for me to say something.

"You didn't open it?" I asked. I walked over to the desk and picked up the envelope. I brought it over to where he was standing and held it out to him. He let me place it in his hands. Then he looked up at me the way he used to, and for a moment I thought we might kiss, I thought maybe things hadn't changed so irreparably after all, but he looked back down at the envelope and went over to sit on the edge of his bed.

I sat down next to him, leaving an arm's length between us, because I knew things had changed. I watched as he peeled back the sticky closure of the envelope and pulled out the photo. I'd wrapped it in a sheet of white tissue paper and placed it between two pieces of cardboard to keep it flat. He unwrapped it and carefully set the pieces aside.

"That was one of Mallory's," I explained as he examined the black-and-white photo of that place where I'd taken him, that place that had changed us both.

I watched as he turned it over in his hands and read the note I'd written on the back for him.

"What does it mean?" he finally said, looking at me once again.

"I think it means that there's not one truth, not one way to love and be known, but . . ." I paused, trying to think of a word big enough to encompass everything I'd learned about him and Mallory and my parents and myself.

"Infinite ways?" he finished.

"Yes."

"I like that," he said quietly.

"And it also means I'm sorry," I whispered. "And it means that all those things I said to you, all those things I did—they were about me and my stuff, not you."

"I know." He nodded, and then said, "Me too."

As we stood in his driveway waiting for Hayden and Gabby to pick me up, I wanted to tell him how I thought he was the best person I'd ever known or ever would know, and that what we had had healed something in me I hadn't thought could be healed, and that I didn't have a clue how I'd ever get over him and, most of all, I wasn't sure I even wanted to.

When the car pulled up, we looked at each other, and I hoped he knew all of those things already without me having to say them out loud.

I threw my arms around him because I couldn't let this end without one last embrace.

He hugged me back, and as he released me from his arms, I felt the ground beneath my feet begin to shift. I held on tighter for just a moment, and he let me.

But nothing holds still that long; nothing holds that still long enough.

I let go.

I forced my feet to walk away from him. When I got into the car and looked back at the house, he was already gone.

CHRIS

LIVE OR DIE. I USED TO THINK IT WAS SO SIMPLE—A
choice, really. Live authentically or die pretending. I thought
once I chose to live, I'd finally start my life. What I didn't
know is that it's not a choice you make just once; it's a choice
you have to keep on making. Because life doesn't wait until
you're perfect, or better, or out of pain, for you to be alive.
You have to choose it every minute of every day.

That's what I was thinking about as she turned away
from me.

I went back into the house because I couldn't stand to
watch her leave. I ran up the stairs to my room before my
parents could ask me any questions. My heart was pounding.
There was something more I needed to do, something I still
needed to say, but I didn't know what.

My eyes drifted to the photo sitting on my desk, to the
discarded envelope still on my bed. I jerked open my desk

drawer and rifled through it, throwing its contents on the floor, until I was holding it—the necklace I bought for Maia.

I raced down the stairs with my fingers working to pry the necklace out of the little plastic bag. As I swung the door open, I heard my mom calling my name, but I ran, not even bothering to close it behind me.

The car was sitting at the stop sign on the corner.

"Wait!" I yelled, waving my arms over my head. "Maia!"

The car started moving again, then stopped abruptly, the taillights glowing red in the dark. The door opened, and Maia stepped out of the car.

It felt like I was running through water; my legs just couldn't get me there fast enough. When I finally reached her, I was out of breath, and she was standing there, waiting for me.

"Here," I said, holding out the necklace. "I wanted you to have this."

She let me place it in her open hands—and she cradled the locket in her palm, smiling at it like it was something living, fragile. Then she undid the clasp and held one side of the necklace in each hand, bringing it around to the back of her neck.

"Will you?" she asked me.

I had to step in close and reach around her to latch the chain, and as I smelled the citrus in her hair, I wished so badly we could just return to the way things were. But I knew we couldn't.

I backed up a step, and tried to memorize the way the locket looked against her skin. We put our arms around each other once more, and her lips brushed my cheek, as we stood there under the streetlight.

I watched the car drive away, getting smaller and smaller in the distance. And I realized then that Maia was never the right person at the wrong time, and she wasn't the wrong person at the right time. We were both the right people, in exactly the right place, at exactly the right time.

AUTHOR'S NOTE

When I am writing, I always try to think about the kinds of stories I really needed when I was a young person, the ones that would've made me feel less alone in the world. While I am not transgender, I connect to what trans and nonbinary youth are going through right now as being parallel to my own coming out and coming-of-age experience. I grew up during a time when things felt pretty bleak for LGBTQ people, when I did not have the rights I do today, and when my future and my safety as a lesbian felt very uncertain. One thing I have learned to believe in along the way is the transformative power of love—love of any kind. Love is what heals us and gives us hope, and that is something no one should ever be without.

There is nothing I know of that opens minds and hearts better than sharing our stories, and my wish for *Something*

Like Gravity is that it can, in some small way, give hope to those who may be struggling with some of the same things as Chris and Maia.

To you, I say this: You matter. You are not alone. You won't be erased.

ACKNOWLEDGMENTS

This book was years in the making. It has changed shape many times along the way, and there were moments when I thought it would never come together. Without the following people it never would have.

First, I thank YOU—my readers—for joining me on this journey and inspiring me every step of the way. Some of you I've been fortunate enough to meet face-to-face and others online, through the personal stories you have entrusted me with in late-night emails, messages, and posts. These moments we share are what keep me going—thank you for always reminding me why I must continue writing.

To my agent, Jess Regel: I remember first telling you about the idea for *Something Like Gravity* over a slice of pizza in 2017, and from that moment on, your support of this book has never wavered. I feel like the luckiest author in the world to have you and the team at Foundry Literary + Media by my side.

Deepest thanks go to my editor, Rūta Rimas. For your belief in Chris and Maia's story, for loving these characters like I do, and for helping to bring the vision I had of them to life. Your guidance, insight, and support shaped this book into what it is today, and for that I will be forever grateful.

Thanks are also due to Justin Chanda, Nicole Fiorica, Margaret K. McElderry Books, and the entire Simon & Schuster Children's Publishing Division—so many talented, dedicated people had a hand in making sure this book came safely into the world, and I am grateful to each and every one of you. Mia Nolting, as a longtime fan of yours, I could not have asked for an illustrator whose work I admire more—thank you for bringing Chris and Maia's world to life through your incredible artwork.

Many thanks to my early readers for bearing with me through the crappy first drafts and helping me to see more clearly the story I was trying to tell. To Samantha Gellar— for reading each and every version of each and every draft, many times over—as well as Holly Summers-Gil and Bryson McCrone, for your careful reading of portions of this book. Robin Constantine and Rebecca Petruck, thank you for your early encouragement and enthusiasm (not to mention the amazing plotting brainstorm session we had on retreat). Dr. Angela Mazaris at the LGBTQ Center at Wake Forest University, I cannot thank you enough—your guidance, feedback, and thoughtful reading of this book made all the difference. Thanks also to Mike Brotherton, Christian Ready, and the Launch Pad Astronomy Workshop at the University of Wyoming, for helping to kindle my inner astronomy geek.

It is often said that writing is a "lonely profession," but I am lucky to have such amazing author friends who disprove that adage: Amy Reed, Jaye Robin Brown, Brenda Rufener, Robin Roe, Kathleen Glasgow, Julie Buxbaum, Brendan Kiely, the Nebo Retreaters, the Sweet16ers, and so many others. (I could fill a book with each of your names.)

As always, an enormous debt of gratitude is owed to my family and my dear friends.

Finally, last but never least, thank you, Sam—my love, my heart—without you, there would be no Chris and Maia, no *Something Like Gravity*, no love story to tell.